CW00739655

'Isabella M Smugge is bacl[...]influencer, with millions of f[...]the country. But Isabella has[...]four, estranged wife, daught[...]of the PTA comes with a who[...] Isabella is struggling to juggle it all, and is vulnerable to the same stresses as any lesser mortal. She needs her friends more than ever, but also needs more than even her friends can give her.

'Ruth Leigh has done something extraordinary with this chapter of Issy's story. Among the familiar fun and frivolity, the pomposity and ridiculousness, she weaves a heartfelt, poignant and beautifully written story of deep spiritual awakening. The best book yet, IMHO. **#issyandGod #perfectmatch**'
Joy Margetts, author of The Healing *series of books and* Christ Illuminated

'Once more unto the breach, dear friends, and fill the gap with a philandering husband and lashings of pomegranate and sumac essence! Issy's back, and so is the wonderful array of friends, frenemies, enemies and family that attend her in this brilliant and breathless instalment of Issy's life. Get your copy now and buy one for that special person who needs a bit more *Ansbach and Powdering Gown* in their life.'
Andrew J Chamberlain; speaker, podcaster, and author of The Creative Writer's Toolbelt Handbook *and* The Centauri Sequence

Dee Sallyann

Enjoy!

The further adventures of Isabella M Smugge

Ruth Leigh

instant
ap☐stle

First published in Great Britain in 2024

Instant Apostle
104A The Drive
Rickmansworth
Herts
WD3 4DU

actual persons, living or dead, or actual events is purely coincidental.

British Library Cataloguing-in-Publication Data

A catalogue record for this book is available from the British Library.

This book and all other Instant Apostle books are available from Instant Apostle:

Website: www.instantapostle.com

Email: info@instantapostle.com

ISBN 978-1-912726-82-0

Printed in Great Britain.

September

This morning I woke at 6.50 after a night of blissful, uninterrupted sleep, flexed and pointed each foot ten times (maintaining flexibility and mobility is so important as one heads into one's forties), stretched, yawned and said to myself, 'Isabella, you're a lucky girl. You've got four beautiful children, this lovely house, quite a lot of real friends and a wonderful career.'

I luxuriated in the gentle autumn breeze caressing me through the open window, allowed myself to relax into my ludicrously comfortable king-sized, beech-framed bed with its hand-tied hourglass springs and enjoyed the silence. My youngest child, Milo, was not requesting company or refreshment via the baby monitor and my three older ones, Finn, Chloë and Elsie, were presumably wrapped in peaceful slumbers themselves. The other occupant of my gracious Grade II listed Georgian house, my mother, had just returned from a spa weekend with a clutch of sixty-something ladies, preparing herself for her forthcoming wedding.

I can't quite believe that it was three years ago that we moved from London to the country. It was early August when my husband Johnnie, the children and our Latvian au pair Sofija made the trek from our double-fronted Victorian home in West Brompton to this former rectory in a Suffolk village.

Back then, I had romantic dreams of living out our lives in rural bliss, growing old together (while remaining supple and attractive) and launching our children on to rich and satisfying careers and well-balanced personal lives. On the advice of my terrifying agent, Mimi Stanhope, I had eschewed the lure of private school for the little Smugges and enrolled them at the village primary, fondly believing that it would be good for my brand and would win me a whole new horde of followers. I remember walking on to the playground in my carefully curated on-trend outfit with Sofija trotting along behind me and realising that I had seriously misjudged the situation. In London, people expected me to be living my best life, to wear a different outfit every day and to be well groomed at all times. In Suffolk, not so much.

Taking some deep, cleansing breaths, I mused on the last three years. True, I had made two enemies, one of whom, the forthright Liane Bloomfield, had transitioned to a frenemy; the other, fellow playground mother Hayley Robinson, remaining very much anti-Smugge. But I could count the startlingly good-looking vicar, Tom, and his wife, Claire, as real friends, as well as my lovely fellow parent Lauren and a whole bunch of other school mums. I had mended my fractured relationship with my sister, Suze.

In other family related news, my mother had had a stroke, come to live with me and, as a result, interactions had become infinitely more friendly.

All this aside, I have been a single parent for nearly three years. Ever since Johnnie broke my heart by having an affair with Sofija, Isabella M Smugge has been the sole occupant of her beautifully dressed former marital bed. A brief and ill-advised bout of make-up sex with my husband led to the accidental conception of my fourth child (not that I'd be without him), and thus, in spite of a number of attempts on Johnnie's part to woo me back, I am alone.

I'd be lying if I said I never got lonely or yearned for someone to cuddle at night. All my friends, my mother and my sister have told me, categorically, never to take my cheating husband back, and so far I have been strong. His incredibly handsome chiselled features, piercing sapphire eyes, top-level grooming regime and personal charm are hard to resist, however. I fell so passionately in love with him all those years ago and it's been tough to stay focused.

Sleepily doing my Kegel exercises (as a woman passes into the dreaded Middle Years, it is ever more important to maintain really good pelvic floor health), I listened to the sound of soft breathing in my ear and felt the warm weight of a sleeping body next to mine. Is it so wrong to crave some company? I spend so much time writing about my life and sharing inspirational content with my followers across the socials, and while I have watched my brand grow ever more relatable as I navigate life without Johnnie at my side, still I yearn to be with someone, to be adored, to come first for a change.

I felt the tickle of whiskers on my cheek and the rasp of a tongue against my ear. The smell of fish was strong on my companion's breath, which was strange as the family had enjoyed an Ottolenghi Puy lentil and aubergine stew for supper last night. I rolled over and planted a kiss on my bed-mate's furry little head. She began meowing and bumping her head against mine, a sure sign that it was breakfast time. I swung my legs out of bed, did a couple of roll downs, pulled on my floral, lace-trimmed, stretch-woven dressing gown and super-comfy open-back textured metallic slippers and descended to the ground floor with the cat trotting eagerly at my heels. **#catowner #breakfast #bedsharing**

As one of the UK's most beloved lifestyle influencers and the woman that *Gorgeous Home* magazine once called 'Britain's Most Relatable Mum Designer', I need to stay at least three steps ahead of all the competition. Every week of late, it seems, a new, young and perky would-be competitor pops up on the 'gram or TikTok. I am trying not to mind. Yes, I did invent lifestyle blogging as a valid career, and it's true that I have a devoted following, all of whom hang on to Issy Smugge's every carefully curated word. However, the road to oblivion is paved with bad decisions and unwise outbursts on Twitter (or whatever it's calling itself these days) and I cannot afford to rest on my sustainably grown laurels for a minute.

With only the cat for company, I enjoyed my first double-strength cappuccino of the day in peace. Walking across the Indian sandstone kitchen floor, I took a deep breath and tried to ground myself in the now. I am constantly racing ahead to the next achievement, the next product placement, the next glittering prize, and if three years in Suffolk have taught me anything (and they have), it is that life is precious. My dear friend Claire was at death's door when she had her fourth child, Ben, the year I arrived in the village, and the shock of nearly losing her, plus the trauma of Mummy's stroke the August before last, really made me think about what I value in life.

Sunlight was streaming through my sparklingly clean windows as I walked outside and sank on to the reproduction Edwardian garden love seat by the pond. Birds were singing melodiously, the sun was warm on my freshly exfoliated face and a gentle breeze was whispering in the branches of the birch tree. I had left my phone in the kitchen deliberately, although this was an excellent opportunity to take a few of my justly famed images to post across the socials with a handful of appropriate hashtags. As my life continues to depart from the plan Johnnie and I laid out for it when we first met, I'm finding that I'm less keen to show off. Coming from the UK's premier Instamum, that may sound baffling. But as I try to be a better parent, friend and daughter, and continue to dip my toe into church life, I'm changing.

Facing up to the trauma of being sent away to boarding school at seven, the long-buried pain of losing my father and my godmother in an accident abroad at the age of twelve, and the realisation that I have been in a relationship with a coercively controlling (albeit dazzlingly handsome and charming) man for most of my adult life has taken its toll. I used to think my life was perfect and I certainly gave that impression on my social media. These days, I'm far more likely to post a funny story about a broken nail or a wonky cupcake or a parenting fail than to pump out wall-to-wall images of my carefully curated life. Yes, I still have standards, and yes, millions of devoted followers look to me daily for advice on the correct paint colours or how to tablescape really well. But I'm letting my slip show a lot more, and that's something I never thought I'd hear myself say. **#authenticity #realme**

My mother is getting married next month, and having hosted my friend Kate's nuptials in the summer, I am very much in the zone. The Old Rectory is mood board central at present! I will shortly be acquiring a stepfather, two stepbrothers and a stepsister, and while three out of four of them are pro-me, the fourth is certainly not. Harry Cottingham, my mother's fiancé, has three children by his late wife, and the youngest, Karen, is not a fan of any of us.

At the Grand Meeting of the Families in August, Mark and Karl, their wives and children all made a huge effort to be friendly and welcoming. Karen, however, is quite another matter. She scowled pretty much throughout the entire meal, sat next to her father and sighed loudly every time he spoke to Mummy or held her hand. The man is seventy, for heaven's sake, and he's been a lonely widower for several years.

I admit, I struggled when I first met him. Seeing my mother giggling and playing footsie under the table raked up all kinds of painful feelings. I loved my father very much and I never got to say goodbye to him or have him walk me down the aisle, nor did he meet his grandchildren. The pain of that, I suspect, will never really go away. However, in my constant attempt to become a better person (albeit it via several screaming rows with Mummy), I have now accepted Harry and he is a lovely man.

Harry's had a significant effect on my mother's general health. Not only does she smile far more regularly these days, but also, after many years of fruitless nagging from me and Suze, she finally gave up her cigarette habit. It seems that Harry's wife was a heavy smoker and died from pneumonia, having had a lung complaint for years. Give Mummy her due, once she decides to do something, she sticks to it, and although she often admits that she misses the joy of sucking a cocktail of addictive and toxic substances into her lungs, she has not yet fallen off the wagon. Which makes her a much more pleasant housemate. Karen, on the other hand, is an enthusiastic consumer of the evil weed and is trying to lure Mummy back into her old habits.

In addition, I came face to face with my arch nemesis, the muck-raking gossip columnist Lavinia Harcourt at our school reunion. Things got a little out of hand, but after a stern talking-to from our former headmistress and a promise from both of us never to engage in fisticuffs in the sacred precincts of St Dymphna's ever again, we agreed to meet on neutral ground to talk about our considerable differences. But more of that later.

And as if my life as a single parent of four and internationally renowned lifestyle blogger and mumfluencer wasn't complex enough, my husband has started going out with a twenty-four-year-old work colleague called Paige (I ask you!), got himself a tattoo and inadvertently started a new family. Young Paige is now two months pregnant and suffering from rampant heartburn plus sickness which refuses to confine itself to the mornings but continues for most of the day. I know this, and quite a lot more besides, since he is a chronic over-sharer.

From the top, then, my to-do list looks like this:

1. Prepare nutritionally balanced breakfast every day for four children who all like different things.

2. Ensure three of said children have everything they need for a full day of education while thinking about potty training for the fourth (is he too young? I must consult Claire).

3. Help Mummy to pull off a stunning, on-trend wedding celebration.

4. Reach out to Karen.

5. Make Karen like me.

6. Make Karen like Mummy.

7. Meet Paige.

8. Introduce Paige to children.

9. Deal with inevitable fallout of introducing Paige to children.

10. Manage not to give Lavinia Harcourt a smack when we meet at a chi chi cocktail bar in town.

And that's before the everyday grind of school runs, homework, after-school clubs and what are laughingly called enrichment activities! Do I need any more in my life? I think not! **#busymum #newterm #blendedfamily**

I can't quite believe that I have children going into Years Eight, Five and Three. It seems like yesterday that I was dropping my little Finn off at nursery on the first day and crying all the way home. I'm looking forward to getting back into the school routine, if I'm honest. Trying to juggle work and children is no joke. I don't know how people without staff and plenty of disposable income do it.

I was taking the jug of mango, pineapple and passionfruit juice out of the fridge (packed full of vitamins, so good for the growing child) and putting out my navy-blue crackle glaze breakfast set when Finn appeared. He's inherited his father's dark hair and blue eyes but, as yet, none of his less attractive qualities.

'Morning, Mum. Fancy some toast?'

He poured himself a glass of juice and put two slices of organic granary bread in the toaster.

'Go on, then. I think we've got some of Wendy's blackcurrant jam in the fridge.'

When we bought the Old Rectory, we inherited the gardener, Ted Ling, as well as a Victorian greenhouse and a thriving vegetable garden. The Smugge larder is kept well stocked with fresh tomatoes, salad greens, courgettes, cucumbers, beans (French, runner and borlotti), radishes, sweetcorn and pumpkins, and most of the contents of the fruit cage go straight to Wendy and Sue, the jam makers at church, who turn it into jars of the most delicious preserves.

I sat next to my boy at the island as we munched on our toast and jam.

'So, are you OK about today, darling?' I enquired, taking a sip of my second single origin cappuccino of the day.

'Yeah. It's all good, Mum. Don't worry.' Finn glanced at the clock. 'I'd better go. I'm meeting Jake and Zach at the bus stop.'

I leaned over and kissed him. 'Have you got everything? Pencil case? Geometry set? Lunch?'

'I had it last night when you asked me and nothing's changed since then. See you!'

Slinging his rucksack over his shoulder, he walked out of the front door and slammed it before I could set up the traditional back-to-school shot. I'll have to do it when he gets home and put a filter on it so it looks like early morning. What kind of multi-award-winning influencer forgets to take a picture of her own son on his first day of school? I'm off my game.

I could hear the tap of Mummy's stick on the stairs, Milo's voice on the baby monitor and Elsie calling from upstairs. As I was stirring Mummy and Milo's porridge, whizzing up a fruit smoothie for Chloë, putting two more slices of bread in the toaster and getting out a jar of organic *Ricca Crema Spalmabile al Cioccolato, Arancia e Nocciole* chocolate spread (Italian, rich, indulgent and one of my new paid partnerships), Mummy appeared.

'Good morning, darling. Has Finn gone already? I wanted to wish him good luck for his first day. Milo's shouting for you. I think he's done something in his pants. There's the most frightful smell drifting down the landing.'

My eye darted involuntarily to the chocolate spread with which Elsie is obsessed. Another day of parenting was upon me and I honestly didn't know if I was ready for it.

Walking onto the playground with Chloë stalking ahead and my little Elsie clutching my hand, I spotted Lauren with her three girls.

'Hi, babes! Nice shoes.'

I realised, to my horror, that I was still wearing my super-comfy open-back textured metallic slippers. I'd meant to change them before we left, but in all the flurry of trying to find Elsie's bookbag and realising that the kitchen clock was five minutes slow and that we were therefore in danger of being late on the first day back, it had completely slipped my mind.

'Yes,' I lied, thinking quickly. 'All the rage this season. Ideal for autumn/winter transitioning and so comfortable.'

'They look a bit like slippers to me, but what do I know about fashion? Are yours all excited about coming back to school?'

'I wouldn't say excited exactly. Finn was OK this morning, but I never get much out of him. How about the girls?'

She sighed. 'Crystal couldn't sleep last night for worrying. She doesn't do well with change. She settled great last year but now she's gone up into the next class, she's got herself in a right state. I'm half expecting a call from Mrs Hill before I get home.'

Mrs Hill is the friendly and efficient powerhouse who runs the school in conjunction with our head teacher, Mrs Tennant. I never used to worry about anything to do with lunch payments, school trips or forms when Sofija ran the show at the Old Rectory, but these days, with only a housekeeper, gardener, part-time nursery nurse and manicurist on the staff, I have to be a lot more hands-on.

The playground was filling up with parents holding the hands of tiny children dressed in over-large school uniforms. The start of the autumn term is the time when mothers (and sometimes fathers) hand over their four and five-year-olds and realise that they are at both the beginning and the end of a new season of life. Miss Moss, the kindly Reception teacher, was bending down to speak to her new students and tactfully ignoring the sobbing women holding their hands. Looking back to when my little Elsie started Reception, I remember feeling a sense of relief that another of my children had been fed into the omnivorous maw of full-time education. The very notion of dressing my precious baby boy in little grey trousers, a white polo shirt, navy-blue sweatshirt and black school shoes, however, brought the tears rushing to my eyes.

'Look at them!' Lauren was gazing across the playground. 'I was a mess when Pearl went up from nursery. It's always worse when it's your last one.'

I squinted over at the Reception line. A woman dressed in skin-tight jeans, high-heeled ankle boots and a leather jacket and sporting a pair of over-sized gold hoop earrings was embracing a little girl with two neat blonde French plaits tied with navy blue ribbon. As the bell rang and the line of minute people trotted off to their classroom, their mothers surged to the glass window of the corridor, waving and blowing kisses.

'Is Liane's youngest going into Reception? I didn't realise she was old enough.'

But Lauren had broken into a trot and was heading at top speed for Crystal's line where her daughter was sitting on the ground with her arms folded and her head down, scowling mutinously. My PTA enemies Hayley and Chris Robinson scuttled past, making sure to avoid making eye contact, which was absolutely fine with me. Standing alone in my slippers, I felt a little isolated, but just then, Maddie, Kate and Lovely Lou appeared.

'Ooh, nice shoes! They look as comfy as slippers. Is that the trend this autumn?'

I came out with the autumn/winter transitioning line again which my friends swallowed without question. We were catching up on the news when I spotted Liane walking quickly past. There has been a summer cold going around (I never catch anything thanks to my high vitamin intake, balanced diet, good exercise routine and daily echinacea capsule) with which she has clearly come down. Her eyes were red and puffy, the eyeliner and mascara around them smeared and her nose running.

'Liane! Have you got that cold that's going round?'

I let out a muffled yelp as Maddie's foot connected with my ankle.

'I'm fine, Smug. Double eye infection if you must know.'

Issy Smugge never misses a chance to share the bounty which life has poured out upon her.

'I've got some amazing eyedrops back at home. *Yeux Pétillants de Beauté.* They're wonderful. Do you want me to bring them for pick-up time?'

My frenemy shoved her hands into her jacket pockets and sped away towards the gate. I was somewhat taken aback. While I wouldn't say that we were friends, exactly, still our relationship is relatively amicable and she has gone so far as to say a few nice things by accident over the past few months.

Lauren appeared back in our midst, looking grim.

'Great start to the term. I pretty much had to drag her into the classroom. So, what's all the news and schmooze, ladies?'

We walked slowly out of the playground, none of us that keen to get back home.

'What's up with Liane?' I asked. 'I offered her some eyedrops and she barely spoke. Have I done something to upset her?'

The girls exchanged looks.

'No, babes, it's not you.' Lauren was the spokeswoman. 'Her little one started Reception today and it's hit her hard. Plus the anniversary of her dad's death's coming up. She's not in a good place. When she's like that, we know to leave her alone. She'll talk when she's ready.'

Not for the first time, I realised that I live in a community that is loosely stitched together with intricately woven relationships, dynamics and a shared history. Try as I may, I will never truly be a part of it. The smell of coffee was drifting enticingly out of the new café on the high street and I yearned to leave my responsibilities behind for an hour and enjoy my friends' company. But I couldn't. Over the summer break, I allowed myself some downtime with the children and didn't schedule every single day of the school holidays with a mixture of enrichment activities and work. I had a lot of work to catch up on.

At the village centre, we divided, Lauren to go to the Post Office to stock up on party bag fillers for her daughter's upcoming birthday celebrations, me heading back home. My friend gave me a brief hug and a side eye.

'You forgot to take your slippers off this morning, didn't you?'

I sighed. 'Yes. Of course I did.' **#losingit #platespinning**

Returning home, I found Mummy and Milo constructing what appeared to be a multi-use modernist building with a large box of sustainably made educational bricks in the family room. I never thought I'd see the day.

I walked down to my studio and unlocked the door. I had a Zoom call scheduled with Mimi. My agent is wonderful at what she does and has advanced Isabella M Smugge's career no end. However, she is not exactly relaxing company and she can spot a creeping uncertainty or a moral quandary a mile off. I checked my lipstick, tidied my hair and prepared for the onslaught.

'Darling! How *are* you? Looking incredible. I simply *loved* your latest blog about plate spinning in your forties. Honesty really sells, in moderation.' She let out a hoarse laugh and took an enthusiastic drag on her cigarette.

'Now. Sweetie. I'm in talks with the people at the *Sunday Times* and *Vogue*. They both want you for serious lifestyle and fashion spreads. *Ascendancy* magazine wants to do a feature on you – working title 'The Influencer's Influencer'. And I have some terrific news. Brace yourself.'

I had been bracing since the moment her corrugated features appeared on my screen, and felt it was time to take a breath.

'Fire away, Mimi. I can't wait.'

My agent leaned forward and puffed out a cloud of smoke.

'I've been keeping a weather eye on the shenanigans at Belle Peinture. I saw Bill Stoddart and Hugo Parker in the smoking room at my club the other night. They were obviously having a private conversation, but nothing gets past Mimi.'

She paused for a second, giving me a chance to reply, which I declined to take. It's best to let Mimi spill all her beans before commenting, I've found over the years. Belle Peinture, as you no doubt know, is the gorgeously expensive mineral-based paint company used by anyone who's anyone and several who are aspiring to be. Bill, Hugo and Hugo's brother-in-law Mark Power are the founder members and run a very tight ship. For years, Mimi has been angling for a paid partnership with them but to no avail. She coughed and stubbed out her cigarette.

'I hid behind the chiffonier and listened in. Wonderful news, darling! Mark has left the company and is starting his own paint firm! You know what a maverick he is. I can't believe he's lasted as long as he has. It all came to a head with his attempt to drive through his Hanoverian paint range. I heard whispers about it around town and it's even more exciting than I thought.'

My heart missed a beat and I felt a surge of excitement run through me from my gorgeous gel pedicure (deep Burgundy, so this season) to my freshly lowlighted hair. I had all but decided to source the paint and wall coverings for my second-floor renovation from Belle Peinture and jolly well foot the bill myself. In order to pull off a truly show-stopping reno, the savvy influencer must think through every tiny detail and overlook nothing. The paint, of course, is the foundational element but the correct flooring, storage, light fittings and decorative touches are also absolutely vital if one is to stay on top of the trends while being sustainable and relatable. My followers simply adore it when I redecorate, and I must confess that I do love the whole process.

I took a sip of my skinny latte and settled back to hear what Mimi had to say.

'I know you're far too stylish to fall into the obvious decorating traps, darling. No muted Regency shades for *you*! I went straight from the club to have a late-night drinkie with Venetia. She's finally gone ahead with the surgery and got her elbows done while she was at it, and I have to say she's looking almost human.'

Venetia Portarlington is almost as terrifying as Mimi, a hugely successful agent who manages Daisy Finch, the cleaning blogger, along with a whole host of other influencers and media tarts. Of indeterminate age, with a dowager's hump, beady eyes and a sixth sense for juicy gossip, she is not a woman you would wish to fall out with. They say that she could bring half of London's CEOs to their knees if she so chose.

Mimi lit a fresh cigarette.

'Venetia heard that he's calling the company Bitter and Twisted. So gorgeously dark and unpleasant, just like him!'

She laughed in a rasping baritone.

'Venetia's still in touch with her second husband's step-niece. You know, the head colourist at Belle Peinture. Mark's poached her and she told Venetia all about the Hanoverian range. Lots of deep, dark, vintage colours with amusing names and a few lighter ones to break it up. Perfect for you to use as accent colours and for your reno. No good at all for those dreadful little boxes that normal people live in, and of course far too expensive for the everyday market.'

I was feeling a little unsure. While my readers and followers love me revealing new and exciting trends, most of them don't live in vast Grade II listed former rectories with unlimited decorating budgets. Call me old-fashioned (although no one ever has), but what your everyday house owner really wants is a nice reliable selection of pale hues with the odd pop of colour.

'I don't know, Mimi. It all sounds very now, but is he going to do anything more down to earth? You know, something my followers will actually buy.'

My agent waved her scarlet-tipped hand dismissively.

'Don't give it another thought, darling. That's what you pay Mimi for. I'll call as soon as I've got the colours out of Venetia.'

As you will know if you follow twenty-first-century paint trends, Michaela Gotts was the head colourist at Belle Peinture, the woman *Paint Chips Today* called 'the mineral-based wizard of her generation' and the co-founder and presenter of the 'Gottcha!' podcast which covers the gorgeous and far-reaching world of paints and wallpapers. There's nothing that woman doesn't know about interiors. For some time now, Mummy and I have been thinking about having her on our podcast and now that she's finally jumped ship, she'll have even more fascinating paint gossip for us.

Mimi and I wrapped up our conversation. I could almost hear the cogs whirring in her head. A new paid partnership, an achingly trendy product and the potential to lure a high-octane guest on to our podcast. Say what I will about my agent, she certainly is 100 per cent behind my brand. She stubbed out her cigarette and waggled her nicotine-stained fingers at me.

'Love you, sweetie, miss you, mwah, mwah!'

And with a final bone-rattling cough, she was gone, leaving me to ponder how on earth I was going to stay calm and focused with a to-do list that would put anyone to shame. **#busybusy #trendscout**

In the old days, I raced through the week in a flurry of carefully curated gorgeousness, scheduling blocks of quality time with the children which involved a few heart-warming and wholesome family posts and never thinking that they might be missing out on something. Or that I was. I honestly believed that I was living my best life and being an amazing mother. Back then, living in London with my devoted husband, wonderful au pair and right-hand woman Sofija, huge circle of friends and glittering social life, I thought my life was perfect.

These days, my routine is quite different. Yes, I am almost entirely housework-free (unless you count wiping crumbs and blobs of random stickiness off the island and using my multi-head mini vacuum cleaner to run along the skirting boards). Yes, Ali, my devoted housekeeper, does all the washing, drying and ironing for me. Yes, I have a team devoted to keeping Issy Smugge looking dewy, fresh and radiant at all times. But apart from that, I'm just a normal, everyday mum, making breakfast, loading the dishwasher, doing the school run, checking bookbags, sorting out packed lunches (OK, Ali does them, but I do get them out of the fridge), helping with reading and homework and generally maintaining the emotional well-being of four children.

As the evenings got slightly darker and my Virginia creeper began to turn from vivid green to a bright shouting red, the smell of woodsmoke and the crunch of fallen leaves became the backdrop to my twice-daily walk to school and back. I do love autumn, but this year, rather than focusing on doorscaping and planning my menus and starting to think about the perfect Christmas, I have a wedding to get through.

When I was still a happily married London-based mother of three, I'd have laughed in your face if you'd told me that my mother would ever be:

1. Getting married again.

2. Happy and relatively positive much of the time.

3. An evangelical non-smoker.

4. Actually pleasant to me and the children.

When we first moved to Suffolk, she was cold and judgemental to me and ultra-critical of the children. Being forced to spend a year together under the same roof has worked wonders for our relationship. The children actively enjoy spending time with her, she simply adores Milo, and she has become infinitely warmer and more loving. True, she has, by some miracle, found a man who has voluntarily offered to spend the rest of his life with her and that's made quite a difference, but I think that actually getting to know me as a person has changed her entire outlook on life.

Milo calls her 'Gandy', which is as close as he can get to 'Granny', and it's become a general nickname with the children, which is rather sweet. That said, she hasn't changed completely. She is still prone to loud, embarrassing comments in public and to interfering in my life. I was enjoying a rare moment of peace in the family room post-school run, sipping my coffee and leafing through an interiors magazine when she appeared.

'Now, darling. Don't be cross. I'm coming with you when you go to meet the Harcourt girl in London.'

I let my magazine slide to the floor.

'What? I don't need *you* there breathing down my neck. Lavinia and I are old enough to deal with our own affairs.'

Mummy frowned. 'That's clearly not true, Isabella. Look at what happened when you met up for the first time since school. You screamed at each other like a pair of fishwives and ended up having a fist fight! So common! I think it's far better if we stay at my club and I sit quietly in the cocktail bar and keep an eye on things.'

'Come on, Mummy! She's harboured a grudge for years because I cut off her plait, which she deserved.'

My revenge on my sister's school tormenter had been to sneak into her dorm as she slept and snip off one of her precious long golden plaits. Lavinia had never forgiven me and, as a top gossip columnist, used her paper to disseminate horrible stories about me.

Mummy and I wrangled for some time, but she would not be moved. Great! I'm going to be forty-two next June and my own mother thinks I need a babysitter. **#cringe #helicopterparenting**

The weeks trundled on without incident and the day of my meeting with Lavinia Harcourt drew ever nearer. I was trying to remain calm but at night, fast asleep in my beautifully dressed bed, my head nestling on my self-plumping, lavender-scented

Plump No More pillows, my overactive brain took refuge in the most alarming dreams.

I was skiing down a black run, being pursued by Lavinia wielding a machine gun, when Mummy suddenly appeared and told me she was marrying Joey Essex. Then the scene switched to my old house in London with Johnnie telling me that he had a second wife and family down the road in Fulham and that I mustn't mind too much. The next minute, I was back at St Dymphna's in front of the class trying to read from a book of Latin poetry which had unaccountably been translated into Russian. It was a huge relief when I awoke at 5.45 to the sound of Milo crying.

By the time I'd got him back to sleep, I was wide awake myself. I pulled on my dressing gown and walked downstairs. I flung open the boot room door to commune with nature and got a faceful of the most unpleasant odour. I couldn't place it, but it was most noxious. Deciding that I'd had more than enough fresh air for the day, I closed the door again and made myself a comforting hot chocolate. No one else was up and I didn't feel inclined to start work just yet, so I curled up on the sofa in the family room and closed my eyes. Our startlingly good-looking vicar Tom always encourages us to pray at all times, so I thought I'd give it a go.

I was halfway through my list of requests when I lost consciousness. I woke, dribbling slightly and with my half-drunk chocolate stone cold, to the voices of my children quarrelling in the hall. Sighing, I heaved myself off the sofa and commenced another day of desperate overachieving in the face of some considerable opposition.

One of the great things about being self-employed is that if you fancy downing tools and having your bestie over for coffee and a chat, you can. I lured Lauren back from drop-off with the promise of high-quality caffeine and home-made ginger snaps.

Slumped on the sofa with our feet up on the ottoman and talking enthusiastically about what I was going to say to Lavinia, our conversation was interrupted by a chirrup from both our phones. I don't know about you, but there is no respite from emails about delayed buses, behaviour policies and the urgent need to buy textbooks and scientific calculators at one end of the spectrum right down to bump notes and invitations to class assemblies at the other. This one was from the primary school and was sharing the news that Elsie's class was suffering from an outbreak of nits.

As far as I know, none of my children's scalps have ever been infested. Or if they were, Sofija dealt with it in her usual efficient way without bothering me with the gruesome details. The point is that they are very clean and that it is next door to impossible that head lice could have become part of the Smugge family.

I shared these thoughts with Lauren.

'They never say who it is. Trouble is, at that age, there's a lot of contact and it only takes one untreated kid for it to spread. Are you honestly telling me yours have never had nits?'

I assured her that to the best of my knowledge, this was the case. Her phone rang.

'It's the school. Hang on, babes.'

There was a short pause while a voice at the other end imparted vital information which made my friend leap to her feet and grab her bag.

'I've got to run. Crystal's in the office with Mrs Hill in a right old state. See you later.'

And with a brief hug, she was gone, leaving me with my second half-drunk beverage of the day. Oh well.

On the playground at pick-up time, I found Lauren being comforted by our fellow mums Maddie and Lovely Lou. It seemed that Crystal had reacted badly to the teasing of one of her classmates. He had been needling her since the beginning of term and while Lauren had been working with the teacher to keep things on an even keel, today it had all been too much and her daughter had punched her enemy square on the nose in the middle of Literacy. This had led to a number of outcomes, namely:

1. From the huge amount of blood spurting from the said nose and the rapidly swelling nasal membranes, the teacher had diagnosed a broken nose and called the child's mother.

2. Said mother had come up to the school breathing out vengeance on Lauren and her entire family and threatening to sue the school for negligence.

3. The child had been rushed to A&E from where his mother was issuing regular bulletins via social media.

4. Liane Bloomfield had threatened to go round to the child's house and put his mother straight.

Poor Lauren was beside herself. Maddie handed over mopping up and comforting duties to Lou and filled me in.

'It's that new mum. You know, the family who moved into one of those big posh houses on the new estate? The Whitmores. She's the one that works in Ipswich at some office or other three days a week and is always going on about how she juggles her family and her fabulous career. Right braggy. I've tried talking to her but she's not interested. Her kid is a horrible little so-and-so.'

I was righteously indignant on Lauren's behalf.

'What can we do to help?'

Maddie looked grim.

'Well, for a start, we need to talk Liane down. She's never liked Sally, ever since she sneered at her in a singing assembly for being late. And she's mates with that Hayley Robinson. *She* wants to try working a week of night shifts and looking after five kids single-handed with no support from anyone.'

It seemed an ugly situation, violence spilling out in a safe space where our children went to learn and grow. I felt powerless. And all the more so when my little Elsie's class appeared and her teacher came up to me to share the shocking news, *sotto voce*, that my daughter's head was playing host to a full-on infestation. She handed me a leaflet.

'This will give you all the information you need. We ask that you treat Elsie immediately, then re-treat in a week's time.'

Clutching my leaflet, I gazed in horror at my daughter who was scratching her head enthusiastically and looking under her nails with great interest.

'I'm trying to see the eggs, Mummy. Becky says they're teeny-tiny. I can feel the lice wriggling on my head. It tickles!'

'Go and have a little play, darling. Mummy's a bit busy at the moment.'

I hoped that by encouraging my daughter to dash about the field with her friends, the Robinsons, standing uncomfortably close, might forget about what they had just heard. Not that that's very likely! **#nits #itchy #cringe**

My forthcoming meeting with Lavinia, headline news with the girls until Crystal punched Oliver Whitmore and nits came calling at the Old Rectory, had been bumped to Any Other Business. The mums' WhatsApp group was at fever pitch with constant updates on Crystal and Liane and the nit situation. Maddie took control and started a new group, 'Nit Help', to answer my increasingly desperate questions. It seems that you can apply a stinky lotion overnight then wash it out thoroughly the next morning, or you can apply another stinky and much runnier lotion and comb out the little critters with a nit comb an hour later. A number of mums also recommended investing heavily in tea tree oil products, which nits hate. Who knew? I opted for the first choice and sent my poor little girl to bed with a shower cap on her head complaining that liquid was running down her neck. I can only hope and pray that none of the other children get it.

Liane has been dissuaded from going round to the Whitmores and having it out with Sally, although what will happen when they see each other on the playground is anyone's guess.

Crystal is refusing to go to school ever again. Lauren is in despair. Oliver Whitmore is recovering at home. My suggestion of a mums' group breakfast at the new café for an emergency summit is being considered.

My head is itchy. Can adults get nits? I sincerely hope not. Lying, sleepless, in my lovely bed, I tried to banish images of hugely magnified head lice from my mind. I can never unsee the contents of that educational leaflet. Never!

I got up half an hour early to tackle my poor little Elsie's head. Naturally, Mummy has lots to say about the situation. She is being almost supportive, in an out-of-touch kind of way.

'Clean heads don't get lice, Isabella. That's what Nanny always used to say. She had a special comb and a bottle of olive oil in case you girls ever got them. Not that you did, of course. The very notion!'

I pushed the leaflet across the island.

'That's a myth, Mummy. Anyone can catch them. I'm going to the pharmacy this morning after drop-off to pick up some tea tree oil, shampoo and conditioner then I'm off for breakfast with the girls. Can you look after Milo for me?'

She agreed, idly scratching her head as she did so. Can it be…? We can only hope not. **#nithorror #playgrounddrama**

October

I am absolutely exhausted! A less driven and successful woman would have admitted defeat. However, Issy Smugge is not one to give up, and although I am at present unhealthily dependent upon caffeine and late-night bingeing of comforting boxsets about people in Regency times (such fun!), I know that the storm will pass.

My little Elsie is presently nit-free, as am I and Mummy. Thank heavens the other three didn't catch them. Mummy's remarks on the subject are seemingly endless. The family bathroom and my en suite are full of anti-louse products. I suspect that I am suffering from some kind of post-traumatic stress disorder as I only have to smell tea tree oil to feel an eye twitch coming on.

The week of my meeting with Lavinia, I took the girls to school and left Milo at home with Mummy. I walked on to the playground and there was Lauren, looking pale and drawn, with Ruby and Pearl in attendance. There was no sign of Crystal or the Whitmores. Chris and Hayley Robinson were lurking eagerly on the edge of a huddle of parents, drinking in poisonous nuggets of gossip. Nearly all of the girls in Elsie's class were sporting tightly plaited hair, or buns like miniature Victorians. There was a strong aroma of tea tree oil in the air.

Once we'd dropped the girls off, we walked up to the new café in the village for a much-needed Mums' Emergency Breakfast.

Thank heavens for the smiley lady who has decided to bring good coffee and a limited but excellent menu to our community. She has decorated in soothing tones of blue and grey with on-trend pendant lighting and mirrors. Mismatched vintage tables and chairs and distressed oak floorboards all add to the welcoming vibe. We bagged the big table by the window and ordered without restraint. Now was not the time to count pennies or calories. As plates of granary toast with bitter marmalade (me), full English breakfasts with extra beans and mushrooms (Liane and Lou), scrambled egg on toast (Maddie and Lauren) and a sausage bap with brown sauce (Kate) arrived, we gulped down our coffees and addressed the matter at hand.

'That woman's threatening you on Facebook, Loz! We can't have that. Who does she think she is?'

Liane was cutting savagely into her fried egg.

'Violence breeds violence. That's what they used to tell us at school.' Lou is the eternal peacemaker, but her calming words were having no effect on Liane.

'Moving here, strutting around like she owns the place, showing off about her big house and her fancy job and her perfect kids. She's worse than you ever were, Smug. She'd better hope I've calmed down a bit before she comes back on *our* playground.'

This was as close to a compliment as I was ever going to get from Liane. I beamed and tried not to feel too self-satisfied that she found Sally Whitmore considerably more annoying than me.

Poor Lauren was wiping away a tear.

'I feel so helpless. Crystal isn't sleeping and she's really suffering with anxiety. I don't want to have to move schools, but what else can I do? If I got her a place at a different primary, I'd have to take Ruby and Pearl out and they're both really happy in their classes.'

'What about calling a meeting with the mother and having Mrs Tennant there?'

I am known for my incredible problem-solving skills.

'What about letting me go round there to tell her what's what and then slashing her tyres to send a message?'

Liane had finished her breakfast and was eyeing the bowl of organic sugar crystals on the table as if it had done her a terrible and unforgiveable wrong. Try as I might, I couldn't seem to come up with a solution that worked for everyone. After a second round of coffees and some desultory chit-chat about how I was going to manage Lavinia ('Punch her in the eye, Smug, if she tries anything. Show her who's boss'), we walked down to the pharmacy to stock up on tea tree products. Most of the girls have at least one child with nits, some not, but as Lou says, prevention is better than cure.

The bell on the door rang as we walked in and the woman being served at the counter looked up, startled. She had a large carrier bag in each hand and had clearly been stocking up.

'Hello, Hayley. How are you?' Lou was smiling determinedly at my enemy while Liane folded her arms and scowled.

'I'm all right. Just taking steps to protect my Lysander.'

She attempted to scuttle past us but was stopped in her tracks by Liane.

'Been stockpiling, have we? I hope you've left something for the rest of us.'

She marched over to the shelves where the shampoo and conditioner stood.

'Raspberry and mango? Mint and chia seed? Coconut and lemon? That's it? Have you honestly bought every single bottle of tea tree, you complete selfish loser?'

Hayley shuffled rapidly towards the door, pursued by Liane. I could see that there was going to be an almighty row and that I wasn't going to be buying heavily scented anti-louse shampoo and conditioner from my local provider any time soon. **#fight #takingitoutside**

I don't know what I'd do without my lovely Claire. She was the first person to reach out when I pranced on to the school playground with Sofija three years ago, and she has been a loyal support to me ever since. She's not doing too well at present and I really want to make sure she knows that I am there for her. The day after the row between Hayley and Liane (eventually broken up by one of the boys from the butchers' who could see it was going to end in violence), I dropped the children at school and lured her back to the Old Rectory for coffee and toast. Milo and Ben get on very well and we were able to leave them playing with the contents of a large wicker basket of educational toys while I fired up the coffee machine. Mummy was upstairs talking to her friend Veronica Madingley on the phone and all was calm. Which makes a pleasant change.

'How are you? I haven't seen you really to talk to since we came back to school.'

Claire sighed and looked down at her hands.

'Tom and I are trying to get a diagnosis for Joel. It's been incredibly stressful and I know I've been hiding away. I'm sorry – it's not what everyone expects the vicar's wife to do – but I can't face up to all the everyday stuff when I'm trying to get my little boy the help he needs.'

In Issy Smugge's world, many problems are solved quickly and easily by the application of a large wad of cash. If I had a suspicion that any of my children had additional needs, I would be straight on the phone to the best private people in the country with my gold debit card at the ready. Saying this was pointless. And it would also be unkind. I contented myself with getting up and making Claire another latte.

'What are the school saying?'

My friend looked sad.

'Delayed global development for sure, but that covers a vast range of conditions. They think he does have a learning disability, but he's so young they can't really be sure. Tom and I want to get a diagnosis now so that we can get the right help for him. The school is being super-helpful, but there's no funding really and they're already so stretched.'

I could think of absolutely nothing to say that would be of any help, so contented myself with squeezing my friend's arm and sending good vibes her way.

'Anyway! Enough gloom and doom. How's the wedding prep?'

Claire's question was answered by Mummy appearing in our midst with her mobile clutched in her hand.

'Honestly! That woman! Only she could catch a disease like this! Oh, hello Claire. How are you?'

Pleasantries exchanged, Mummy sank into my statement teal velvet cocktail chair and shared the latest news. Her friend Veronica Madingley had been a hard yes on both the daytime and evening celebrations and had requested a twin room en suite in the quiet part of our local hotel (she suffers very badly with her tinnitus apparently), but had just rung to say that following a week away in the Cotswolds, she had developed Hot Tub Folliculitis, which is apparently A Real Thing.

Claire is the soul of politeness but this latest revelation caused her to choke on her latte and have to be banged on the back.

'Hot Tub Folliculitis, Mrs Neville? Surely you're joking.'

Mummy looked grim.

'I certainly am not! Only Veronica could get an illness from wallowing in a hot tub.'

I tried not to laugh. I really did. Most unfortunately, I looked over and caught Claire's eye, which set us both off. We threw back our heads and went off into peals of laughter with which Mummy joined in. Living with me has improved her sense of humour no end. We laughed heartily for some time as tears streamed down our faces and our coffee went cold.

When we'd pulled ourselves together, Mummy filled us in on the symptoms of Veronica's condition.

'It's quite common, apparently. There can be a lot of bacteria sloshing about in hot tubs and it makes your hair follicles go all red and itchy. Veronica has got loads of side issues associated with it – she would! – she's running a fever, she feels sick, she's got a sore throat and she's spending half her life in the loo. She already has issues in that department and I really don't want her having one of her episodes halfway through the speeches. I'm starting to wonder if the Jerusalem artichoke purée with the main course was a mistake. That woman's a martyr to her bowels.'

After a bit more chit-chat, Claire got up to go and gave me a hug.

'You're such a good friend, Isabella, thinking of me like this. And especially when you've got so much going on yourself. When's the meeting with Lavinia?'

Just the mention of my arch-enemy's name was enough to put my stomach into knots.

'Tomorrow. I can't say I'm looking forward to it.' **#confrontation #summit #enemy**

Not only do I have the long-awaited meet-up with my deadly enemy to look forward to, but I am also up to my eyes in wedding prep. Mummy spent much of her summer sitting outside by the mock orange or perched on a stool at my kitchen island ploughing through guest lists and table plans. Harry, her fiancé, is a willing and devoted sidekick but, like any sensible man, is letting her make all the big decisions.

'You just tell me what to wear and when to turn up, sweetheart,' he said, kissing her hand and gazing at her with affectionate devotion. 'You've got such marvellous taste that I know it will all be lovely. All I care about is that we're going to be together forever.'

I had to walk into the pantry and rearrange my cans of artisan tinned fish at this point (piquant little spiced sprats and Devon cuttlefish braised in ink, tomatoes and aromatic herbs – perfect for a kitchen supper), partly because I wanted to give them their privacy and partly because my eyes had filled with tears. I don't begrudge Mummy her late-flowering happiness, I really don't. But living with a woman who is passionately in love and who knows, absolutely, that that love is returned in full measure presses on all my sore spots. When Johnnie and I exchanged our vows on that sunny Saturday all those years ago, I honestly believed that we would be together forever. But it wasn't death that had come between us. It was another woman.

I allowed myself to let out a few quiet sobs, leaning my head against the pantry shelf neatly packed with store cupboard essentials such as organic cannellini beans, extra virgin olive oil from Puglia, spelt flour and jars of sustainable tamarind paste. It is sometimes painful watching Mummy fill her diary with breakfasts *à deux*, manageable country walks, romantic strolls by the sea and intimate suppers. I thought my future held endless vistas of bliss, but instead I'm alone and often overwhelmed, although I'd never admit to it.

I wiped my eyes (being careful not to smudge my two-toned eyeliner and Endless Luscious Lash mascara), took a deep breath and returned to the kitchen where Mummy and Harry had their heads together and were giggling over the guest list.

Their wedding coordinator, Lucinda Moss, an incredibly efficient woman who is never seen without a clipboard in one hand and a mobile phone in the other, has been a marvel. With infinite tact, she has steered Mummy away from several unwise choices and managed to persuade her that no one in their right minds is having pâté, chicken and lemon tart at their wedding feast any more. There was a brief spat around reception drinks and the pros and cons of sherry, but Mummy has now rubberstamped Lucinda's suggestion of a gorgeous contemporary botanical cocktail (gin-based, natch) mixed with organic elderflower cordial, lemon juice and apple juice, mildly bruised mint leaves and strips of fresh cucumber artfully arranged in a sturdy short glass. Which is, of course, ideal for the older, more trembly hand. Many of the wedding guests will be of riper years and I have been having nightmares about fragile champagne flutes being smashed to smithereens by those who have, quite literally, lost their grip.

I can only hope and pray that there are no unfortunate incidents with posh ladies who fell out decades ago over something stupid, and that Karen behaves herself. Fat chance! **#weddingstress #weddingplanner #sherrynosherry**

The day of my meet-up with Lavinia dawned cold and wet. Peering out of my bedroom window, I watched as sheets of rain lashed the trees in the garden and the wind sent leaves flying all over my reproduction Edwardian love seat and into the pond. I peeled off my *Masque Hydratant Intense Pour Elle* overnight extra-dewy face sheet to reveal a glowing complexion. Apart from an ill-advised puff on a menthol cigarette behind the lacrosse shed in Year Nine at St Dymphna's, I have never ingested tobacco and I am sure that this is at least part of the reason for my flawless English rose complexion. Lavinia looks to be on about eighty a day and will soon have a face like a map of rural Norfolk. I turned on the shower and stood underneath it for ten minutes thinking calming thoughts. It seemed as convenient a time as any to commune with the good Lord, who presumably knew all about my assignation.

'Dear God. This is Issy Smugge. I hope You don't mind me getting in touch while I'm in the shower. I won't lie to You, I'm quite nervous about this meeting with Lavinia. And also about Mummy coming along. She's completely in the wrong (Lavinia, that is), but she won't have it. And I don't want a loud drunken row in a cocktail bar. I'd be terribly grateful if You could intervene in some way. I know You've got world peace and so on to deal with, and this seems fairly insignificant in the grand scheme of things, but I really would be so very appreciative. With many thanks.'

I seized my organic biodegradable loofah, squeezed some rosemary and cracked black pepper cleansing wash on to it and gave myself a jolly good scrub. Since Johnnie left, I have let myself go a lot more *au naturel* but I still have standards. Just because no one sees the bits of me between neck and knees is no reason not to exfoliate, cleanse and moisturise daily. **#selfcare**.

Remembering poor Claire's struggles, I added a PS to my prayer.

'Oh, and please can You help Claire and Tom with the whole business with getting a diagnosis for Joel? I mean, You can do anything, right? When You look at everything else going on, this isn't a biggie. With very best wishes.'

I rinsed off my intensely nourishing conditioner, turned off my raindrop shower and wrapped myself in a luxurious Egyptian cotton bath sheet. Only an application of extra rich eye cream and a slick of lip scuffing balm, the perfect outfit and shoes, fragrance layering and immaculately styled hair stood between me and the meeting with my old enemy.

I worked like crazy for the rest of the day and by the time I collected the girls from school, I was as ready to face Lavinia as I was ever going to be. I kissed the children goodbye, gave Lauren her final briefing (she's staying over with the girls and holding the fort) and helped Mummy into the back seat of the car.

As the gleaming car drove out of the village and onto the A12 (I always use the most marvellous service which sends me such charming drivers), Mummy pulled her wedding planning notebook out of her on-trend soft textured leather tote bag and began making copious notes. Having disappointed her aristocratic parents by refusing a marriage proposal from a marquess and disobliged them yet further by insisting on getting engaged to a man with no title, no estate and a pair of happily married parents with a complete set of fish cutlery, her Big Day, apparently, was not exactly filled with joy. The second time around, marrying a man she truly loves and with nearly everyone absolutely delighted about it, she is giddy with excitement.

Leaving her to annotate her seating plan and fuss about colours, I gazed out of the window at the bright blue autumn sky framed with trees whose leaves were gradually turning ruby, bronze and golden. Since becoming friends with Claire, I have found myself speaking to the Almighty on a relatively regular basis (although generally fully clothed and not in the shower), and He has been most helpful in answering many of my requests. I sent the third one of the day up now.

'Dear God. Isabella Smugge again. Sorry to bother You. I know I mentioned this before, and sorry to repeat myself, but I'm really worried about this whole Lavinia thing. What if she gets drunk and attacks me, or one of her people paps me or Mummy embarrasses me? I don't suppose she believes in You, but if You could see Your way clear to keeping things on an even keel, I would hugely appreciate it. Also, I know Lauren is brilliant with the children, but if You could keep an eye on the Old Rectory as well, I'm sure I could see my way clear to giving a chunk of cash to the fabric fund at church. Kindest regards. Amen.'

Having alerted God to my immediate needs, I carried on working while Mummy rustled around with sheaves of paper covered in notes. It's a good thing she's got one of the UK's premier lifestyle experts on her side. I've helped her to buy exactly the right wedding dress (cornflower blue in a very forgiving material with lace detail), talked her through floral looks, persuaded her not to have a traditional wedding cake with pillars (I ask you!) and agreed to walk her down the aisle. Suze is holding her up on one side while I even things up on the other. The guests will see two strong women marching a third to her fate, while Suze and I know that she's far too proud to use her stick in public. Compromise is a wonderful thing. **#herecomesthebride #family #support**

We were coming up to Colchester when she finally spoke.

'Now, Isabella, I know what you'll say so don't interrupt me. I've invited Audrey Harcourt along tonight. It will be super to catch up (Rupert hardly ever lets her leave the house, from what I understand) and we can sit discreetly at a table at the back and keep an eye on things.'

I gazed at my mother in horror. Whole weeks can go by without me fantasising about maiming her or dreaming of the day she moves out. But this was completely unacceptable.

'You've done *what*? How old do you think I am? I can manage to have a civilised conversation without my mother sitting there looking over my shoulder with my nemesis' mother right next to her. You're *so* embarrassing!'

Mummy tutted loudly.

'Nonsense, darling! You don't know how lucky you are to have me. Imagine being landed with a mother like poor Audrey, weak as water and with no get up and go at all! Heaven only knows how Lavinia's managed to get as far as she has in life. I'm doing this for *you*. I don't want to have to sit there drinking cocktails and making small talk. I'd much rather relax at the club with a G&T and sort out the guest list.'

'Well, why don't you, then? Tell Audrey your sciatica's flared up and you can't meet her. I don't want you there breathing down my neck.'

She responded in the old, angry, spiky way and I found myself having a most unseemly fight with her and trying not to notice the driver's eyes wandering to the back seat.

'Honestly, Isabella, you're so ungrateful sometimes! All the things I do for you.'

'And how about me? Taking you in and arranging care for you after the stroke and sorting you out a social life. It hasn't been easy, you know.'

'I'm sorry I've been such a burden to you, Isabella. Thank heavens Harry came along when he did and that soon I'll be out from under your feet.'

I sighed heavily. 'That's all very well, Mummy, but you *are* going to be under my feet tonight. Literally. In the same cocktail bar staring at me as I try to act like an adult with that terrible woman who lives for gossip and scandal. I can just imagine what she'll be writing in her column.' I put on an impression of Lavinia's drawling voice. '"Which middle aged has-been influencer was recently spotted in town with her mother, washed-up interior designer Caroline Neville? Are the rumours true? Is Isabella M Smugge so over that she has to take her mother out for dinner with her? Watch this space, dear readers, as I reveal how all of the babbling blogger's friends have dropped her like a hot potato." Honestly, Mummy, you're playing right into her hands!'

My mother's lips thinned and she narrowed her eyes.

'Washed up? Charming! I'll have you know that several glossy magazines have approached me and asked me to write a column for them. You're not the only cat in the litter tray, you know!'

There was nothing more to be said. I folded my arms and turned away and, judging by the icy silence that descended over the car, so did Mummy. The rest of the journey passed by without incident and as we drew up at the bar, instructing the driver to take our luggage on to the club, I could see that I would have more to contend with tonight than a bitchy arch-enemy and the potential of being papped. **#embarrassing #ohmummy**

Even allowing for a rapidly consumed continental breakfast sent to my room at Mummy's club and minimal packing (Issy Smugge is surely the queen of the packers – check out my blog series on 'Stress-Free Weekends Away and Beyond' if you don't believe me), it was gone eleven o'clock in the morning when our car finally nosed gratefully back up the drive of the Old Rectory. Mummy had spent most of the journey with her eyes closed (either in a light doze or unconscious due to overconsumption of alcohol, I couldn't tell you which) and had accepted my offer of two extra-strength painkillers shortly after we left the club.

I had been bracing myself for a difficult evening spent in the company of my arch-enemy, but nothing could have prepared me for what actually happened. I was so distracted that I only managed to draft half a blog and post some gorgeous images of cocktails and small plates. I spent the rest of our journey back to Suffolk gazing out of the window and allowing my mind to whirl.

Back home, all seemed to be well. Mummy made herself a double-strength black coffee and went upstairs to lie down. I found Lauren in the snug with her feet up on my thrillingly modish velvet swivel navy footstool (incorporating hidden storage). She had a coffee in her hand and was reading what appeared to be a novel. I had begged her to stay in the peaceful surroundings of my lovely home once she had done the school run.

Entreating her not to get up under any circumstances, I went into the kitchen to make myself a much-needed double-shot cappuccino. Steaming mug in hand and back in the snug, I sank on to the footstool's companion, my wickedly comfortable fluted Art Deco style navy-blue sofa with its on-trend hand-tufted cushions in dusky pink.

Lauren closed her book and fixed me with a beady eye.

'So? How was it? I managed not to text you but I am *dying* to know what happened! Was there a punch-up?'

I launched into the preamble of my row with Mummy in the car before recalling that I should at least ask if the children were all right. Lauren clapped her hand to her mouth and gave me a full rundown.

'What are we like? All good last night, kids ate their tea fine, we played on the Xbox together, no rows, Milo went down like an angel, slept through the night, no probs this morning. I took him to the park and we had a good runaround. I love staying at yours. It's like a luxury hotel. Carry on.'

I had just got to the bit where Mummy told me that she was bringing Audrey Harcourt to the bar to keep an eye on me and Lavinia ('No actual *way*! You're kidding, babes!'), when we were interrupted by the unwelcome sound of our phones beeping. It was testament to the quality of Lauren's devotion to Issy Smugge and all her works that she merely glanced at the screen, murmured, 'Nits again,' and begged me to continue.

Naturally, I arrived a full fifteen minutes early at Freudian Sip, the pretentious cocktail bar chosen by Lavinia for our discussion. And of course, my old enemy was already there, dressed in a black jersey dress with a poison green leather jacket and spiky silver bracelets. I had selected an embellished evening skirt, crisp white shirt, structured bag, a pair of authoritative heels and a simply fabulous pair of earrings.

Lavinia was sitting in the window drinking a Long Island Iced Tea and scowling at me.

'Well. Isn't this a treat. It's the Plait Stealer herself.'

I rearranged my features into what I hoped was a gracious smile.

'Hello, Harcourt. Nice outfit. I can see it's not new.'

Because, honestly, who wears that shade in the winter? This season is all about soft emeralds and pops of lime green. In retrospect, I should have kept my thoughts to myself, but old habits die hard.

Lavinia was opening her mouth to respond when Mummy appeared. Behind her was a cowed-looking woman in an ill-advised fawn two-piece and court shoes which had seen better days.

'Ma? What are *you* doing here?'

The woman, who I took to be Audrey Harcourt, gave her daughter a nervous kiss on the cheek.

'Don't be cross, Lavvie. Caroline and I thought it would be fun to stay at the club and catch up on the old days. You know we were at finishing school together.'

She let out a nervous giggle and fiddled with her clip-on earring (old gold and pearl – so horrifically out of fashion).

'No point in standing around here like a couple of spare parts, Audrey. I've booked a table and those cocktails won't drink themselves.' Mummy took Lavinia's mother firmly by the elbow and marched her over to a table near the bar. I took advantage of Lavinia's temporary paralysis to beckon the waiter over and order myself an Aperol Spritz. I settled myself on the insanely comfortable orange velvet padded stool and looked my enemy in the eye.

'Where do we start?'

Now, in essence, I have nothing against cocktails. They are perfect for a girls' night out, date night or (strictly in moderation) at weddings. However, for those of more mature years, they are often a Bad Idea. But more of that later.

Lavinia and I had sunk three each and were actually starting to have something approaching a conversation. I listened patiently as she ranted on about the emotional trauma caused by the loss of her long golden plait. She tapped her fingers impatiently on the table as I explained my side of the story and my protective instincts towards my sister. She made some catty remarks about my weight as I nibbled on a small plate of spicy poussin bites and I rolled my eyes as she went outside for yet another cigarette. I couldn't see that we were ever going to be BFFs, but if we could at least find some common ground, the constant backbiting might be reduced.

I was in two minds whether to mention Lavinia's father. Having decided to have the meeting in the first place, I consulted my friend Charlene about the whole knotty topic. Mother of one of Finn's closest friends, Jake, she has suffered from anxiety for many years. Since gaining access to the wisdom of lovely Tony the counsellor, her life has completely changed.

'It's a tricky one, Isabella,' she had said to me thoughtfully. 'She's obviously had a very traumatic childhood and that's affected her whole life. Lots of father issues too. Tony says that we all have scripts that were written for us before we had the choice and we often live by them even when we're adults. In her mind, you made her father stop loving her and that's a huge deal for her.'

As an angry schoolgirl protecting my bullied sister, I had known nothing of scripts and trauma and ego states. As a well-educated and empathic lifestyle blogger and influencer, however, I could see where Charlene was coming from.

'OK. But what about what she did to Suze? I can't just let that go.'

'Tony would say that you need to speak out your truth and tell her the consequences of her actions. As long as you stay calm and adult, it'll be fine.'

In principle, I couldn't argue. But this was Lavinia Harcourt we were talking about, fearless, entitled, angry and with a pen dipped in the highest-quality vitriol. Trauma in childhood (so Charlene told me) is deeply embedded in the psyche and very tough to sort out. She reminded me of Tony's never-fail techniques for dealing with tricky conversations (leave lots of silences between remarks; murmur, 'Interesting,' when something particularly frightful is said; never accuse or blame; maintain a calm tone; etc) and wished me well. It seems that her own mother and ex's awful behaviours have improved very slightly with this treatment, and since violence and shouting hadn't worked for Lavinia and me, I was ready to try something new.

With Charlene's advice in mind, I kept my hands folded in front of me and put my head slightly on one side as Lavinia, under the influence of three Long Island Iced Teas, innumerable cigarettes and no food at all (what state must her insides be in?) began, in an almost imperceptible fashion, to Open Up.

I learned that she had always been made to feel inferior to her older brothers, told to keep her mouth shut, smile and look pretty, never had her talents acknowledged or encouraged. As she spoke, the very slightest of quavers in her voice, I gazed at her furrowed brow and clouded eyes and remembered Charlene's last nugget of wisdom.

'It's helped me to think of people who are horrible to me as wounded children. Tony says that my mum and my ex are stuck. They never got what they needed when they were little and the only way they know to get through life is by acting up and bullying people into submission. When you're with this woman, try to remember what she looked like at school. A child. A child who never had her basic emotional needs met and who is sad and angry and doesn't know what to do.'

I listened as Lavinia told me about the time she wrote a story and got it published in the parish magazine.

'I suppose that was the start of my career. I wrote it so carefully, in my best writing, and checked it loads of times. I showed it to Ma and she said she'd ask her friend Patsy Fosker to look at it. She was such a kind woman. No children of her own but she did so much in our village. Always smiling. Always pleased to see me.'

She paused and took a swig of her cocktail.

'Funny what you remember. I haven't thought about Patsy for thirty years and I can see her in front of me as clear as day. We ran into her in the village and she said she couldn't believe a child of my age could write so well. "You must be so proud of this dear little girl, Audrey," she said. "Make sure you nurture this talent. And any time you've written something, you let me know, Lavinia."'

My enemy's eyes were full of tears. I remembered Charlene's advice and stayed silent.

'Nurture my talent! That was a laugh. I was so stupid. I actually thought my father would be proud of me. Ma showed him the magazine and he skimmed it and said I'd spelt a word wrong and I'd be better off playing with my dolls and helping her around the house. "Men don't like an overeducated woman who shows off, Rapunzel," he said, pulling my plait. "This is all very nice, but it won't get you anywhere in life." I'll never forget that. Ma didn't stand up for me. She never did. I took the magazine upstairs and put it in my school trunk. I used to read my article when I couldn't sleep at St Dymphna's. I was always top of the class in English, you know, Neville. Always. I never made a spelling mistake again and I wrote and wrote. It was my escape.'

She stopped speaking and gazed into the middle distance. I was feeling an alien emotion.

'Lavinia, that's awful. What an unkind thing to do to a child. Well done for not giving up. You didn't listen to him and now you make your living writing. That's amazing.'

I waited for my enemy to throw her drink in my face or make an acid comment. To my amazement, she looked down and I could see tears falling slowly down her over-made-up cheeks.

'I did listen to him, though. I hear his voice in my head every single day. You could say that's what drove me to succeed. I suppose I should be grateful to him. But I've never been able to trust a man again. If my own father can't be proud of me, who would be? I've watched my brothers have careers that aren't nearly as successful as mine, get married and have babies and they've had more praise from Ma and Pa for that than I ever have.'

There was a short silence. I took a sip of my Aperol Spritz and considered switching to Negronis. Although really, strictly speaking, a couple of cocktails are more than enough for a woman midweek. Lavinia gestured to the waiter and a fifth Long Island Iced Tea appeared.

'So you see, Neville, when you decided to play your little prank on me and cut off my hair, you put an end to any chance of me having a relationship with my father. And I couldn't forgive you for it. I hated you so much. I used to lie awake at night fantasising about finding the plait and shaming you in front of Miss Trent and everyone at school.'

Lavinia had bullied my vulnerable little sister unmercifully, made her life at school miserable and given me a huge amount of stress via her column. But the woman who sat in front of me didn't look like a nationally renowned gossip columnist and award-winning journalist. She resembled a sad little girl who just wanted to be loved. My heart went out to her and I took a huge risk and put my hand over her own trembling, nicotine-stained claw.

'I'm sorry, Lavinia. Truly. If I could go back and undo what I did, I would. I had no idea what you were struggling with.'

Now, surely, she would lash out and begin shouting or give me a slap. To my astonishment, however, she put her other hand over mine and gave it a squeeze.

'Can't believe I'm saying this, Neville, but I'm sorry too. I didn't know your parents had such a bad marriage. It all looked completely Little Miss Sunshine from where I was sitting. I shouldn't have bullied your sister. All right?'

I nodded. Bizarrely, it *was* all right. We sat in silence, two successful women at the top of our careers, returning briefly to childhood and trying to bridge a vast chasm of misunderstanding and bitterness that had lasted for thirty years. I couldn't think of anything to say and apparently neither could she. Which was absolutely fine. **#makeup #reconcilation #unexpected**

Goodness only knows what would have happened next (a drunken embrace, possibly? Protestations of undying friendship?), but the silence was broken in the most unexpected way by the noise of raised voices from Mummy's table.

We spun round and, to our joint horror, saw that our mothers were having a confrontation. Their glasses had been knocked over and a tide of viscous yellow liquid (a Snowball if I'm any judge of cocktails, which I am) and a brown frothy stain (Espresso Martini?) was spreading across the bleached wood table. I've never seen Mummy in an actual full-on fight, but if I were a betting woman (and I'm not), I would have put a tenner on her to win.

'You wicked woman, Caroline de Courcey! You knew I liked him and you sneaked out of the chalet after lights out and went dancing with him and got him fired. I hate you! I'll never forgive you!'

The mousy, dowdy little woman who had crept into Freudian Sip at the beginning of the evening was now a red-faced, raging creature who meant my mother some serious actual bodily harm. Mummy tutted loudly.

'Oh, do shut up, Audrey! Franz would never have looked at *you*. It was only a flirtation. We used to sneak out for a few schnapps and had a dance and a cuddle. He'd been eyeing me up from the minute he started giving us ski lessons and you know it.'

'I was in love with him, you selfish cow! I just wanted to be with him and get married and have his babies and never go home again. He was so handsome and charming and he used to always sit next to me on the chair lift and pick me up when I fell over. I should have known you'd come along and steal him for yourself.'

She followed up her words by pouring the remains of what looked like a double gin and bitters over Mummy's head. Lavinia and I had been frozen in our seats watching our mothers' fight unfold, but as the violence escalated, it seemed that both the bar manager and the combatants' daughters had the same idea.

'Ma! What do you think you're doing? Put that fork down.'

'Mummy, for goodness' sake let Audrey go.'

'Ladies, I'm going to have to ask you to leave. Please settle your bills immediately and consider yourselves barred from this establishment.'

The manager was looking severe, as well he might. The bar was full and we were the centre of attention. Lavinia and I have spent our professional lives in the spotlight, but I would have put good money on the theory that we were both yearning for the floor to open and swallow us up. Which, of course, it didn't.
#embarrassing #fistfight #mumdrama

November

Through sheer hard work, dedication, good genetic make-up and a work ethic that is second to none, Isabella M Smugge has climbed to the very uppermost branches of the Tree of Success. The trouble with being at the top is that it's an awfully long way down, and you do pick up quite a few scars and scratches in your mad scramble to the top. I've always been proud of my achievements, but not so much that I didn't want to carry on reaching out for the next thing and the next and the next. Am I the UK's premier mumfluencer, celebrated for my accessible and engaging lifestyle blogs? I am. Do millions of ordinary people look to me on advice on decorating, homeware, culinary and cultural matters? Why yes, of course they do. Was I the first person in the UK to realise that you could make a very good living indeed by showing off? Apparently. Or so said Lavinia's column the week after our meeting at Freudian Sip.

I'm a realist. I might deal in dreams and aspirations and fairy dust, but like any influencer worth her Pink Himalayan Rock Salt, I know all too well that behind the smiles and the immaculate surfaces and sparkling windows there is a whole heap of unresolved conflict. I had no idea about any of it before I moved to Suffolk and my life began to unravel, but the longer I live here, the more I understand that everyone has a story. And of course, I was all too aware that Lavinia would continue to mention me in her column. However, there was considerably less venom in the paragraph she wrote about me, and I felt there had been a sea change.

If my life were to be serialised on a well-known streaming platform with exceptionally high production values, a glossy cast and brilliant dialogue (and they could do a lot worse, let me tell you), my meeting with Lavinia would end with us embracing each other while Mummy and Audrey looked on misty-eyed. In no possible version of said scene would the bar manager threaten to call the police while barring two intoxicated sixty-something posh ladies. Everything was going rather Channel 5 post-watershed until we managed to extract our mothers' debit cards from their purses, pay their bar bill and, gripping them firmly by the arms, frogmarch them out on to the street.

Once there, the usual backdrop of sirens, polluted air and discarded takeaway wrappings brought us both back down to earth. Lavinia put her fingers to her mouth and let out a piercing whistle. Immediately, a couple of dodgy-looking middle-aged men in grubby coats appeared. I closed my eyes and prepared to be mugged, but within seconds, they had flagged down a black cab and were pouring us all into it.

Audrey had stopped shouting and was sobbing quietly. Mummy was staring out of the window, her hair soaked with gin and bitters, a cut on her hand from a broken glass and a grim look on her face.

It was a mismatched and unlikely foursome who exited the taxi at the club and made their way unsteadily into the entrance hall. In our different spheres of influence, Lavinia and I are both used to taking charge. The concierge looked rather taken aback but, within seconds, we had discreetly explained the situation and were escorting our respective parents to their rooms, which fortunately were at different ends of the building.

Ten minutes later, having helped them into their nighties and into bed, we reconvened in the cosy members' bar where a fire was crackling in the grate and various ladies, none of whom appeared to be:

1. Drunk

2. Injured

3. Deadly enemies

were sitting in comfortable armchairs reading and chatting to each other. Lavinia and I sank back into two expertly upholstered wingback chairs.

'Well. I didn't see that coming, did you?'

Lavinia had waved away the offer of an alcoholic drink and was sipping at a glass of iced lemon water.

'Definitely not. Who on earth is Franz? And what was all that about your mother being in love with him?'

My enemy appeared to be stone-cold sober in spite of the vast amounts of alcohol she had ingested that evening. 'I've never seen her like that before. Pa rules the roost and she just goes along with what everyone else wants. I don't think I've ever heard her raise her voice. What do you think we should do, Isabella?'

I took a minute before replying. We've always been 'Harcourt' and 'Neville' to each other. To hear my Christian name coming out of my enemy's mouth was a bit of a shock.

'Let them sleep it off and then talk to them separately about it. I don't know if you know, but Mummy's getting married in ten days. She wanted to have the wedding at the beginning of the month, but her stepdaughter-to-be works in education and she insisted on having it in half term.'

Lavinia nodded. 'Maybe that triggered something in Ma. I need to get back to my flat tonight but I'll come back here early tomorrow and take care of her. I don't want to leave you trying to manage the two of them solo.'

It's so easy to form a view of someone and believe it 100 per cent. Lavinia Harcourt had been my sworn enemy for thirty years and if you'd asked me, I would have told you that she was a hard, bitter woman incapable of change. Watching as she cried and shared the most painful of childhood memories with me had altered my opinion. Half of me wanted to sit up and talk until the fire died and the birds outside began singing, and the other half wanted to go upstairs, get into my PJs and snuggle down into my comfy bed to sleep what was left of the night away.

Lavinia, too, seemed to be struggling with conflicting feelings. After a short silence, she said, 'Look. I didn't know how this was going to go and I didn't come here to forgive you or hear your side or make friends. I don't like you. I never have and I know you don't like me. But you've surprised me. And people don't tend to do that in my line of work. I could sit here and tell you that I'll never write anything nasty about you in my column ever again. But we both know I'd be lying. I appreciate honesty. And you said you were sorry about what you did and I accept that. All right?'

I nodded. 'All right, Lavinia.'

We sat in a silence that seemed more comfortable than I had expected. The question I'd been dying to ask since we were ejected from the bar burst from my lips.

'Who were those men? And where did you learn to whistle like that?'

She smiled wryly.

'Part of my information network. I've got people all over town ready to take shots and overhear private conversations and spy for me. How do you think I get all my news? And the whistling? I've learned all kinds of things since I went to Fleet Street. Ma would pass out if I told her a tenth of them. None of them are ladylike and some of them are borderline illegal, but they got me to the top of the tree.'

She stood up, stretched and stuck out her hand.

'Night, then. And it goes without saying that you'll never publish anything about tonight and neither will I. Deal?'

I shook her hand.

'Deal. Goodnight.'

Back at home, I had precious little opportunity to think about the surreal evening I'd spent in the company of Lavinia Harcourt. The nits were back with a vengeance and the family bathroom smelled strongly of tea tree oil. Chloë had a brief but catastrophic falling out with Liza Bennet, one of her best friends, and my little Milo got an ear infection. A combination of broken nights, constant delousing and the run-up to Mummy and Harry's wedding were enough to make even an organiser of my calibre start to feel a little overwhelmed.

A couple of days passed before Mummy thawed out enough to speak to me in a civilised manner. There had been raised voices the morning after the night before, as she sat up in bed in her room at the club, her hair uncharacteristically tousled and unkempt. Lavinia and I had exchanged numbers the night before and at 7.45am I had received a text.

'Getting Ma up and pouring black coffee down her. I'll put her on the train home at nine. Hope your mother is OK.'

I replied that as far as I knew she was and that I would be returning to Suffolk with what remained of her post-haste. I sat on the end of the bed.

'What on earth were you thinking, Mummy? You couldn't have showed me up any more if you'd tried! A drunken shouting match with that poor woman in a crowded bar! You should be ashamed of yourself.'

Mummy, propped up against her pillows with a limp hand clutched to her forehead, let out a snort.

'I should be ashamed? *You* should be ashamed! I wouldn't have had to come chasing all the way up to London and meet up with Audrey in the first place if you and Lavinia hadn't had that row at the school reunion. I was doing what any good mother would to look after her daughter.'

'What, by shouting abuse at Audrey in a bar? And who's Franz? Are you really telling me this all blew up over some man from fifty years ago?'

Mummy tutted impatiently and took a sip of the extra-strong black coffee made by me several minutes earlier.

'Not that it's any of your business, but yes. I was simply making polite chit-chat. Audrey's always been a shy little mouse, and being married to Randy Rupert for all of those years hasn't made her any more interesting. She never did have any conversation and she never knew how to dress. When we met at finishing school in Switzerland, I suppose you could say I took her under my wing.'

I bit my lip and remained silent while the tale unfolded. It seemed that Mummy, sent away to Switzerland by her distant, aloof, aristocratic parents was one of the social kingpins of her year, vivacious, lively and keen to embrace every opportunity that the land of cuckoo clocks, fondue and snow-capped peaks could offer (her words, not mine). Finishing school, in case you are not aware, is a thankfully outdated concept where young girls are polished to a high sheen and provided with a clutch of accomplishments such as skiing, baking, hostessing and deportment. Mummy was abroad for two years and her parents' hope was that she would return home as an exceptionally marriageable young lady and snap up a titled husband and estate.

'I took to skiing at once. Poor Audrey was terrible at it. She spent more time on her bottom than upright. Scared of everything, always crying, always falling off things. The steeper and icier the slope, the more I enjoyed it! Our ski instructor was called Franz. Goodness me, he was dishy! I became so adept at skiing that my parents paid extra for me to have private lessons in the afternoons. We would go down black runs, off-piste, anywhere really. He was tall with blond hair and his eyes were cornflower blue.'

Mummy giggled and gazed into the middle distance. I took the opportunity to help myself to a Lapsang Souchong teabag from her hospitality tray and pour boiling water on to it. Time was ticking on and I didn't want to leave London late and put any more pressure on Lauren, holding the fort back at the Old Rectory.

'Yes, so – he was dishy, you fancied him, you went off-piste. Go on.'

Mummy shot me a dirty look.

'We didn't go *off-piste* if that's what you're implying, young lady! But, of course, I flirted with him. Audrey was always mooning over him, gazing at him during lessons, burbling on about him after lights out. We shared a room, you see. But she was so wet that I didn't really think she was serious.'

I waved my hand impatiently.

'And…'

'All right, all right. One night, I waited until Audrey was asleep and climbed out of the window. Our room was on the first floor so I slid down the drainpipe and dropped into the snow. Franz and I met at a little bar on the other side of the village and drank schnapps and chatted and laughed and danced. Everyone in the village knew that the girls at the finishing school had pashes on the ski instructors. We were teenagers, away from home for the first time. What did they expect? He walked me home and we had a lovely time saying goodbye by the funicular. After that, he only had eyes for me. I think he had a bigger crush on me than I did on him. I hadn't realised that Audrey honestly thought she had a future with him. I sneaked out a few more times, but then I got caught and he was transferred to another branch of the ski school at a village on the other side of the valley. Audrey cried herself to sleep for weeks.'

I took a sip of my Lapsang and glanced at the clock.

'But she didn't know the reason he left?'

'Well, no, obviously not. *I* wasn't going to tell her. We finished our two years and went home. I turned down Eddie Bathgate's proposal and my parents were hopping mad. Poor Audrey didn't have many suitors (you can't count her second cousin. Intermarriage is always such a bad idea), and when Rupert came along, she jumped at the chance of being the Honourable Audrey Harcourt. We all warned her against him, but she wouldn't have it. He was very handsome and charming, until you really got to know him. As you know, I married your father and my parents never forgave me and I never thought of Franz again.'

I was confused.

'So how did all this come up in conversation?'

Mummy drained her coffee cup and rearranged her pillows.

'We'd both had several cocktails and Audrey never could hold her drink. We started reminiscing about how we met and I mentioned Franz. Audrey clutched at my sleeve and launched herself into a great long emotional rant about how she'd always loved him and never forgotten him and how her marriage had been a mistake. With the benefit of hindsight, I should have kept my mouth shut, but I'd had three Snowballs and you know how they affect me. I agreed that he was the dishiest ski instructor in the village and told her what a marvellous kisser he was. I know, I know! But I was a little intoxicated and it was fun looking back at the good old days when I was young and carefree. Audrey completely lost it. I didn't think she had it in her.'

I stood up.

'Well, I hope you'll be apologising to the poor woman, Mummy! I'm shocked at your behaviour. And to think you were there because you thought *I* couldn't behave myself!'

This went down as well as you might expect, and we had our second row in twenty-four hours. I left her clambering shakily out of bed to have a much-needed shower and returned to my own room where room service had delivered my continental breakfast. What a night! I could hardly wait to get home to Suffolk where the worst I had to contend with was itchy scalps and playground fights. **#confrontation #offpiste #slipperyslope**

Back at the Old Rectory, having told Lauren all the juicy details about Mummy and Audrey's row, I thanked her for being such a good friend.

'Babes, honestly, it's my pleasure. It's like Liane says. You never disappoint. Am I allowed to tell the girls when I get to the playground this afternoon?'

I gave her permission to share every last enticing crumb of news and she departed. Silence from upstairs seemed to indicate that Mummy was either catching up on her sleep or engaged in writing a six-page letter of apology to poor Audrey Harcourt.

I called my florist and ordered a large bouquet to be sent to Lauren. Before doing so, I texted Mummy.

'Getting some thank-you flowers for Lauren. Do you want me to order some for Audrey from you while I'm at it? x'

There was a short silence, then she replied.

'I'm perfectly capable of dealing with Audrey myself, thank you very much, Isabella.'

That was me told. I scheduled some posts, did a few stories and tweets and wrote the other half of the blog. Time flew, and as I strapped my little Milo into the pushchair, wound my gorgeous vintage-style block-printed chiffon scarf round my neck and shrugged myself into my go-to trench coat, I allowed myself a brief moment of panic about the vast amount of work I still had to do before Mummy's wedding. So many things to worry about.

1. Could Mummy and I reconcile before Suze and I walked her down the aisle?

2. What if Randy Rupert appeared on the doorstep, thirsting for revenge?

3. How would it be if Lavinia used her new knowledge to blackmail me?

Not for the first time, as I walked briskly down the hill towards the school, I wondered what it would be like to be a normal person.

In the playground, large puddles had formed around the blocked drain by the benches and piles of fallen leaves were being kicked around enthusiastically by toddlers. I headed for the knot of eagerly chatting mums. Liane saw me coming and broke free from the group, almost cantering up to me.

'Smug! Tell me it's all true. Was Lauren exaggerating? Did your mum really have a proper row last night?'

I confirmed that, if anything, Lauren had played it down. Liane sighed ecstatically and closed her eyes for a second.

'What did I do before you came to town, Smug? How did I live? Is she at yours? I'm going to have to have a good old catch-up with her. I'll WhatsApp her now.'

She began stabbing enthusiastically at her phone. I felt it incumbent upon me to warn her of Mummy's enfeebled state.

'No offence, Liane, but she's not in a great place. She's got a cracking hangover, she's in a really bad mood with me and I don't think she fancies any company.'

Liane held up a restraining hand.

'Trying to concentrate. Shut it, Smug.'

Her phone beeped and a smile spread over her face.

'She says she'll meet me at the café first thing tomorrow and tell me all the gory details. Go Mrs N!'

Honestly!

In the glittering and gorgeous world of Isabella M Smugge, late October is usually the time when I start the big build-up to Christmas. My followers simply adore my mood boards, my décor, my meal ideas and my advice on planning the perfect Yuletide for all the family. This year, I'm not feeling it. Mimi and I had our usual meeting on a cold, dark, wet Monday morning, the day after three out of my four children had been returned from the weekend by their father. Finn was moody and silent, Chloë shredding her nails and Elsie uncharacteristically whiney and miserable. I was too tired to dig into their feelings, but promised them a rare treat of fish and chips from the village chippy and the chance to eat their dinner off trays on their laps while watching TV. I saw them off to school with reluctant smiles on their faces. I've realised how easy it is to make children happy and I'm determined to be the kind of parent who puts them first at all times.

I fired up the heater in my studio, lit a Cuban Tobacco and Fig candle (the ideal fragrance for a miserable autumn day) and braced myself for my agent's frantic enthusiasm.

'Darling! There you are. Looking – well, not your usual stunning self, to be honest. How is everything in your fabulous world? Tell Mimi.'

I tried to rearrange my exhausted features into a natural and radiant smile.

'Bit of a to-do with Mummy and her friend in London when I met up with Lavinia, I'm stressing out about the wedding on Saturday, Johnnie's being very annoying and I'm tired.'

In principle, Mimi is a big fan of honesty, but it has to be carefully controlled and curated and get me lots of likes and shares. Her brow furrowed.

'That's not good! You're the spectacular face of the almost achievable aspirational lifestyle for millions – we need to cheer you up, pronto! You haven't changed your mind about selling your mother's wedding pictures to *All Right!* Magazine, have you? They came back to me this morning and upped their offer. Enough to keep her in European river cruises and on-trend knitwear for the rest of her life.'

I confirmed that I had not. Mummy's comments on the subject were unprintable, and whereas once upon a time I would have thought only of the reach and engagement that a twelve-page full-colour spread in one of the UK's most fawning and celebrity-packed periodicals would bring me, now I could see her point.

'You know best, I suppose, sweetie. Tell me that at the very least you'll post some adorable images of the tots and close-ups of old hands with bright shiny new wedding rings on them and arty shots of blistered Hispi cabbage and dessert cocktails?'

I confirmed that a carefully selected collection of pictures would appear on my platforms, having first been checked through by the bridal pair. My agent puffed out a dense cloud of cigarette smoke.

'That's something, at least. Now, darling, Christmas! Who's round the table this year? Which look have you gone for?'

I confirmed that after a brief flirtation with Winter Tradition (all deep red and green tones with a warm colour palette and classic cable-knit stockings in cream wool, snow-dusted spruce trees and silver glitter tree baubles), I had plumped for the Royal Fairytale look. Mimi gasped and clutched at her chest. For a moment, I was concerned that she was having a coronary, but once she got her breath back, I realised that she was expressing extreme joy.

'Marvellous, darling! You're so clever and that's why you're my favourite client. Can we call on your mother's royal connections to get any of them in the pictures? Even a minor duchess or two would do the trick.'

I assured Mimi that while Mummy was on nodding terms with several of the more junior branches of the Royal Family, they weren't exactly mates.

'I had to ask! And you never know what might come up next year. So, what are we talking? Jewel tones, lashings of gold, regal motifs?'

I confirmed that I would be hanging rich, jewel-coloured baubles in navy blue, deep purple, gold and forest green on my classic fir Christmas trees, placing eye-catching fairy tale green glitter wreaths packed with foliage on all my exterior doors and festooning my windowsills and banisters with natural swathes of spruce, pine and twinkling gold fairy lights. Mimi clapped her hands together.

'That's my girl! Last week of November as always? Harpreet will be delighted. You know he always waits to see how you decorate and then copies you exactly. Scaling it down, of course. We can't all live in a Grade II listed Georgian rectory in the country!'

61

She laughed croakily and lit another cigarette. Harpreet is my socials man, an absolute genius. I don't know what I'd do without him.

'So, spoil me. Who's round the Smugge Christmas table this year? I'm seeing happy little faces lit by candlelight, perfect organic sustainable food, flutes of champagne, smiling guests. Who have you got for Mimi?'

She appeared to be salivating slightly. Not for the first time, the thought occurred to me that if I were starting out on my career now, I wouldn't pick Mimi as my agent. But like a weak pelvic floor or an infected ingrown toenail, she's hard to shake off.

'Mummy and Harry want to spend their first married Christmas alone together. At the moment, it's looking like me and the children, Amanda and her daughters (you know, Natasha and Kitty) and Davina, Toby and their two. So that's twelve around the table, and I might have a New Year's thing this year and have Suze and the family up for it. Mummy and Harry will be there too.'

Mimi was nodding and making rapid notes.

'OK, OK, so we've got the horsy sister-in-law, but she has at least got little children who always dress up a Christmas table no end. Any teeth yet? Hair? Can they sit up unaided or are we talking high chairs? I'm hoping for some simply stunning shots.'

Amanda and Davina are the two sisters-in-law to whom I am closest. Johnnie's youngest brother, Rafe, is married to a stunning, internationally renowned businesswoman and events organiser of Russian heritage. Xenia and I get on well, but she inhabits a very different world from me. Amanda is divorced from Johnnie's older brother, Charlie, who turned out to be a serial adulterer and all-round Bad Egg. She left him a year ago when she found out that his latest squeeze was only two years older than their eldest son. Her daughter, Kitty, is suffering from anorexia, and seeing her gaunt body, empty eyes and the suffering in her mother's face has driven a sharp little knife deep into my heart. I often find myself thinking about it as I drift off to sleep. My girls are so healthy and full of life, and of course they're still so young, but I don't know what I'd do if the stress of life got too much for them and they started starving themselves.

Johnnie and I used to make Toby and Davina the butt of our jokes and I blush to think of how shallow and judgemental I used to be. They are the kindest, most compassionate people I know and I simply adore them. They've suffered a string of miscarriages throughout their marriage and it gladdens my heart to see them so happy with their two little children, Matthew and Florence. Amanda and Davina get on very well and neither of them is a Johnnie fan.

I love seeing my children interacting with their cousins and I want my Christmas to be all about love and comfort and security. For the first time ever, this year I contemplated just putting up any old decorations that came to hand and not even bothering with a tree in every room. I didn't share this with Mimi, but it may be that next year I cut right back on what you might call my professional showing off.

After many wrangles and rows with Finn over the past couple of years, I'm not insisting on the usual images of family togetherness with the children dressed in coordinating outfits by the main Christmas tree in the entrance hallway. It's not fair on them. I chose this life, posting constantly and influencing people I'll never meet, but I'm starting to get an uneasy feeling that it might not be the thing I'm meant to do forever. Still, I won't think about that now. January is traditionally the time for dwelling on gloomy thoughts and giving things up you like. Plenty of time then to think about where I go next.

'Your *Issy Smugge Says* book series is still selling marvellously, darling!' Mimi's rasping voice broke into my thoughts. 'Are you quite sure you won't start it up again? People love it.'

I've never regretted laying down my book series. It gave me my start and people did adore them, but enough is enough.

I gave Mimi a brief rundown on my meeting with Lavinia and assured her that not a word about the row would be making it into her column ('Well, that's something, darling!') and that some kind of rapprochement had been reached. We rounded off our conversation with insincere good wishes and, with a final wracking cough, Mimi disappeared in a cloud of smoke. **#royalfairytale #sparkle #yuletide**

Last October, I would never have thought that such a glittering occasion as my own mother's wedding would be overshadowed by a nit outbreak, a fight in a cocktail bar and various primary school dramas. I had to take lots of deep breaths and reset my brain and put myself in the correct celebratory zone as the big day approached. Thank heavens that Mummy and Harry are now safely married. It was all simply perfect. Apart from the weather. And Karen, her new stepdaughter. But apart from that, flawless.

The glowing, smiling woman in cornflower blue, holding a simple bouquet of sea holly, cream rose buds, Amaranthus and cotoneaster berries and gazing down the flower-lined aisle at Harry was almost unrecognisable as my formerly uptight, chain-smoking, gin-swigging, bitter mother. Suze and I took an arm each and whispered, 'Ready?' as a beautiful piece of baroque music began playing softly. It was a surprisingly emotional moment.

We walked slowly past the rows of modish cross-backed Chiavari chairs with cornflower-blue seat pads and gauze ribbons (gold is *so* over!) relishing the fragrance of the flowers, the smiling faces and the beautiful music.

The peace was shattered by an insistent voice shouting, 'Gandy! Gandy!' and my little Milo broke free of Amanda's restraining hand and rushed towards us, arms outstretched. Mummy smiled and bent down to give him a cuddle. The final leg of the journey was considerably impeded by the presence of a chatty toddler clutching at his grandmother's skirts as her daughters fought to keep the whole shebang going, but finally we were there and Mummy was standing unaided with Milo holding her left hand and her husband-to-be gazing adoringly into her eyes. I had selected Extra Waterproof mascara and eyeliner that morning as I could see that I would be needing it. **#emotion #love #secondtimearound**

My new stepbrothers Mark and Karl, along with my stepsisters-in-law, Freya and Nikki, and my stepnieces and nephews (I'm going to have to think of a new way to refer to them! Blending families is jolly hard work) could not be more welcoming or ready to bond with me, Suze, the children and Mummy. Plus, of course, the extended family (bevvies of cousins and second cousins whom we only see at weddings and funerals) and all of Mummy's friends. Veronica Madingley, to no one's surprise, developed complications around her Hot Tub Folliculitis and was unable to attend. **#shockhorror**

Karen, Harry's daughter, had a face like a slapped bottom all day. When the bride and groom exchanged their vows, the magic was shattered by loud nose-blowing and sniffing from her direction. I could see that her brothers were working hard to contain her venom, but she shot us so many dirty looks that I actually considered taking her to one side and Having a Word. Suze talked me out of it.

I kept an eye on the children, charming in their wedding finery, kept a discreet eye on the reception drinks and canapés and ensured that everyone was chatting and mingling. By the time we sat down, I'd had a couple of botanical cocktails and the edge was well and truly off.

Once the main course had been cleared away, it was speech time. As it was the second time around for the bridal pair, it had been agreed that they would both speak and that anyone else who wished to stand up and say a few words would be most welcome. Harry was first to go.

Younger grooms are often paralysed with fear and turn to drink to get them through the ordeal. In this case, not only was Mummy's new husband stone-cold sober, but he was also a gifted and moving speaker. He managed to speak about his first wife, his children, Mummy and us in an entirely loving and appropriate fashion and finished by saying that Mummy had brought him a life-giving joy that he never thought he would experience again. There were tears in everyone's eyes as we all raised our lead-free crystal champagne flutes and toasted the new Mrs Cottingham. Then it was Mummy's turn. Harry helped her to rise to her feet and she stood, flute in hand, and gazed out over the assembled masses in the delightful Palladian dining room bedecked with flowers and smiling faces.

'When my daughter Isabella rang me up and told me she was leaving London with her family and moving to Suffolk, I told her I thought it was a ridiculous idea and asked her what on earth she thought she was doing.'

She paused as an appreciative ripple of laughter ran round the room.

'When I first visited her, I wasn't terribly polite about her new house. The truth was, I was jealous. She had taken a rather tired, shabby old place and turned it into a beautiful family home and she was surrounded by her own loving family. Back then, I pretended I wasn't lonely and bitter, but I was. And I took out my feelings on both of my daughters. And for that, girls, I'm truly sorry. But this is a happy occasion and I don't want to make all of you cry for the wrong reasons. If Isabella hadn't taken that leap and moved to this beautiful county, I wouldn't be standing here today, married to this lovely man.'

There was a short silence as Mummy gave everyone a chance to fumble about in their bags for a tissue and dab at their eyes.

'I've been given a second chance at happiness and I intend to seize it with both hands. None of us knows how much time we've got, but I am going to make the very most of every day bestowed on me. Isabella, Suzanne, I am so proud of you both, and without you I don't know what I'd do. Harry and I are so privileged to be able to blend our two families and I would like you to all raise your glasses and drink to my wonderful new husband. To Harry!'

I never stir out of the house without a full make-up kit stowed in my bag, and today of all days I could see that I would need to reapply nearly every element covering my beautifully made-up countenance. The applause was thunderous as Suze stood up and gave a short but emotional reply to Mummy's words.

Karen nearly spoiled it by staggering to her feet (she had been hammering the cocktails and wine, I noticed) and opening her mouth to speak. Fortunately, her brothers leaped up at the same time and delivered a speech on behalf of their family, which was more than acceptable.

I foresee trouble ahead with my new stepsister. **#blendedfamily #jealous #angry**

Most single parents of four children would have enough to worry about trying to keep everyone fed, watered and nit-free, plus working and juggling all the responsibilities of a household. I've always been known for my incredible capacity for work, which is just as well. My fellow playground parent Kate is stepping down as chair of the PTA after four hard years in post and is grooming me as her successor. As the former chair of the Beech Grove PTA back in London, I was known for my superb organisation of events, infinite capacity for running fundraisers and natural flair with people management. So, as Kate says, it makes sense for me to step up. People aren't exactly clamouring to take over the role.

We have Chris Robinson, husband of the frightful Hayley, as our treasurer and, say what I might about him, he does do a solid job of managing the accounts. Rebecca Bennet, a fellow playground mum and relatively new member, is happy to step into my shoes as secretary and Kate has hoovered up two new members from the eager ranks of the Reception line. Our AGM is coming up, at which we must conduct all the boring business of officially recognising the resignation of the chair and the appointment of a new one. Mrs Tennant, our efficient head, will be there and we have put out flyers and a note in the school newsletter about the huge amount of fun that can be had from being a member of our merry band. It's unlikely that anyone will believe us, but as Kate says, it's always worth a try.

The children were with Johnnie the weekend after the wedding, and yet again I had to remind him that I am not happy about them meeting his permanently puking partner until I am ready. Our last conversation did not go well.

'Look, Iss, I understand how you must be feeling about all this. It's natural to be jealous. I'm with another woman and starting a new family, but you'll always have a special place in my heart.'

I dug my beautifully manicured nails into the palms of my hands and took several deep breaths.

'Not jealous. Not even a little bit. This is not about you or me. It's about our children. Remember them? The ones we had together and who you said you'd always be here for?'

There was an indulgent chuckle from the end of the phone.

'Protesting a bit too much, I'd say! But OK. You're not jealous. Paige wants to meet the kids and I don't see what your problem is. Why don't you drive them down to the house on Friday and we can all have a meet-up. You'll love Paige. She's so young and full of life. Well, she was. Once the vomiting stops I'm sure she'll be back to the way she used to be.'

Slowly and patiently, as if to a small, dull child, I explained yet again that his appalling behaviour since he went off with Sofija had damaged our children and that it was our duty, as adults, to protect them and put their feelings and needs ahead of our own. This did not seem to sink in. I always put my husband on such a pedestal but in the cold light of day, I can see that his emotional intellect is set permanently to zero and he cares only about himself. Eventually, I extracted a promise that

Paige would not be at the house on the coming weekend and that he would wait for me to be ready to meet her.

How do primary school teachers cope, I wonder? When I was in London and my children were enjoying the benefits of a private education at Beech Grove, I never even thought about the hard work and challenges their teachers faced on a daily basis. Maybe it's not so extreme in the private sector, but once you get involved with state education, the gilt is most certainly off the gingerbread. Lauren tells me that the government, in addition to putting hurdles and stumbling blocks in the way of the teachers on an almost daily basis, constantly makes cuts to their budgets. It seems that the roof on the gym and the hall at school has needed replacing for more than five years, that the library is perilously short of books and that even with the efforts of the PTA, many parents struggle to pay for their children's enrichment trips.

Isabella M Smugge to the rescue! I booked an appointment with Mrs Tennant and offered her a goodly chunk of cash. I can put it through the books as a charitable donation, tax deductible. However, that wasn't the reason I was doing it. I didn't mention it to Mimi as she would have insisted on lots of photos of grateful children holding books, and probably made poor Mrs Hill shin up a drainpipe for a dramatic shot of the new roof tiles.

Mrs Tennant was enormously grateful.

'We do our very best, Mrs Smugge, and our prime concern is keeping the children safe. Your generous donation means we can get the roof replaced over February half term and that will save so much money on the heating. I assume you would like to keep your donation confidential?'

I confirmed that this was the case. However, I was more than happy to make a separate contribution towards new books and this I suggested I put through the PTA as a gift. I walked out of the school feeling truly good about life. Tom preached a sermon about radical generosity a few weeks ago and I believe that I am practising it in my own community. I hope God will be pleased with me. **#giving #generosity**

PTAs are the same the world over. You get a small group of people doing all the really hard graft with a few hangers-on. And no one ever wants to be the treasurer, which is why when you get one, you need to hang on to them at all costs.

So imagine my surprise when Kate announced her resignation and asked if anyone would like to take on the position of chair. I opened my mouth to offer, but before I could get a word out, none other than our own revered treasurer spoke.

'I'd be happy to step up to that role, Kate.'

He looked around as if waiting for a round of applause. None was forthcoming. Kate looked thunderstruck.

'Oh. Gosh. Well – thank you, Chris. What a kind offer. But we do value your role as treasurer so much and personally (although of course it is entirely up to you), I'd be more comfortable seeing you continuing in that position. Was anyone else interested in being chair?'

She raised an interrogatory eyebrow and tried not to look at me. I cleared my throat and raised a perfectly manicured hand.

'I'm more than happy to take over the role of chair. I've been the secretary for a while now and I feel that I really understand how the committee works.'

Chris Robinson frowned. 'Are you implying that I don't? I believe that *I* would be the obvious choice for chair once Kate steps down. I'm an organic part of this community in a way that you can never be. No offence.'

I felt my cheeks reddening. It's true I haven't been in the village for as long as the Robinsons, but I do have twice as many children as them and am much more popular. Apart from snotty Sally Whitmore, I've never really seen anyone chatting to them of their own free will on the playground.

'I may not have been here as long as you and Hayley, but I do believe that I've invested in the village and in our community. I'm here for the long haul and I think my life experience and connections would fit ideally with the role of chair.'

Chris Robinson let out a nasty little laugh.

'Invested. Is that what you call it? Hayley and I are not alone in our concerns about your "investment".'

He made the universally recognised hand signal for speech marks and looked around as if expecting a standing ovation. Kate intervened.

'I'm sorry, am I missing something here? What are you implying?'

'It's pretty obvious. We all know that *she* bought her way on to the PTA with lavish gifts. My wife was a loyal, hard-working secretary to this group and she was ousted by a newcomer who forced herself in where she wasn't wanted. What have you got to say about *that*?'

He sat back and folded his arms. I had lots I wanted to say, but was stopped by Mrs Tennant.

'It's no secret that Mrs Smugge has made several generous donations to the school. She has recently offered to buy new books for the library which I think we can all agree are desperately needed. Nothing underhand or dishonest has gone on. And of course we all recognise and acknowledge the hard work that Mrs Robinson put in during her time on the PTA.'

This would have been enough to silence most people, but not our weaselly treasurer.

'This is just the latest move in her campaign to buy herself popularity and power. We're sick of it. I refuse to vote for her to become chair.'

Maddie, crimson in the face, leaned forward and waved her finger at him.

'You're chatting waz, Chris, and you know it! Hayley resigned at the school fête over the whole loo roll issue. We all heard her. She'd been complaining about the way things were done for some time and she left us in the lurch. If Isabella hadn't stepped in, I don't know what we would have done. She might not be your cup of tea, but it's incredibly rude and ungrateful of you to try to block her becoming chair just because you and Hayley are jealous of her. And do I have to remind you about how you got that new kitchen of yours? *Do I?*'

This was a sensitive point. It had come out that the Robinsons' top-of-the-range new kitchen had been paid for with blood money. Hayley had been selling toxic nuggets of gossip about me to Lavinia. A less forgiving and kindly woman would have confronted them about it long ago, but I'm all about building bridges.

That said, I've served as an officer on two primary school PTAs in my career and never ever did I think I would live to see a power struggle for someone to become chair. Every outgoing chair pretty much has to beg someone to become their replacement and the mood in the room was getting pretty ugly. Our head stepped in again.

'I think more than enough has been said on this subject. I'm going to bring this conversation to an end. Mr Robinson, Mrs Smugge, you both wish to be considered for chair? Am I correct?'

We nodded.

'And is anyone else prepared to nominate themselves?'

It seemed unlikely that a third candidate would step forward, but to my amazement, Rebecca Bennet put her hand up.

'I'm very happy to become chair if Isabella is prepared to remain as secretary and Chris as treasurer. They're both doing an amazing job and we'd be lost without them.'

This, it seemed, was the stuff to give our treasurer.

'I appreciate that, Rebecca. No one truly sees or appreciates the hard work I put in. I work full-time, you know, and I co-parent two young children. Running reports and composing spreadsheets takes up a lot of my leisure time.'

Most of the committee and Mrs Tennant assured him that his efforts were greatly appreciated. I couldn't speak, and Kate and Maddie were both making involuntary strangulation movements with their hands. Mrs Tennant proposed Rebecca as chair and Maddie seconded her. Chris and I were proposed and seconded as treasurer and secretary. We went through the rest of the agenda with the minimum of chat and, jobs having been assigned for the clutch of Christmas events coming up, we disbanded, Chris Robinson scuttling straight home to his wretched wife and the rest of us (minus Mrs Tennant) heading straight back to my house for a much-needed glass of Pinot. A power struggle! On the PTA! Allegations of financial misconduct! I ask you! **#enemy #pta**

The rest of November was relatively event-free. I hosted a pamper party and sleepover for twelve of Chloë's friends and nothing went wrong. Unless you count one of them having a mild allergic reaction to the bubble purifying charcoal face sheet. Mummy came back from two weeks in Madeira suntanned and glowing with happiness. Johnnie managed to keep his mouth shut about Paige. I had coffee and a catch-up with Claire and agreed to host our new homegroup at the Old Rectory from January. I went to church twice and got lots of extra holy points by donating some high-end tinned products to our food bank. I had no idea that people went hungry these days, but apparently they do. I've got a lot to learn.

Only twenty-four shopping days left till Christmas! After such an eventful three months, I'm looking forward to some peace and quiet. **#jinglebells #dingdong #christmasprep**

December

I worked extremely hard for years to become an overnight success and I never thought that once I reached the dizzy heights of universal acclamation as the UK's premier mumfluencer, lifestyle blogger and universally revered trend scout I would ever want anything to change. I pretty much wrote the instruction manual on being an influencer and, as you know, many have followed in my footsteps. What no one sees is the constant slog that goes on behind the scenes. For every perfect, polished image, every carefully thought-out hashtag, every beautifully written piece of content, hours of deep thought and constant editing are involved. It's exhausting. And for the first time, as I sat at my rose quartz kitchen island making the final amendments to my scheduled Christmas posts and ticking off items on my ludicrously long and sprawling Mum To-Do List, I wondered if the game was worth the creamy musk and sandalwood candle.

I'm aware that I'm in a fortunate financial position. I was born into a wealthy family, I benefited from an expensive private education, doors were open to me which remained resolutely closed to others and I have sailed through an enormously successful career which has made me even more money. Most are not so fortunate. I see that now on a daily basis as my friends on the playground struggle to make ends meet, pay the bills and cope with an ever more stressful life. If it were appropriate, I would gladly hand over a sizeable chunk of cash to them all. But I can't. I made the mistake of giving Lauren's girls some spending money at the Christmas Fayre last year and our relationship was ruptured for a few painful days. While it's so tempting to swoop in and make everything right with a wave of my Magic Influencing Wand (and wouldn't that be a great piece of merch?), I've learned that it's not the way.

That said, I am obliged to keep on keeping on, for now at least. Contracts have been signed, paid partnerships entered into and Isabella M Smugge is not only a woman, a mother and a daughter, but also a full-on award-winning brand. She cannot just walk away from all of her responsibilities, however much she would sometimes like to.

If one has children, December is a month full to the brim with school activities, spilled tubes of glitter, overpacked diaries, nativities, angel costumes, wonky tinsel haloes, headdresses made from tea towels and lengths of cord, Secret Santa gifts, seasonal round robins and a constant sense of running to keep up. This year, for some reason, I am really struggling to keep all my plates in the air. I miss Sofija more than ever. She came to Chloë's birthday party and, as always, when I saw the way my children's faces lit up, a tiny little dagger stabbed me in the heart. The exception was Milo, who seized me by the legs and buried his face in my dress every time he saw her. My treasure of a housekeeper Ali and I decorated the entire house (I don't know what I'd do without her), and I took all the images with which Harpreet is embellishing my socials all through the merry month of December. The stats are looking good. Mimi is beside herself with joy. I'm pleased, I suppose. But really, how much longer can I stay in this privileged position? Everyone's posting content about wreaths, garlands and baubles. I'm getting tired of all the glitz and surface happiness. What lies beneath? **#deepthoughts #whatnext**

New levels of awkwardness on the playground! We now have a stand-off between Liane Bloomfield and the Whitmores, anyone who's related in any way to Liane (and that appears to be half of the village plus surrounding districts) and the Whitmores, Lauren and the Whitmores, me and the Robinsons, Liane and the Robinsons, Maddie and the Robinsons and Kate and the Robinsons. The trouble with having children at primary school is that you are thrown together with a random group of people you'd never choose to socialise with in real life. As Lauren says, it's sheer bad luck that various bouts of unprotected sex have put me and Hayley Robinson together. In spite of the many wrongs visited upon me by Hayley and her frightful husband, I am still smiling at them every time we meet (which is all the time! How many more seasonal events is a woman expected to attend?) and trying to be an adult about it all.

Crystal has, reluctantly, come back to school. There have been high-level talks between Lauren and Scott, Sally and David Whitmore, Mrs Tennant and the class teacher. Oliver Whitmore has been moved to the back of the class and Crystal to the front. As far as is possible, they are observed during the entire school day and any issues dealt with immediately. All this along with the daily grind of teaching, making attractive decorations for the corridors and common spaces (leaning very strongly towards snowflakes and paper chains, as far as I have observed), trying to keep a classroom of overstimulated and excitable children quiet and doing all the paperwork the government insists upon. Who would be a teacher?

No one currently has nits, for a mercy.

Rebecca Bennet, our new chair, broke all the records at the Christmas Shopping Afternoon. She wrote to all the other primary schools within a ten-mile radius to invite them along, managed to fit in thirty-five stalls by utilising both the gym and the hall (we prayed for dry weather as constant leaks from the ceiling is not a good look at a PTA event), pulled together an incredible selection of cakes, sausage rolls and mince pies and raised a vast amount of money for the school. Chris Robinson sent some pass-agg messages on the PTA WhatsApp group which she effectively squashed in a courteous and determined fashion. I love her!

We now have the Christmas Fayre, our new Wreath Making event and the Christmas Disco to get through, but I have swerved festive performances as three out of four of my children are now too old for them. My little Milo will be the final young Smugge to tread the boards as Shepherd #3 or Lead Angel or even Joseph. But that's in the future.

I am, once again, running the Chocola at the Christmas Fayre and have agreed to be on the wreath-making team. Back at Beech Grove, I participated in seasonal events where we wound wire around pre-mossed wreaths and studded them with fragrant oranges, pine cones and bundles of cinnamon sticks while quaffing high-quality mulled wine. However, these days, my door garlands come pre-made by toiling local artisans. Charlene has come forward to offer her services. As well as running an increasingly successful textiles business, embarking on a glittering round of events on the craft fair circuit and apparently making curtains and blinds around the clock, she is also a gifted wreath-maker and designer.

I have agreed to host the event at the Old Rectory. The menu has been nailed down. We will be offering:

1. Mulled wine with plenty of fresh oranges, cinnamon, allspice, berries, star anise and bay leaves.

2. Mulled apple juice, as above.

3. Tiny star-topped mince pies made with Kate's mum's homemade mincemeat.

4. Ottolenghi mint and pistachio chocolate fridge cake (so simple and delicious).

5. Organic turkey, cranberry and stuffing sausage puffs.

6. Plant-based vegetable tartlets.

Half the tickets have already been sold. Mummy and Harry are coming over that night to babysit, the other three are at Johnnie's and once Milo is in bed, Mummy will be making her own wreath for the marital front door.

On that note, the wedded bliss of the new Mr and Mrs Cottingham has had a little bit of a dent put in it. Understandably, moving into the former family home of her predecessor means that Mummy has to be extremely sensitive. While Mark and Karl are absolutely fine about the few changes that have been made (new curtains in the reception rooms, made by Charlene, some new hanging baskets filled with winter pansies and ivy and the transformation of the cloakroom from a fusty little space painted in a most ill-advised shade of yellow (I mean, who thinks *that's* OK?) to a clean, modern room, Karen has been most put out.

'I've never seen anything like it, darling.'

Mummy was perched on a stool at my island sipping a much-needed G&T while Harry dozed in front of the fire in the snug.

'Crying, saying her mother would turn in her grave, insisting Harry went into the garage and got the old paint out and returned the cloakroom to the original shade. I put my foot down at that point, and Harry backed me up, but they were out by the front door whispering for ages once I'd said goodbye to her. I've got lots of plans for the spring. The garden's a disgrace. I've drawn up some plans and Harry says he's happy if I am. But *she's* got it in for me.'

It's a tricky situation. Mummy has moved into another woman's house (although of course she's dead and therefore presumably doesn't mind), and quite rightly is trying to improve it. She's certainly got her work cut out. The location is excellent, on a quiet estate an easy ten-minute walk from Woodbridge town centre. However, the house is an ugly box with no outstanding architectural features and the garden is laid mainly to lawn with a few bedraggled shrubs and bushes, an elderly greenhouse and a couple of tired-looking sheds. It's simply crying out for some intelligent planting, a new front door (I suspect that the current one is made from a substance known as UPVC) and an extensive programme of redecoration. Mummy is planning to put in some frothing pink *clematis montana* to train up the walls in the spring (the perfect way to cover an unattractive house and so much prettier and less destructive than ivy) and has ordered a number of plant catalogues over which she is currently poring. Surely Karen can't object to the garden being improved.

'I wouldn't be so sure, darling.'

Mummy drained her G&T to the dregs and refreshed her glass.

'That woman could take offence at anything. She kept texting poor Harry on our honeymoon. My next battle is Christmas. I want it to be just the two of us on the day itself. I'm perfectly happy to go along with their family traditions on Christmas Eve and Boxing Day and New Year's Day and any other blooming day. But I don't think it's too much to ask to have my husband to myself when we're newly married.'

I expressed my support and asked her if she'd like to come and stay for New Year. Suze, Jeremy and Lily will be joining us, with great relief, I suspect, as they are hosting the frightful Carole (Jeremy's mother) over Christmas. A woman who struggles to process brassicas and many other foodstuffs, yet fills her face with them at every opportunity, she proved a difficult house guest at the Old Rectory last Christmas. I had to replenish the scented oil in my diffusers at an alarmingly rapid rate and my luxurious quilted loo rolls got quite a hammering. But the gracious and welcoming hostess must rise above such trials. Poor Suze. I am also asking Silvia, my mother-in-law. Our once warm and loving relationship has changed, and I feel a bit awkward, but I'll worry about that closer to Christmas.

'If it means a break from Karen, I'm there!'

Mummy crunched on a handful of spiced nuts and took another sip of her drink.

'Blended families, don't they call it, darling? I'm all for building bridges and being a good stepmother, but she's not making it easy for me.'

I foresee trouble ahead. **#newlyweds #friction**

The next morning, I was looking forward to a really good day's work. I have so much to do, what with all my Christmas content, the Chocola donations to label up with raffle tickets, menus to be planned, blogs to be written, a couple of new collaborations to work on and, of course, the Christingle at church to be organised. As last year, I am in charge of all the design and costumes and I am hoping and praying that we do not have another outbreak of sickness and diarrhoea and/or nits this year. Last Christmas, we had a large heavenly host who were decimated by head lice, stage fright and poor toileting. Our cast of shepherds, wise men and even members of the Holy Family themselves were also taken out by a virulent bug sweeping the village.

I had a summit at the vicarage with Claire, Lauren and Sue Thompson, the recently retired dynamo who did so much good work on our production last year. In addition, as we have an even larger cast this year, swelled by some of the families who have recently moved to the village, we have added to our team.

Everyone seemed ready to fall in with my suggestions for staging, backdrops and decoration. Since I moved into the Old Rectory, I've decorated it four times for Christmas. Everything I used from previous years – fairy lights, baubles, fake gift-wrapped presents, ribbons, etc – is safely stored in the attic. I got Finn to help me bring it all down and spent a happy morning with Claire and the efficient Sue turning the church into a winter wonderland. A local farmer always provides the tree which, I was glad to see, was a sturdy spruce with evenly matched branches and just the right height to work in such a vast space.

Though I say it myself, I do have quite the eye for décor and by the time I'd finished, the medieval interior was gently illuminated with golden fairy lights, the tree was exceptionally tastefully decked and all the stone windowsills were covered with artful arrangements of holly, bay leaves and other foliage helpfully picked by the ladies over the last day or so.

I can't bear waste and I'm beginning to realise that my house is full of things that could (and should) be repurposed. I must think about how I can use them to benefit my friends Jess and Andy's charity in Kenya. They're such lovely people who could be enjoying a comfortable life here in Suffolk but instead have chosen to live in a very different way, rescuing and restoring young girls and looking after them and their babies.

I mentioned this to Claire as we wove fairy lights into the greenery and she beamed at me.

'I'm so proud of you, Isabella! Lots of people would have got really bitter after what happened between you and Johnnie, but you're always looking for ways to help others. I can't tell you how happy I am that you moved here. You're a gift from God.'

She gave me a hug and I felt tears start into my eyes. I normally deflect remarks of this nature (yes, I am a famous influencer and God has clearly heard of me and also follows me, but really, why would He allocate time to work with me on various life issues when He has such a vast global to-do list?) but on this occasion, I was willing to take it. Maybe there was some kind of divine intervention that led me to choose this particular village for my new abode. Who knows? **#lifechanges #coincidence #thanksgod**

I am so incredibly busy that I went to bed twice last week without removing my make-up (unheard of!) and I've forgotten to take my multivitamins three days on the trot. December is a crazy month. I keep feeding the Yuletide publicity machine with beautifully posed shots and enticing content, and on top of all that I've got the PTA events, children's activities, the Christingle and some fairly complex family dynamics to negotiate.

I always read around my subject and now that I have been plunged into the choppy waters of not one but two blended families (Angry Stepdaughter Meets Accidentally Pregnant Mismatched Couple), I'm working hard to find an adult way through the many difficult situations facing me. Mummy and Karen are scrapping daily over a wide variety of subjects, mainly how the Cottingham Christmas is going to play out. Her brother

Mark has offered to host Karen this year, but she is insisting that the precious memories of her mother cannot be trampled upon (her words) by any change to routine.

Mummy and I met for breakfast in the café in the village. I have decided that I will start to address my creeping weight problem in January. I am struggling to get into some of my size ten clothes and the thought of ballooning to a size twelve horrifies me! I do have some standards. The trouble is, I'm so short on time, constantly, and it's so easy to grab a slice of granary toast or spoon some tuna mayonnaise into a baked potato rubbed with olive oil and rosemary. I realised the other day that I've run out of both pomegranate seeds and sumac essence and really, can there be a clearer sign of mental confusion than that?

I didn't want to slide down the slippery slope of over-calorification (if that is even a thing), so I scanned the menu for healthy food. I had almost decided to order some chilli-infused smashed avocado *sans* toast with a side of scrambled egg when the tall, red-haired young waiter walked past me balancing not one, not two, but three full Englishes, destined for a group of chattering women on the big table by the window.

'Isabella,' I said to myself, 'you deserve that breakfast! You've earned it. Why are you always saying no to yourself? Swap out the toast for a grilled Portobello mushroom, ask for your eggs to be poached and go for a run later.'

The door opened with a blast of chilly air and Mummy came in, minus her stick. I suspect that the poor young waiter was not expecting to be seized by a posh, elderly lady in desperate need of caffeine, but so he was.

'Now. Young man. If you could just give me your arm to that table over there so that I can join my daughter, I would be obliged to you. And a double shot black Americano, please. We'll order our food in a second.'

There was a sign by the till reminding customers that table service was not offered, but the young man did as Mummy said without a murmur.

'Hello, darling! What are we having? I'm starving!'

She looked exceptionally buoyant, wearing a new outfit, well accessorised and with a twinkle in her eye. Marriage is agreeing with her.

'I thought a full English. I can go for a run later and if I don't have toast and ask for my eggs to be poached and add a mushroom, it won't hurt.'

Mummy tutted loudly.

'Oh, for goodness' sake! You modern girls! In my day, we lived on cigarettes, coffee and fry-ups. I'm having the lot. Fried egg, extra toast, butter, bacon, sausages and a pot of beans. I've given up smoking and I'm getting lots of exercise (that walking group Harry and I joined is simply marvellous), so why on earth shouldn't I start the day right?'

She had a point. However, I can't remember the last time I indulged in a fried egg, so when the waiter reappeared with Mummy's coffee, I went for the works minus the toast and plus two eggs, scrambled. And a large cappuccino. **#bestmealoftheday #breakfast #fullenglish**

'You're looking perky!' I sipped on the iced water thoughtfully provided by the management and waited to hear Mummy's latest news.

'I had lunch with Mark and Karl yesterday. Such lovely boys. Very loyal to their mother's memory, of course, but they let a few things slip.'

I pondered this while enjoying my perfectly cooked and locally sourced back bacon. Delicious! On the rare occasions I'd been at Harry's house, it had struck me as rather cold and bare. Apart from the family photos everywhere, there were few ornaments or pictures and the décor was stuck firmly in the past. Everything was decent quality, but faded. Colours were muted and the whole place was screaming out for a makeover. Most people evolve with the times. There's only so long a person can live with patterned carpets and woodchip painted in magnolia, surely. I appreciate that I am the doyenne of interior design and on-trend paint colours, but you don't have to be me to know that a coat of on-trend paint and some new curtains can really revitalise a room.

Mummy chewed enthusiastically on her bacon.

'I understand that change can be frightening. And I do appreciate that Karen was very close to her mother. I've no wish to replace the woman, or obliterate her memory. I've tried telling Karen that but she doesn't seem to get it. Karl told me that Karen is very like her mother. If that's the case, I don't know that she would have been the best company in the world.'

'I'd say, take it easy, keep trying to build bridges with Karen and see how it goes. How are the plans for Christmas going?'

'We've had a breakthrough. I had a long chat with Harry about it and I've managed to work out a compromise. They're all coming to us on Christmas Eve and we're going to do a lovely lunch and evening buffet. Karen was making noises about staying over, but Mark has managed to persuade her to join him and the family the next day.'

Mummy popped to the loo and I ordered her another coffee. As I was standing at the counter and eyeing up the homemade cakes (I mustn't indulge, but they do look rather yummy), the door opened and a familiar voice rang out.

'Oi, oi, Smug! Morning off?'

I explained that I was having breakfast with Mummy and talking tactics on her stepdaughter issues.

'Haven't seen Mrs N for ages. Mind if I join you? Double shot Americano, mate, hot milk and extra sugar. You know how I like it.'

The young waiter gave her a half-smile and fired up the coffee machine. I assumed that he was a member of the extended Bloomfield/Ling tribe. We returned to our table and Liane flung her bag to the floor and sank into the chair next to me with a sigh.

'Whole week of nights. I'm on the edge. I'm going to have a couple of coffees, chat to Mrs N, then go home and sleep till pick-up time.'

I was quietly impressed that my frenemy's system was so evolved that it could take on four shots of caffeine first thing and still let her sleep. Mummy appeared, freshly lipsticked and patting her hair.

'Liane, dear! This is a nice surprise. Are you joining us?'

I kissed Mummy goodbye, wished Liane a deep and peaceful sleep and went to settle the bill. Her voice rang out, clear and entirely discernible over the background chatter and the noise of coffee beans being ground.

'Oi! Mate! Get me some toast, will you? White, lots of butter and jam. Strawberry if you've got it.'

The red-haired waiter coloured slightly and rolled his eyes. I smiled sympathetically.

'She can be a bit much, but she's got a good heart. Take no notice.'

He grinned at me, his eyes twinkling, and too late, I realised my mistake. The resemblance was unmistakable.

'I know. She's my mum.'

Oops.

December is my busiest month of the year and without Sofija's help and support, my extra workload is untenable. Thank heavens I didn't step into Kate's shoes as chair of the PTA. Being the secretary is more than enough, thank you very much. I was just about managing to get through the days, but my sleep patterns and nutrition habits were taking a hit.

My routine is punishing. Get up at 6am, do some work before Milo wakes up. Hoist him out of his cot when he calls for me at the top of his voice. Change his nappy, dress him, give him breakfast, put him in the family room with some toys. Finn does his own breakfast, God bless him. Do breakfast for the girls, school run, home, work solidly until pick-up time. Squeeze in some more work time by letting the children watch television/play video games (oh, the guilt!). Make tea. Feed everyone. Load the dishwasher. Put Milo to bed. Spend an hour of quality time with the older ones. Do some more work in the kitchen so that we are at least breathing in the same oxygen (does this count as detached parenting?). Say goodnight to them. Do some more work. Fall into an exhausted slumber at around midnight. It's not sustainable, but then neither is December! I never thought I'd hear myself say this, but roll on January.

I can only manage to get through everything with the help of the fabulous Ali and my wonderful agency nursery nurse Sue Parkin, who takes Milo three days a week. As a single working parent, it's not unreasonable to need help, surely. On Friday morning, I came back from the school run with a massive to-do list and found Ali in the kitchen wiping down the island. I wished her a cheery good morning.

'Morning, Mrs Smugge. I'm afraid I'm feeling a bit peaky. I hate to ask, but would it be all right if I left early today?'

I looked at her properly for the first time. Her eyes were dull, her complexion pale and her brow bedewed with sweat. I took the cloth out of her hand and insisted she sat down while we went through her symptoms. Which were:

1.   Intermittent stabbing pains in her abdomen.

2.   Nausea.

3.   Loss of appetite.

4.   High temperature.

None of this sounded particularly good. I questioned her on the severity and longevity of her ailments. Halfway through a detailed exposition of exactly where the pain was and how it felt, she doubled up and went as white as a sheet. Fortunately, I had placed her in my gorgeous statement teal velvet cocktail chair which has a wide seating base and capacious arms. Had I offered her a kitchen stool, we might have added concussion to her woes.

'Can – you – ring – my – husband? Quicker – than – ambulance.'

The poor girl was forcing out her words in between gasps of pain. It was no time to argue. I seized her phone, pressed her finger against the unlock icon and found her husband's number. There was a brief and awkward moment when he addressed me as 'baby cakes', but once we had established that it was his wife's employer rather than Ali herself on the phone, things got back on to an even keel. I described her symptoms and suggested he made haste to the Old Rectory. Five minutes later (he must have come up the bypass), he screeched to a halt on the drive, scattering gravel everywhere. We helped poor Ali into the car and I asked him to keep me updated.

'I'm – so – sorry. Know – how – busy – you – are.'

To the last, my housekeeper was demonstrating the remarkable work ethic that keeps my abode sparkling and tidy and my freezer so well stocked with homemade meals. I assured her that her health came way before any of my First World concerns and watched as the car raced down the drive and indicated left up the lane, clearly taking the shortcut to Ipswich. I said a brief prayer ('Dear God. It's me. Please help poor Ali. If at all possible, could You arrange for her to be seen the minute she gets into A&E and for her husband not to get a parking ticket? Kindest regards, Isabella M Smugge') and opened the freezer to find something to defrost for tea.

And then I shut it again.

Don't I have enough on my plate without having to cook meals? We have a Chinese takeaway and a fish and chip establishment in the village, and since I am pivoting away from self-serving, inward-looking content and towards more community-based work, what could more appropriate for the UK's best-loved mumfluencer than to support her local fast-food establishment? Also it would make the children incredibly happy and it's becoming ever more difficult to find things that work across their age range. Finn is getting too old for the park *en famille*, Milo's too young for nearly everything truly fun and

Chloë is rapidly turning into a teenage girl (although she has only just started Year Five). Food is the one thing that brings them all together.

Also, it's Friday.

And I have been working jolly hard and neglecting my poor children.

I broke the good tidings to them upon their return from another full week of education and supervised leisure activities and was touched at the response.

'You're the best mum in the *world*! Maisie's had two Chineses and a drive-through burger already this month and she didn't even do her reading every night like her mum told her. Can we have loads? Can we have the banquet. Please?'

It's not often my elder daughter is so effusive. Finn was beaming, Elsie was shouting, 'Prawn crackers! Seaweed! Ribs!' and Milo was joining in with the general exultation by seizing me by the legs and bellowing incoherently.

As I have observed before, it's so easy to make children happy. I held up my phone.

'OK, you lot. Here's the deal. I have till 5.30 to work in peace, you three keep Milo happy, then I turn off the laptop and the phone, we get the Chinese, eat it in front of the telly and you get to choose what we watch.'

Of late, choice has caused issues since Finn, at nearly thirteen, has a quite different taste in televisual entertainment from his sisters and brother. However, the lure of exotic food presented in foil containers had apparently caused him to forget this, and at 5.30, all promises having been kept, I had managed to plough through all my most annoying jobs, post some fun Mum Fail content ('Hey Mamas! Anyone else caving in and ordering a takeaway tonight? **#fridayfun #nocookfriday #chinese #makingmemories**') and cross off a reasonable amount from my to-do list.

Fair's fair. I switched my phone off, unplugged the laptop and stowed it away in its case where Tabitha the cat couldn't get to it (she has taken to nibbling leads of late, which is adding greatly to my stress) and hustled everyone out of the door, Chinese-bound. **#familytime #lovemyfamily #yumyum #takeway #littlewins**

It's a mummy weekend, which would normally cause me quite a bit of anxiety. It's not that I don't love spending time with my children (I do), but with so much on my plate and any number of deadlines coming up fast, it's becoming harder to get everything done. Strangely, taking the night off and enjoying a takeaway seemed to revitalise my poor exhausted brain. I fell into bed at ten o'clock and slept incredibly well, waking only as Milo's gentle murmurings over the baby monitor seeped into my dreamless repose. There was a text from Ali's husband.

'Ali's been rushed into theatre. Her appendix was massively inflamed and on the point of bursting. Being operated on now. I'll keep you posted.'

Perhaps it's a sign of how much I've changed that my first thought was for the pain and anxiety Ali and her family were going through, rather than how on earth I was going to manage all the cleaning and cooking and washing by myself. That was my second thought.

I sent up a quick emergency prayer asking for help, swung my legs out of bed and commenced my day.

Saturday passed fairly painlessly. Finn was out with friends most of the day and I fell on my own sword and took the three younger ones, plus Claire's daughters, Hannah and Becky, to our local soft play centre, the lavishly misspelled Kiddiez Fun Korner (I thought about mentioning the lack of an apostrophe after the 'z' in 'Kiddiez' to the teenage staff but decided against it).

Once you get past the smell of fried food and socks, plug in your noise-cancelling earphones and fire up your laptop, it's amazing how much you can get done. Milo had a marvellous time in the ball pit and toddler section, with me perched at a table nearby keeping an eye on proceedings. I bought a large jug of squash and some crisps which kept everyone happy for a couple of hours. At lunchtime, I purchased meals where everything seemed to be in the shape of something else and insisted on sides of what the menu optimistically described as 'fresh garden peas' (and the alternative to that would be what? Stale indoor peas? **#smileyface**) as a sop to good health. Most of them ended up on the floor anyway. I got myself a jacket potato with tuna, mayonnaise and cucumber, with a limp side salad which looked as if it had had a fairly hard life.

I arrived at ten o'clock and managed to string out proceedings until three o'clock. I got a two-hour nap out of Milo, who collapsed into his pushchair clutching his beloved cuddly lion and fell fast asleep in spite of (or perhaps because of) the incredible racket all around him, and only had to break up two fights between the girls and some older, mean children. This could be the answer to my work/life/parenting balance issues!

I dropped Hannah and Becky back at the vicarage and accepted Claire's invitation to come in and have a coffee and a catch-up. Milo, fresh from his nap, was up for playing with bricks and a toy train layout with Joel and Ben. The girls all rushed upstairs and we were left in peace in the cluttered front room. I filled Claire in on the Ali saga.

'I feel so sorry for her. But I just don't know how I'm going to manage this month without her. I suppose I'll have to go back to the agency, but then I need to break someone new in. I know it sounds selfish when there are people who can't afford to pay the bills, but I've got loads of guests coming for Christmas and all the rooms to do, plus all my work. And I tried praying about it. So far, nothing.'

Claire looked sympathetic.

'I'll pray that God sends the solution. In fact, do you want to have a pray now while the children are all happy?'

I have not yet mastered the art of speaking to God aloud. I tried once, last year, in church when a random woman asked me for help and messed it up massively.

'Errr – I suppose so. But I'll feel silly. And you might laugh at me if I get it wrong.'

My friend gave me what you might call an old-fashioned look.

'Isabella Smugge. You appear on national television, cool as a cucumber, you reach out to millions and do a podcast with your mother. You do things I never could. What on earth could you do to make me laugh at you?'

I agreed, reluctantly, to Have a Bash. Although Claire assures me that there is no hierarchy in the Christian world (the good Lord looks upon archbishops, bishops, vicars and ordinary entry-level types like me in the same fashion, apparently), surely it can't hurt to have a real live vicar's wife interceding alongside you. Also, I need to practise out-loud praying as Lauren tells me that a lot of it goes on at homegroups. Gulp.

Claire kicked things off with a general introduction to the issue, thanks for Ali and her family, fairly specific requests for speedy healing, quick recovery and protection from infection and then, to my amazement, by telling God that she wanted to thank Him for me! I was touched. When she'd finished speaking, I waited for a minute for her to say, 'Amen,' thus signalling that it was my turn. However, she didn't, and I realised that I had got myself embroiled in Freestyle Praying, something Lauren has given me notes on.

I cleared my throat.

'Dear God. Errr – thank You for Ali. I am truly grateful that she is such a nice person and a good housekeeper and that she helps me so much. Please can You make her better and not let any awful side effects happen like those infections people get in NHS hospitals. Also please bless her husband and her boys and send help to support them. And could You please find someone quickly who can clean my house to the same standard as her and who understands how to dress a bed properly. I would be terribly grateful. Thank You very much in advance. Amen.'

Once, many years ago, before the children came along, I was on a skiing trip in Colorado with Johnnie. We were having a marvellous time, enjoying amazing food, fine wines and wonderful snow conditions. I was hammering down a red run behind him when I skied over a lump of ice and everything went wrong. I can still feel the panic that descended upon me as my skis stopped responding and I picked up speed with no control. As I hurtled down towards the valley with the wind whistling in my ears waiting for the inevitable crash, I felt stupid and frightened. Me, the woman who could take on any terrain, skiing like a novice.

Take away the snow-covered mountains, the clear blue sky and the pine trees and put Isabella M Smugge in a shabby Suffolk vicarage, and you have pretty much the same experience. What was I thinking? There's nothing wrong with being direct, but why did I blurt out that snobbish remark about the NHS? Why was I so ludicrously specific about what I needed in a temporary replacement housekeeper? What would God (and more importantly, Claire) think of me? My cheeks were burning hot and my heart beating at double speed. What next? Did I open my eyes? But what if Claire was still communing with the Lord? Why hasn't someone written a manual on this kind of thing?

Claire sighed quietly, said, 'Yes, Lord, hear our prayers,' and then shuffled her feet. I took the risk and opened my eyes.

It seemed the praying had come to an end.

'That was rubbish. I can't believe I said those things. I feel like an idiot.'

Claire smiled and put her hand on my arm.

'You were fine. No one's judging you. You don't worry about what you say to me, or Lauren or the girls at school, do you? It's exactly the same. More coffee?'

I felt pretty sure it wasn't the same, but bowed to her superior knowledge. She herself, appearances to the contrary, had not been brought up in a churchy domestic environment, singing hymns and going to holy events as I believe many religious people do. To my amazement, shortly after we met, she had revealed that she'd grown up in a dysfunctional and violent home and been fostered after a particularly traumatic incident. Separated from her siblings, wracked with guilt and shame and extremely vulnerable, she had rebelled against her foster parents, become a habitual school refuser and taken enthusiastically to drink and drugs. When she met Tom, then a trainee lawyer, she was at her very lowest ebb, genuinely considering suicide. Whenever I doubt that there is an actual deity up there who cares about me, or question the way my life is going, or wonder if all that churchgoing is actually doing me any good, I remember what she told me in the self-same front room three years ago. She was on the edge, she was saved, and her life was transformed.

Gazing out at the rain lashing against the windows (November and December have been incredibly wet and gloomy with lots of flooding in the surrounding countryside), I pondered the way my own life is going and decided to trust in God as Tom is always telling us to do at church. I sent up a quiet prayer.

'OK. I'll leave this one in Your hands. You know I like doing everything myself, but I could really do with the help. Thanks in advance. Amen.' **#trust #freestyling #outloud**

Johnnie came to collect the children after school the next Friday as I was preparing for the wreath-making event. I promised that I would arrange a meeting with Paige in January and kissed my three eldest goodbye. Mummy managed to be almost civil and Johnnie pretty much kept his mouth shut, which was a blessing.

As yet, no one has stepped forward to offer to be my temporary housekeeper. I am continuing to trust in the good Lord through gritted teeth. I am giving Him until close of play next Tuesday and then I will be taking matters into my own hands.

The wreath-making event was a triumph! Rebecca is delighted. Fortunately, Hayley didn't come, but a number of school mums I don't know did, and it was good to have a chance to chat to them and show that I am not an unrelatable posh mum, but very nearly one of them. Result! Only the Christmas Fayre and the Disco to get through now. I have not volunteered for any jobs at the latter. I will be sitting in the dark with my noise-cancelling earphones on handing out money for snacks, sweeties, carbonated drinks and glow sticks for two hours. Lauren says that's the only way to get through it. Then we're having fish and chips. The PTA has an alcohol licence so there will be wine and beer on sale. I may allow myself a small glass of whatever's on offer.

On Tuesday in the playground, exhausted and fairly sure that I was wrong and that all those other so-called answers to prayer were coincidences, I was waving my children off when Liane came marching up to me.

'I hear you've lost some of your staff, Smug.'

I confirmed that this was the case.

'I've just finished my dementia course and I've got some spare time. I could do with some extra cash for Christmas. What do you pay?'

Somewhat taken aback (Liane is so direct), I told her.

'OK. Stick a tenner on that and call it cash-in-hand with no questions asked and I'll take it on. I love cleaning. Tell me what you want, once, don't talk to me when I'm working and let me have as much coffee as I like from your fancy machine and you've got yourself a deal.'

I stuttered my thanks and agreed to her terms. To be honest, she could have asked for a bag of diamonds and some Class A drugs and I'd have made it work. We agreed that she would join me for coffee after the school run tomorrow morning for a full briefing and start work on Thursday.

I shared the good news with Claire, who smiled significantly and raised an eyebrow.

'All right, all right! An answer to prayer. Excellent. Thank you.'

My day suddenly got a whole lot better. **#answeredprayer #phew**

I am on my knees with exhaustion! The Christmas Fayre is done and dusted. The Chocola sold out in twenty-five minutes. We had record numbers attend and the cake donations only just held out. Lauren was on red alert to run to the shop and buy reinforcements until someone remembered they'd left three boxes of cupcakes in their car. There were no major incidents, unless you count finding that some wretched child had licked an alarming number of jelly snakes and stuck them to the back of the school piano. The Disco was bearable, just. Our treasurer actually smiled when he told us the amount we've raised this term, which has broken all records.

In other news, Liane is proving to be a marvel. I complied with her requests and left her well alone as she sped round my house, cleaning like a woman possessed. Her taste in music seems to err towards heavy rock and metal, judging from the sounds emerging from her earphones. My surfaces are gleaming, my beds beautifully made with hospital corners, all cobwebs banished and the floors so clean you could eat your broccoli and anchovy pasta off them. She works at lightning speed and is managing to keep on top of everything by working three days a week fuelled, apparently, by vast amounts of caffeine and sugar. Poor Ali is likely to be off until at least the end of January. I've briefed Liane on the art of dressing beds and roomscaping and when my Christmas guests arrive, I doubt they'll notice any drop in my remarkably high standards.

I am having to rely on takeaways and variations on Desperation Spaghetti more than I'd like (Ali was about to restock the freezer with homemade meals when she was taken ill), but it's not the end of the world. The children seem happy. Last night I served the following:

Bâtonnets de poisson à la sauce tomate
Frites
Petit pois
Glace à la vanille avec sauce au caramel et pépites

Or, in plain English, fish fingers with tomato ketchup, chips and peas followed by vanilla ice cream with toffee sauce and sprinkles.

Except for the fact that the fish fingers were made with sustainably caught pollock and coated in panko breadcrumbs, I appeared to be feeding my children what 90 per cent of the UK's population eat on a regular basis. Everyone loved it. I swerved the ice cream and added a portion of steamed kale to my main course and it was actually very tasty.

A text from Amanda.

'I hope this isn't going to put pressure on you, but Kitty has switched to a plant-based diet. She still eats virtually nothing, but she's improved very slightly and if it gets her to keep something down, then I'm not going to argue. Of course, I don't expect you to do an entire vegan Christmas dinner and I'm happy to provide all the ingredients for her needs xx so looking forward to seeing you.'

I ran some menu ideas past the children, Davina and Toby. The general consensus seemed to be that they were all fine with a plant-based Christmas dinner as long as they could have all the traditional trimmings and that meat would be served at some point during the festive period. I added, 'Find out what vegans eat for Christmas dinner,' to my vast to-do list and began to plan out who was sleeping where.

My life! It never stops. **#busymum #roomscaping #plantbased**

Kitty has put on three pounds this month and has slowly begun to open up to Amanda about the bullying that caused her anorexia in the first place. Natasha seems absolutely fine, thank God. Matthew and Baby Florence are simply adorable and I am looking forward to a wonderful family Yuletide season.

Johnnie and Paige are spending Christmas together, which is fine with me. The children are going to his for three days between Christmas and New Year (minus Paige who is returning to her ancestral home somewhere in the East End) and being returned to me on New Year's Eve, just in time to meet up with their paternal grandmother, Silvia, their aunt, uncle and cousin and Mummy and Harry. But I shall park New Year for now and concentrate on getting through Christmas. And perhaps even enjoy it.

Standing in church on Christmas morning with my beautiful children, Toby, Davina, little Matthew and Baby Florence, and Amanda, Kitty and Natasha, surrounded by friends and singing joyful Christmas carols, I allowed myself to feel (just the tiniest bit) smug. The school Christmas events were done and the PTA coffers overflowing with fathomless riches. The Christingle had been an unqualified success and there had been no punch-ups, head lice or intestinal complaints. All four of my children were nit-free, my mother was enjoying Christmas with her new husband, my house was gleaming, my guest rooms beautifully dressed with flowers and scented candles, and I myself was resplendent in a fitted black dress with trumpet sleeves and chiffon detail with carefully chosen white-gold and gem jewellery, a smoky eye, red lipstick, timeless dark red nails and a modular handbag which was more than earning its keep. **#ootd**

As we belted out the final chorus of 'Hark the Herald Angels', I looked around me and for the first time understood what Tom meant when he talked about the church family. A mixture of people all with their own stories, secrets and hidden sadnesses, some of whom I knew well, some hardly at all. There were lots of faces I had never seen before, but this was presumably owing to the Annual Christmas Rush, the one time of the year when everyone feels completely fine about walking into a church and singing songs in the company of relative strangers.

I sang the final verse and chorus at top volume and sent up a silent prayer of thanks to the good Lord. I love a houseful of guests and, based on my recent prayer-based success, I am going to really double down on praying for poor little Kitty. It might work. You never know.

Back at home, the makings of Pomegranate French 75 cocktails were in the fridge, my canapés were made and ready to go, in the beautifully clean oven a sweet potato and mushroom wellington and vegan pigs in blankets were cooking gently, my paprika-dusted roast potatoes, Hasselback parsnips with orange and maple syrup were in and all I had to do was reheat my cranberry, orange and rosemary sauce, steam my curly kale and cook my sizzled sprouts with pomegranate and pistachios. For dessert, I'm offering roast figs with sherry and clotted cream ice cream and vegan Christmas pudding with vegan cream and custard flamed in Armagnac.

I poured the cocktails and put out the small plates of nibbles, raising a glass to my family. Issy Smugge says Merry Christmas one and all! **#christmasday #churchfamily #togetherness**

January

Christmas Day was perfect. Kitty looked happier than I've seen her for some time and actually ate some food. As the day wore on and the poor little thing realised that no one was judging her or watching what she ate, she smiled a couple of times and had a chat with Finn. After a light supper (tahini noodles with sesame seeds, chilli flakes and steamed greens, plus Christmas cake and Wensleydale cheese for anyone who wanted it), the two of them went off and started playing Scrabble with Natasha, which was sweet. Matthew, Baby Florence and Milo played adorably together and all went off to bed without a murmur.

Once the little ones were asleep, Amanda, Toby, Davina and I relaxed in front of the fire in the snug with a Christmas cheeseboard and a couple of bottles of good Cabernet Sauvignon.

'That was delicious, Isabella. I can't believe it was meat-free. We probably eat too much of it at home.'

Davina was curled up on the sofa holding Toby's hand, the picture of contented marital bliss. I love them both but it hurts my bruised heart when I think of Johnnie miles away with another woman. Not that I want him back. I don't, but it's still painful.

I refocused my mind on the prospect of a relaxed few days with my family and tried not to think about the moment when my husband would appear on the drive and take my children away. Having consulted with various other separated and divorced mums on the playground, it seems that it does get easier with time. The trouble is, we share four children and there is no getting away from the fact that we will be spending time in each other's company for the rest of our lives.

It's so lovely to have Amanda back at the Old Rectory. We used to have a fairly semi-detached relationship, but since she left her philandering husband, Charlie, we have found that we have more similarities than differences. We chatted about the children, home life, school and current affairs while the fire crackled contentedly and the wine slid down. At half past nine, Davina, who had been letting out violent yawns for some time, announced her intention to turn in for the night. I watched as she and Toby walked out of the snug hand in hand and let out an involuntary sigh. Amanda gave me a penetrating look.

'I know. I feel the same. How come you and I married the rubbish Smugges and Davina bagged the best one of the lot?'

I refilled our glasses. We had well and truly lined our stomachs and if there is a more relaxing activity than sitting in front of an open fire sipping good red wine and nibbling on locally sourced cheese, I don't know what it is. Conversation turned to Silvia, our mutual mother-in-law. I had always thought that she was as perfect as a human being can be. However, last year when Amanda left Charlie, alarming personal qualities began to rise to the surface. My sister-in-law did her degree in psychology and is now retraining as a counsellor. She has an uncanny ability to look at people and analyse their true motives and drives, a bit like an extremely posh X-ray machine.

'She still won't admit that Charlie's done anything wrong. She keeps using phrases like, "Boys will be boys," and, "It doesn't mean anything." I've given up trying to talk to her. And she thinks that Kitty is "going through a phase, like all girls," and isn't putting any responsibility for her illness on Charlie. I've pretty much cut off contact. I wouldn't stop her seeing the children, but she doesn't see much of them anyway.'

I took a reflective gulp of wine. Talking to Amanda is both revelatory and scary. The old me used to pretend that everything was fine, and I have to say I was very good at it. The new improved version of Isabella M Smugge can't overlook toxic behaviour as once she did, and the unpalatable fact is that both Johnnie and Charlie are products of their upbringing. Their father cheated on Silvia, they've cheated on their wives and their children are paying the price. To be fair, mine don't seem to have been too affected by their father's absence, but they certainly still miss Sofija every day, which makes me feel terrible. I shared this with Amanda.

'Hmm. Would you ever consider asking her to come back and work for you? Could you rebuild your relationship, do you think?'

Increasingly of late, I've been thinking about Sofija and wishing things had been different. I pondered Amanda's question.

'Maybe. I don't know.'

Amanda peered into her glass.

'It must be the fire heating the room up. My wine seems to have evaporated.'

Mine had too, so I poured us both another large one. I believe there are a number of recipes that call for leftover wine, but that's never been a problem in my house!

It was gone one by the time the bottle was empty and we rose unsteadily from our seats to stagger off to bed. I glanced at my phone, which was on silent, and saw a WhatsApp had come in on the family group from Davina.

'Stay in bed tomorrow, you two. We'll be up with Florence first thing anyway. I'll bring you breakfast in your rooms when you wake up xx sleep well.'

I am so blessed! I attempted to convey this sentiment to Amanda but it came out a bit wrong. More like, 'Sho bleshed.' How often do I overdo it on the vino collapso and have a lie-in? That would be never. Nighty night! **#wine #latenight #sleepitoff**

Davina was as good as her word. I slept the sleep of the over-refreshed and stirred vaguely at around seven when I heard Milo's little voice on the baby monitor. The next time I came to, my phone told me it was half past nine and my sister-in-law was tapping on my door.

'Tea? Coffee? What would you prefer? Could you manage a fried breakfast?'

I was feeling rather rough and had a cracking headache. My digestive system had presumably spent the night processing far too much cheese and wine, but seemed to be up for a full-on repast. Feebly, I requested Lapsang Souchong and the said full English and fell back on my award-winning pillows. God bless Davina! She had got Milo up, fed him and was supervising the entire tribe of young Smugges downstairs as well as her own two.

Twenty minutes later, I was going head to head with two rashers of beautifully cooked back bacon, two butcher's sausages, a poached egg, granary toast, grilled mushrooms and vine tomatoes and a pot of beans. By half past ten, I was in the shower, feeling restored and ready to face what was left of the day. Clad in barrel-leg jeans, comfy fluffy socks, a structured vest and cable-knit cream jumper, I ran down the stairs feeling rather guilty. What kind of hostess stays up half the night drinking red wine and guzzling cheese and then sleeps in and allows her guests to hold the fort?

I found Toby in the kitchen unloading the dishwasher while Davina played with the children in the family room, from which an unfamiliar sound was issuing. It was Kitty, laughing, sitting on the sofa bouncing Florence on her knee while Finn helped Milo and Matthew to build a wobbly tower out of bricks.

'Davina, I feel so bad for lying around in bed while you're down here looking after everyone. Can I make you a coffee?'

'Certainly not! The very least I can do is to give you a lie-in. Sit down and I'll bring *you* a coffee. Kitty, darling, can I get you anything? You're being an absolute marvel with Flo.'

Amanda appeared in search of painkillers. She joined me on the sofa and we gazed at Kitty, now singing to Florence and blowing raspberries on her tummy. I watched as Amanda's face relaxed and a smile stole across her face.

Outside, it was raining hard and the sky was an unappealing slate grey.

'Mum, I'll do my run this afternoon. It's supposed to clear up later.'

Amanda opened her mouth to speak and I noticed Finn giving his cousin a side eye.

'Mind if I come with you? I'm on the cross-country team at school and I need to work on my stamina.'

Kitty hesitated for a minute.

'OK. But I don't do it for fun. No passengers. You might not be able to keep up.'

My boy is enough of a Smugge to see a challenge and take it on. Assuring her that he was more than capable of running for miles without stopping, he went into the kitchen and started rummaging in the fridge for snacks. The Christmas cheeseboard has got its own shelf. Because, really, this is the one time of the year when you can eat cheese all day while watching glossy, overproduced television and drinking port.

Boxing Day can be a challenge. The excitement of giving and receiving presents is over, but the savvy hostess knows that relaxed yet statement meals bring everyone together. Sticking with the plant-based theme, I was giving my guests butter bean puttanesca, but serving it more as a hearty kitchen supper than a full-on meal. Making the sauce would take minutes, with superior quality butter beans, crushed garlic, tomato purée, capers, olives, chilli flakes and parsley.

I did virtually nothing all day except sit around, play board games and eat cheese. When Finn and Kitty had gone out on their run (the rain was still lashing down, but a challenge is a challenge), I congratulated Natasha on thrashing me at Scrabble and collapsed on to the sofa with Amanda and Davina. Toby was entertaining the little ones, Natasha was having some screen time while Chloë and Elsie played Exploding Kittens.

'Thank you again for having us, Isabella. Last night, Kitty told me she feels safe here. That's a huge thing for her. Being at my parents' is a safe place, but virtually nowhere else is. It's lovely to see her interacting with her cousins.'

Kitty is being home-schooled while she battles her anorexia, and poor Amanda is juggling that along with doing her counselling course remotely.

Davina looked sympathetic.

'It must be so hard for you. How's Natasha doing?'

Amanda smiled. 'She's a completely different kettle of fish from Kitty. Massively into sport, head girl, huge friendship group. I've never had to worry about her. In the nicest possible way, she takes after Charlie. His best bits, that is. She's tough, she doesn't suffer fools gladly and she does what she wants. Boarding school worked brilliantly for the other three but Kitty hated it from the start.'

'How's her therapy going?'

Amanda selected a piece of Baron Bigod, popped it on a charcoal biscuit and spread homemade chutney liberally over the top.

'It's helping to a certain extent. But it hasn't made as much of a difference as I was hoping. As you know, I've based myself at my parents' since I came back from Dubai and with the best will in the world, there aren't that many therapists to the square mile.'

A brilliant thought struck me.

'One of my friends on the playground was pretty much agoraphobic when I moved here. She never went out and had huge anxiety issues. But she sees an amazing therapist and it's transformed her life. I could text her and find out if he does Zoom calls or even if he's got a slot coming up.'

Amanda considered.

'He's not likely to be free over Christmas, is he? I don't want to impose on your hospitality and outstay my welcome.'

I waved away her protests with a beautifully manicured hand (and by the way, glossy dark red nails go with everything. Ideal for anything from a glitzy evening out, cocktails with the girls to an informal dinner party) and offered extended hospitality for as long as she liked.

'You're doing your course online, Natasha will be going back to school, the boys are at uni and work – if your parents don't mind, I'd love to host you here for as long as it takes.'

Space wasn't a problem and Mummy adores Amanda. In fact, the more I thought about it, the more my invitation seemed to be something that would benefit not just my sister-in-law and niece, but also me. I had invited Silvia for New Year because I felt obliged to, rather than because I wanted her company. This was a relatively new feeling and I was uncomfortable with it. Mummy and Harry would be fine and, of course, Suze and Jeremy know Silvia well. The more I thought about it, the more I began to realise that having two extra house guests would dilute the effect of my mother-in-law's resolute blindness to the effect her sons' behaviour had had on the family.

'Let me send Charlene a message and see what she says.'

Am I Mrs Fixit or what? **#christmas #newyear #hostess #sortitout**

Tony the counsellor does not celebrate either Christmas or New Year, it seems. He was more than happy to offer Kitty an introductory appointment on the 30th. Ignoring Amanda's outpourings of gratitude (because, really, why was Issy Smugge put on this earth if it wasn't to be the most gracious and welcoming hostess and best aunt in the world?), I made some last-minute changes to my accommodation plan and ordered in extra food. I had planned roast duck with an orange and Armagnac sauce, braised spicy red cabbage, fondant potatoes, green peas, julienne carrots and a turnip purée for New Year's Day, but by adding in a veggie paella packed with crunchy and vibrant vegetables, I would be keeping Kitty happy too. Mummy and Harry are arriving after breakfast on the 30th, Silvia at tea time the same day and Suze, my brother-in-law Jeremy and niece Lily on New Year's Eve. I'm putting on a relaxed family evening of board games, delicious organic nibbles and on-trend mini cocktails, and foresee an excellent New Year.

Of all the houses I've lived in (and there have been quite a few), the Old Rectory is undoubtedly my favourite. It is the principal dwelling in the village, and with its wine cellar (which Johnnie and I had planned to tank out and transform into a cinema room), generous ground, first and second floors and attics (surely ripe for conversion at some point when I find the time), I never have to worry about space. New Year went jolly well, and apart from a couple of sticky moments around the table when Silvia made comments about Kitty's weight and the possibility of her sons returning to their respective marital homes, things went as well as could be expected.

By 5th January, everyone had been packed off home. Amanda moved into Sofija's old quarters and Kitty into the box room. Having another adult in the house was fabulous. I'd forgotten how much easier it is to run a house and to parent with someone to bounce issues off. It was almost like having Sofija back again.

A miracle has occurred! Kitty has really taken to Tony and they are having weekly sessions. He lives a twenty-minute drive from the village and, while it is still early days, we can see the faintest chink of light at the end of a very long, dark tunnel.

I've organised Finn's birthday event already. He wants to go to an Escape Room with his friends and then have a meal afterwards. As always, I will be the driver and pay for it all. Now I have Amanda at home for the time being, she can look after the other three. And I'm not just assuming that, as I used to in the bad old days. She's so grateful that things are progressing with Kitty that she has offered herself as a temporary housekeeper and co-parent. Which is absolutely marvellous.

That weird smell outside is back. I wonder if someone's drains have blocked.

I'm dreading the meeting with Paige. What if she's horrible and I have to spend the rest of my life juggling childcare with a monster?

Chris Robinson keeps making narky comments on the PTA WhatsApp chat. Thank heavens for Rebecca, who continues to deal with him brilliantly.

I am hosting homegroup in two weeks. Am I nervous? Yes. Do I need to have coffee with Lauren to find out what I should expect? Absolutely! **#newchallenges**

Even with Amanda helping out, I felt tired and drained. I could barely get through my first conversation of the year with Mimi.

'Darling! How's my favourite client? Loving that new pallid look. It's so now. And is that the new eyeshadow style? Smoky and smudged even in the morning?'

It wasn't. I had neglected to cleanse, tone and moisturise the night before for perhaps the first time in my adult life, and had merely added another coat of eyeshadow and mascara upon rising. Mimi continued like a torrent of spring water bursting out of a rock and crashing into the valley below.

'Now, sweetie, I won't lie. I didn't love your new strategy over the holidays. Not nearly enough pictures of beaming tots by the Christmas tree. You're down by 0.08 per cent on engagement across all your platforms. This is not what Mimi expects to see.'

I often forget that I am the boss and that my agent works for me. My nose had developed an irritating sniffle and my throat felt dry and scratchy, but I took a restorative sip of my lime and ginger kombucha and gathered up my courage.

'The children are getting older and they don't want me taking pictures of them and plastering them all over social media. And I read a book with some really frightening stats about the effect social media exposure has on young people. I can carry on doing what I do by implying things, rather than using my family to extend my reach.'

Mimi took a sharp intake of breath, always a mistake when your lungs are more tar than organic matter, and went into a paroxysm of coughing. Wiping her eyes and lighting a fresh cigarette, she leaned forward with a menacing look in her eye.

'But what else are your family for if not to extend your reach and engagement? Why have children if you can't turn them to your advantage? I was looking forward to lots of lovely content about blended families and hilarious teenage misunderstandings. You've always led the pack on trends and whatnot, darling.'

I wasn't having that.

'No, Mimi. My children are not there to be used. I'll keep on posting about the house and the reno and clothes and lifestyle advice, but I'm cutting right down on family images. It's not fair on them. And also, having my niece living here has made up my mind. I'm going to use my platforms to talk more about teenage issues like cyberbullying and eating disorders and mental health.'

Mimi pursed her lips and frowned. 'Honestly, sweetie, why can't you just get yourself a couple of cockapoos and take up paddleboarding like the other influencers? I'm not at all sure about the direction you're taking.'

I suddenly found that I didn't give a fig and fennel flapjack what Mimi thought. Blowing my nose loudly (surely I can't be getting a cold), I went through the rest of the agenda and said goodbye with a huge sense of relief. Half-heartedly, I began writing a lifestyle blog about being your best self in January, but after ten minutes, nose streaming and eyes stinging, I admitted defeat and trudged back to the house, where Amanda made me a pot of peppermint tea (so cleansing) and insisted I had a lie-down.

Isabella M Smugge, queen of the influencers, dozing in the daytime! I could hardly believe it, but as I peeled off my heavenly knee-high chocolate brown suede boots and fell onto my wickedly comfortable bed, the thought of a catnap seemed almost irresistible.

I closed my eyes at eleven o'clock and when I opened them again, to my horror, I realised I'd been asleep for ages. Sitting bolt upright, I seized my phone. Four missed calls from Mummy and any number of notifications. There was a WhatsApp from Amanda.

'I've looked in on you a few times and you were so peacefully asleep, I thought you must need it. I'll do the school run xx'

What have I become? Could this be the onset of middle age? Or worse still, the menopause? I resolved to do a deep dive into the whole business and change my diet, exercise regime and vitamin intake to stave off premature ageing. But before I did that, I lay back on my pillows and closed my eyes again. Just for a minute.

I awoke to find that the cat had decided to take her afternoon snooze on my legs and that Amanda had delivered a tray of tea. Fortunately, I had lapsed into unconsciousness in a semi-upright position and could drink it without disturbing my furry little visitor. I rang Mummy.

'Isabella! At last! Where on earth have you been? I've rung and rung. My marriage is over. I'm leaving Harry and coming back home.'

I gave myself a sharp pinch on the arm to check that I wasn't asleep. My mother still qualified as a newlywed, surely, and had appeared perfectly happy over Christmas. What on earth could have happened in the last week? I sneezed loudly and asked for further information.

'I'm in a taxi. I've got enough clothes to last a week and you can go back to the house and pack up my things in due course. See you shortly.'

'But Mummy, I'm in bed. I don't feel very well. And what do you mean, your marriage is over? It hasn't even been three months!'

But she had gone and I was left with only a sleeping cat, a fragrant pot of tea and a box of extra-soft balm-infused tissues before the storm hit. **#newlyweds #row #atchoo**

I have gone from being a single parent with no live-in help to a marriage counsellor, psychiatrist, taxi driver and entertainment officer in one fell swoop. Milo, always of a rampantly sociable disposition, has not taken kindly to most of his playmates departing. He used to be content with me and the lovely Sue plus his siblings, but has suddenly developed a worrying habit of shouting, 'No!' to every suggestion and waking up at least twice in the night. Could this be the onset of the Terrible Twos? In addition, the children's social lives are full, even in the depths of winter, and they need driving about to various playdates, sporting fixtures and school events. I am helping Kitty with her art and English GCSE schoolwork, which is absolutely fine, but an extra job in my already overloaded schedule.

But, of course, the well-groomed and posh elephant in the room is my mother. My separated mother. My angry, bitter and separated mother who has started smoking again. My life is in ruins! Thank God for Amanda. Without her, I truly do not know what I would do.

It seems that Harry and Mummy had a huge row about Karen. Mummy has been very sensitive and left her predecessor's bedroom as the spare room and turned the big dual-aspect bedroom at the front of the house into the principal suite. It has a rather dated en suite shower room and enough space to put in a dressing room where the old box room was. Mummy and Harry took down a wall and installed a new sleek and contemporary en suite, a dressing room with hanging space and fitted drawers, and redecorated and recarpeted the lot.

All was well until Karen came over when Mummy was out and kicked up a huge fuss. It seems that the box room held many precious and irreplaceable memories (of what I couldn't tell you) and that she was beside herself at the thought of 'that woman' desecrating her mother's home. Harry made the mistake of promising her that he'd put a stop to the changes and when Mummy came home, all hell broke loose.

'It was the last straw. I've been so patient and understanding and I will not have that girl running my life. I told Harry and he got terribly upset. I said he had to choose between me and her, which in retrospect wasn't the best idea I've ever had.'

I was agog.

'Who did he choose?'

'He didn't. He said I had to understand that Karen had emotional needs and that I must be patient. I lost my temper, I'm afraid, and threw a hideous ornament into the fireplace. Harry took it badly so I smashed a vase (that dreadful thing with the handles and the gilt), said some rather unwise things, called a taxi and left to buy some cigarettes and have a boozy lunch by myself.'

All I wanted to do was curl up with a hot-water bottle and be left alone, but Mummy was dabbing angrily at her eyes and scrabbling around in her handbag for her cigarettes. I longed for Amanda's calm presence, but she was out, ferrying various children around the district. Trying my best to be a good daughter, I assured Mummy that everything would be all right.

'I don't know what you're basing *that* prediction on, Isabella! I really thought I'd found happiness but I should have known that Karen would ruin it. And now I've started smoking again. I blame *her*. Always leaving her cigarettes out where I could see them. And we're going to have to cancel our wedding blessing and the party.'

She burst into tears and stomped through the boot room to smoke furiously by the camellia bush outside. Great! As if I need any more stress in my life.

Mummy and Harry had decided to have their marriage blessed at church, and after a meeting with Tom ('So dishy, darling. He'll look marvellous in the photos'), had booked it for the late May bank holiday when the weather could be trusted to behave itself. I'd organised tipis and a caterer and was looking forward to a slightly more relaxed party to which, we hoped, the illness-prone Veronica Madingley could come. And now it was all off! I simply didn't have the energy to start cancelling everything, so I sank into a comfy armchair and closed my eyes. I was feeling tired, peevish and rather put out. I had gone to church repeatedly, prayed a lot more than usual, trusted God with the whole housekeeping business and graciously opened my home to those in need. And this was how I was being repaid! I addressed the Almighty with none of my usual politeness.

'Now, look here! What on earth are You playing at? I cannot believe that my mother and Harry have broken up. What was the point of all that hard work organising the wedding if they were just going to call it a day at the first hurdle? I am not at all happy. And can I just remind You that I am hosting the new homegroup here and will therefore be doing holy activities twice a week? Surely that counts for something. Amen.'

So that's that! I braced myself for Mummy's return from the porch outside the boot room. In she came, smelling of smoke and coughing, just like old times. I handed her a double-shot black Americano and sank wearily on to the sofa. There was a loud ring at the door.

'Oh, for goodness' *sake*! Who on earth is that?'

I heaved myself up again and trotted out to the hall to open the door. There stood my new stepfather, looking angry and dishevelled. I'd never seen him anything but smiling and dapper, but marrying my mother will do that to a man.

'Isabella! Is Caroline here? I've been going out of my mind with worry. She's not answering her phone.'

I indicated that Mummy was at home to visitors and ushered him in. I stood in the hall fiddling with my hair and wondering if I should join them and mediate or keep myself to myself. I decided on option two and walked through the kitchen en route to the back stairs where I had left the colour charts for my reno. As I had expected, there were raised voices. I tiptoed past the island and took refuge in the back hall. Was it wrong of me to eavesdrop? Probably, but I needed to know the way the wind was blowing. Fragments of conversation drifted to my eagerly listening ears.

'... absolutely out of my mind. I rang and rang. Why did you rush out like that?'

'I told you! I can't go on like this! I can't be number two in your life, Harry...'

'... but I love you. You've changed my life. Surely we can...'

'... started smoking again because of her... flashbacks to my first marriage. Why do I never come first with any man? Franz, Isabella's father and now you!'

Either my hearing had suddenly improved or Mummy was turning up the volume. There were three outcomes from the current exchange.

1. It really *was* all over, in which case Harry and Mummy wouldn't want a third person drinking in all the gory details.

2. It wasn't over but some serious marriage counselling/medication/lifestyle changes were required. See above.

3. They were going to kiss and make up. See above.

I was very much hoping for number three. I don't think I can take much more drama in my life.

The next morning, I left Milo at home with Amanda and Kitty, dropped the girls off at school and walked up to the café with Lauren. I ordered a pot of Lapsang Souchong and updated my friend on the latest shenanigans at the Old Rectory.

'But they're back together now, right? They're such a sweet couple.'

Lauren was perched on the edge of her chair looking eager for news, as well she might. Goodness knows how she got through the days before Issy Smugge moved to the village.

'Oh, yes. Ten minutes of shouting then it was all snogging and cuddling and protestations of undying love. I didn't know where to look. She's back home with Harry, thank heavens, all stocked up on nicotine gum and with a plan to deal with Karen.'

I squeezed fresh lemon into my steaming cup of Lapsang Souchong. Lauren recoiled.

'What is *that?* It smells like someone poured hot water on an ashtray. No offence, babes.'

'None taken. Smoky notes, pine-dried camellia leaves. Chinese. I love it. It's so cleansing.'

From the wrinkled nose and narrowed eyes of my friend, it appeared that I was alone in my love of exotic tea. We sat and chatted for an hour with the comforting sounds of coffee grinding and milk steaming in the background. My cold (for I have admitted that is what it is) is getting worse by the minute. Automatically, I took some arty images of my teapot, the lemon slice floating in my cup and some blurred background shots of the café. If the common cold thinks it's stopping Issy Smugge in her tracks, it's got another think coming! **#lovemylife #suffolkinfluencer**

OK. I admit it. I was wrong about the cold. I keep telling myself it's mind over matter, but my joints are aching, I'm exhausted, and limitless wells of mucus and unspecified liquids from somewhere at the back of my nose are making everyday life utterly hideous. I go nowhere without fistfuls of balm-infused tissues and a tube of my Ultra-Hydrating Perfect Pout Lip Balm to hand. Mummy is enjoying a second honeymoon, hard on the heels of the first actual one, and Harry has said enough to Karen to keep her at bay for now. I am holding on by a thread!

I am now up to speed on the phenomenon of the homegroup. Lauren gave me many helpful tips and further explained that when Christians 'feel called' to do something, it means that they have had a good idea but want to give God the credit for it. At present, I feel called to climb into bed with a lemon and ginger infusion and a good book and remain there until spring, but God and I are not on speaking terms, so I have no idea what He thinks.

It seems that homegroups were set up for those who think that going to church on Sunday just isn't enough. They are generally midweek, involve the consumption of tea, coffee and good-quality biscuits and follow roughly the same agenda.

1. Welcome (this includes the said tea, coffee and biscuits).

2. Matters arising – everyone tells everyone else about what's been going on and laughs and make jokes.

3. Holy stuff – this is the portion of the evening where the homegroup leader (mine is Sue T who is running the show until one of us feels led to take over) goes through some notes and we all talk about them.

4. Requests – people say what they need prayer for and pray about it.

5. Any other business.

Lauren tells me that her homegroup has to work extremely hard not to spend all night on points 1 and 2, but is very good at 4. I enquired about the delicate process of praying out loud, something that worries me.

'How do you know what to say and when to start? What if you start talking at the same time as someone else? How do you know when it's finished and you can open your eyes? What about all that muttering that people do at church?'

I was reassured that, as with most things in life, practice makes perfect.

'I kept giggling and mixing my words up when I first did it. You can usually tell when someone's going to pray because they clear their throat and shuffle their feet. At our group, the leader says, 'Amen! Yes, Lord!' and that's how we know we're done. Or you can open your eyes a bit and check out the room if you're not sure. The muttering's optional. It's quite encouraging, though, if you're praying and people say things. Like there's this one guy in our group who says, "Praise the Lord! Yes! Thank You, God," all the time and it makes you feel like you're getting it right.'

I pondered this.

'But what about freestyle praying? When people go off on one and don't say amen at the end. I get really confused.'

Lauren patted my hand.

'Don't you worry. If you're not sure, just nod a lot and say, "Mmm," when other people are praying. That usually does the trick.'

I decided not to mention that I am in a mood with God and have no intention of contacting Him for a while. As if my life isn't complex enough!

January wore on, and with every passing day I felt worse and worse. Even with Amanda supporting me with childcare, Kitty bonding with Milo and Liane whizzing round the Old Rectory like a one-woman cleaning machine, my symptoms became more annoying. My cough is now hurting my chest and I'm barely sleeping. I am relying on evergreen content and even resorted to honesty this morning by posting pictures of boxes of tissues, lip balm and cold preparations.

I was moping around the kitchen in an old tea dress with a cable knit cardigan over it, thick tights and a pair of furry slippers which Mummy must have left behind (completely hideous, but so comfortable!), and with my hair unwashed and no make-up on when the bell rang. I was alone in the house. The children were at school, Milo was being entertained at a local play centre by agency nursery nurse Sue, and Amanda had driven Kitty to see Tony.

I opened the door and saw a small, pallid girl on the doorstep clutching a large brown paper bag. There was a gleaming top-of-the-range car on my drive with personalised numberplates: 'PA1 GE'.

I sneezed explosively, just missing my tissue, and my visitor made a retching noise and vomited into her bag. Suddenly everything made sense.

I've often thought about how the meeting between Johnnie, Paige and myself would play out. At no point in my musings did it commence with one of us spraying snot on to her slippers and the other bringing up the contents of her stomach. Also, whenever I visualised it, I was looking totally fabulous, polished and well put together, not like something the cat had dragged in.

Introductions over, I installed the mother of my husband's fifth child in the family room with a large stainless-steel bowl. I'm going to be redecorating anyway, so even if she pukes on the carpet, it doesn't really matter.

'Look, I'm sorry to take you by surprise. I just had to meet you. You're not like how I expected.'

My visitor was staring at me in wonder. My nose was red raw, my eyes watery and sunken and my hair lank. Anything less like the renowned influencer and lifestyle blogger beloved by millions could not be imagined.

'I don't usually look like this. I've got a terrible cold and I haven't left the house in three days.'

Paige (for it was she), smiled wanly.

'I know the feeling. I'm usually in the office by six every morning to catch the foreign markets. I spend more time with my head down the bog than doing deals these days. I don't know how much longer I can stand it.'

There was an awkward silence. Because, really, what do you say to the woman whom your husband has accidentally impregnated hard on the heels of cheating on you with your au pair? I offered her a coffee but she winced and clutched her bag.

'I can't even keep water down. Thanks, though.'

I took a deep breath.

'So. Paige. What do you want to talk about?' **#awks #girlfriend #sick**

'You're kidding me! She just showed up? What a cheek! What does she look like, babes? xx'

'I think it's quite brave, actually. What did you think of her, Isabella? xx and how are you feeling btw?'

'Did Johnnie put her up to it? Is she still puking? I'd have given her a smack if it was me! x'

The Mums' WhatsApp group had lit up with my revelation about Paige's visit. I was reading everyone's responses from the comfort of my lovely bed. My cold has turned to 'flu and I feel appalling. Amanda has taken over, God bless her. I am starting to bring up catarrh of a light-green hue which is probably quite worrying.

I started typing.

'She's quite pretty, nose piercing, reddish-brown hair, Cockney accent. Not Johnnie's usual type at all. Told me loads of stuff he's said to her which isn't true. Like I'm pushing for a divorce and I drove him away by being a workaholic xx feeling terrible.'

I love a WhatsApp thread, but my eyes were closing and I was burning hot. I turned my phone to silent and went to sleep. You can keep January. I've had enough. **#bigmeeting #januaryblues #ill**

February

One month down, eleven to go! Looking on the bright side, my chest infection has nearly gone, I've stopped sneezing and my gorgeous Extra Rich Moisturising Balm with Colloidal Oatmeal is taking care of my red flaky nose.

We bumped our first homegroup to February. No one seems to mind.

Kitty is still struggling to eat but has cut down her runs to three a week.

Amanda got a First in her latest module.

Mummy and Harry are still married.

Ali is back. Hooray!

Oh, and Sofija is going to start working for me again in March. It's been quite a month.

What do you give a couple who have a combined age of around 135 for a wedding present? It wasn't a question I'd ever asked myself, but it turns out that the answer is vouchers, plants and champagne. Enjoying a coffee and light lunch at the Cottingham marital home, I watched as Harry and Mummy leafed through their pile of remaining gifts, beaming and leaning against each other's shoulders. There was a lot of giggling.

'Look at this, darling. Spa vouchers. I'm getting the girls together for some pampering. You and Suzanne, of course, Isabella, and I've managed to get Liane booked in as well.'

I'd witnessed a conversation between my frenemy and my mother about this very subject and it was clear that Liane didn't want to come.

'How on earth did you manage that?'

Mummy smiled mischievously and, for a second, I got a glimpse of the young, vibrant, fun-loving girl who slid down a drainpipe to go dancing with a handsome ski instructor.

'There's more than one way to skin a cat, darling. I booked her through Caring Touch. I told the owner that I was going to a health appointment with lots of aqua therapy and that I needed a carer all day. She knows that Liane and I get on very well and I told her that she would have to accompany me to a pool so to bring her swimming costume.'

Caring Touch is the agency that employs the Pink Ladies, the team of carers who go out into the community clad in shocking-pink tabards. Last year, when Mummy had her stroke and came to recover at the Old Rectory, I had no idea that so many changes would be set in motion. If I hadn't seen Liane in the playground in her uniform and been put in touch with her boss, Linda Murray, Mummy would never have bonded with Liane and she would never have met Harry.

Mummy's brief flirtation with the evil weed was again over. Determined chewing of nicotine gum and the joy of being back in the marital home had given her the drive to kick the habit for the second time in a year.

'You're still looking very peaky, darling. I hope you're taking care of yourself.'

Once upon a time, I would have taken this as a criticism. As I dug into my pea and prawn risotto and green salad (delicious), I allowed myself to enjoy the relatively new feeling of unconditional love demonstrated by my mother.

'I'll be all right, Mummy. It was horrible at the time, but so much good has come from it. Amanda has been a brick, Kitty did some amazing images when you took my phone away and Sofija's coming back.'

I thought, but didn't say, that I was also back on first-name terms with the good Lord, who seems not to have taken offence at my brief departure from our relationship.

What a month! #newbeginnings #reconciliation

There is no place for illness in the gorgeous world of Isabella M Smugge. Slight sniffles are banished immediately with proprietary blends of vitamins and natural remedies, my excellent diet and exercise regime, plus my good genes keep viruses and infections away, and of course the accident of birth that saw me being born into a wealthy family has given me every health advantage. That said, when a girl has to do the bulk of her own childcare, cooking, cleaning and work, something's going to get over the ramparts and strike her down.

Lessons I have relearned this year:

1. Always take your vitamins.

2. Don't let exercise take a back seat.

3. Try to stick to a balanced diet and swerve carbs and sugar wherever possible.

4. Whatever you do, never ever post across your social media platforms when in the grip of a raging fever.

It seems that at the height of my chest infection, I temporarily lost my mind. Amanda had to take my phone away from me as I was posting complete gibberish under the impression it was my usual high-quality content. Fortunately, Harpreet has control over my platforms and alerted Mimi who told Mummy who WhatsApped Amanda who came racing upstairs and prised the device from my feverish hand. Team Isabella M Smugge was then left in the unfortunate position of only having evergreen content to post (wintry scenes, images of scuffed skirting boards and tired carpets around the renovation project, old stuff to be repurposed), until a most unlikely person came to the rescue.

My niece Kitty is of an artistic disposition. As her aunt lay burning up in her unbelievably comfortable bed, she took a set of photos as good as any I have ever produced. My illness coincided with a light snowfall, preceded by a hoar frost, all of which Kitty captured in an incredibly impressive way. My feed was full of gorgeous shots of icicles hanging from the eaves, early morning sunlight gleaming on the frozen pond, little footprints in the snow and a very small and poorly constructed snow person in the back garden. My followers loved it! With no briefing at all, she also managed to write some copy in my voice, using all the right hashtags and coming up with a few new ones. Harpreet is very impressed. Who knew?

My memories of the chest infection are hazy, but I kept having the most horrible dreams. I was wandering around a huge library, hemmed in by heavy, dark bookshelves while an ominous voice shouted the same words at me over and over again. I was falling from a great height, jerking awake just before I hit the ground. I was running all over my childhood home in Kent, searching for the children who had been snatched away from me. I woke myself up crying in the night and lay there feeling that life held no meaning and wondering how on earth I could go on.

I was wrapped in the clammy tentacles of yet another awful nightmare when I felt a cool hand on my own, smelled an enticing savoury fragrance and heard a voice so familiar that I thought I must have dreamed the last three years.

'Isabella, I have made you bowl of my special *frikadeļu zupa*. Let me help you to sit up.'

As you may know, Latvians love their soups, and Sofija used to serve one of the national favourites at least once a week. This particular one is a hearty broth flavoured with bay leaves and peppercorns with small, intensely flavoured ground beef meatballs floating in it. It could raise the dead and, on this occasion, seemed to have been prepared with just that challenge in mind. I assumed that this was yet another feverish vision, but to my amazement, my former au pair was indeed at my bedside with a tray of soup.

I took a spoonful. Delicious! It was the first thing I'd fancied for what seemed like weeks. I drank in the unexpected sight of its creator sitting on my bedside chair and smiling uncertainly at me. The soup was gone in a matter of minutes and I could feel its delicious goodness making its way through my ravaged digestive system.

'You would like more?' Sofija took the tray from my lap. I nodded and lay back on my pillows as she pattered down the stairs, kitchen-bound. **#dreams #soup #sofijasback**

February is the month of new beginnings! It should have been January (traditionally the time when people make a whole heap of shiny promises to themselves and promptly break them), but my illness put an end to that. This month I will mostly:

1. Be starting the second-floor renovation.

2. Be redecorating the family room.

3. Going to the spa with Mummy, Suze and Liane Bloomfield (and goodness knows how *that* will turn out!).

4. Hosting my first ever homegroup with a bunch of near-strangers.

5. Going skiing, dash it all.

Johnnie and I own a luxurious chalet in Verbier and I haven't been for a while. The last time I even left the country was in August when we flew to Croatia *en famille*. I am in desperate need of a proper holiday. I am going to ask Suze, Jeremy and Lily to come with us. Silvia can lump it. I've texted Johnnie and booked half term week. I can't imagine that Paige will feel up to hurtling down icy slopes in her current state of health, poor girl.

Mimi has been as good as her word and negotiated a fantastic paid partnership with Bitter and Twisted, the new paint company. I am currently the only influencer with whom they are working. My agent is beside herself with excitement. She will be profiting handsomely from the deal, of course.

After much deliberation, I have decided to do the family room as a separate project this month (Kevin and Dave, my reliable decorators, will paint it while we're away skiing) and tease it on my socials, then dive straight into the second floor.

Having pored over the Bitter and Twisted paint charts, I've opted to colour drench the family room in Pretension. It's a gorgeous, light-reflecting statement neutral, ideal for such a versatile space. My accent colour is Irony, a delicate shade of mint green. I'm keeping my plantation shutters (so practical) and changing up the lampshades and cabinetry. The carpet has had a bit of a hammering since it was laid and I'm having it ripped out and replaced with heritage oak floorboards (the original ones can't be restored, sadly). I've invested in a new unit with storage baskets from an ethical brand. Woven jute is featuring heavily. So now! I'll pick out my statement colour with a fabulous rug or two and some throws. **#reno #trends #accentcolours**

I was standing by myself on the playground waiting for the girls to come out, and staring at my phone. I'd just posted a rather fantastic lifestyle blog on redecorating and was checking out the notifications. Liane appeared at my newly exfoliated elbow.

'All right, Smug? What are you looking so serious about?'

I've realised that it's always best to be honest with my frenemy. She can spot a fib or an evasion a mile away.

'I published an article about redecorating this morning and I'm reading the comments. There are a few nasty ones in there.'

Liane frowned. 'About a lick of paint? What's wrong with people? I'm on the list for a house swap but I can't live with my front room the way it is for much longer. What does the Paint Queen recommend?'

This season, as everyone who's anyone knows, it's all about warm beige, feathery neutrals, mid-shade pastels, earthy clay colours and mint-green tones. However, I couldn't say that to Liane. I thought quickly.

'You can't go wrong with a pale, neutral shade. Mind you, there are a lot of dark colours this season. Browns, purples, midnight blue. They don't show the dirt.'

'Hmm. I've got really bad damp in my house and my little one draws on the walls. I like the sound of something dark. Thanks, Smug. Appreciate it. Good to know I'll be "on-trend".'

I waited for the usual sarky remark, which never came. Could it be that I had the chance for a conversation opener?

'Well, listen, I'm getting loads of paint delivered next week. Basically, I'm getting paid to use it. I'll have a lot of dark colours – do you want to have a look when you're at mine? You'd be doing me a favour taking it off my hands.'

Liane rolled a cigarette with one hand and stared at me. My heart sank. I had clearly misjudged the situation and offended her. I opened my mouth to apologise.

'Yeah. All right. I've had to shell out a lot of cash on school trips and I'm a bit skint.'

I assured her that she could have the pick of the paint when it arrived, and breathed a sigh of relief. The conversation over, she gazed at her phone, sucking her teeth and frowning. Lauren and Maddie came up behind us.

'All right, girls? What's going on?'

'Smug's giving me some of her posh paint. I can't stand my front room any more. What I really want is one of the new houses they're building, but that's never going to happen.'

Had it been anyone else, I would have given them a hug and some bracing advice. I contented myself with smiling supportively and letting Lauren step in.

'They only built six social housing properties on the first development. I've heard there's ten on this one. You're in with a chance. Single parent with five kids, born and bred in the village. Surely they'll give you one this time.'

Liane looked glum.

'Yeah, right. I thought I was moving in the spring and then they gave that four-bedroomed to a family from Ipswich. Just my luck. I'll be stuck in that dump till the day I die.' She looked back at her phone. 'Never mind. I swiped right on a few blokes and I've heard back from some of them. One of them even super-liked me.'

I was mystified until Maddie explained that Liane was dipping a hopeful toe into the tumultuous waters of online dating. It seems that you create a profile, like someone else's and match with them. A plethora of men then get in touch with you. You swipe right for yes, left for no. It all seems pretty straightforward.

'If he's thirty, I'm Kim Kardashian!'

Liane was squinting at the screen. A picture of an unshaven man in a baseball cap with a cigarette dangling from his mouth looked back at her.

'Steve, 30. Looking for fun and games. Must love piercings and cosplay. Good SOH essential.'

I grimaced but there was more to come.

'Patrick, 43. A boy's best friend is his mother, but I need someone to share some special grown-up cuddles. If that's you, and you're looking for a fun, no strings attached good time, DM me.'

'Are these for real? And if you're going on a dating site, wouldn't you think really carefully about your profile picture?'

Against my will, I was being drawn in to the murky world of online dating. Steve (allegedly thirty, but looking considerably older) had given up ironing and personal grooming in favour of compulsive tattooing and the piercing of various body parts. Patrick was sporting a hairstyle I believe is known as a mullet and sitting on a tatty leather sofa with a grimy wall behind him screaming out for a repaint.

'That's nothing! Want to see a guy in lime-green cycling shorts with a nipple piercing?'

I didn't, but a second later I was gazing upon the pallid form of Derek, fifty-one, from Great Yarmouth who, according to him, was *'first time here, young at heart and up for laughs lol lifes for living'*. Derek, as well as having no idea how to dress, was a stranger to correct punctuation.

'One more then I'll head home. *"Adam, 32, single guy, attracted by young ladies and older females, likes the bigger girl, if you're dominant or submissive, I'm interested! Let's chat and hook up for some fun."* That's Aidan Ling! No way he's single. Look, Loz. He's still got that wonky eye and the neck tattoo he got done when he was drunk.'

Lauren looked horrified.

'He's with my second cousin! Should I tell her? She's just had a baby and she's got postnatal depression, stuck out in the middle of nowhere while he drives the lorry and does goodness knows what. Disgusting pig!'

Liane slid her phone into her jeans pocket, put two fingers to her lips and let out a piercing whistle which brought her daughters running over from the play equipment. We walked slowly out of the playground digesting the mix of revolting data revealed on the dating site.

'When are you going to start seeing men again, Smug? I can set you up on here, if you like.'

I was horrified, but managed to keep a poker face as I thanked Liane for her kind offer. I couldn't think of anything worse than having strange men messaging me with impertinent remarks and rude pictures.

'She's right, though, Issy. Have you got a type? We could start looking around for someone. You've got to get back on the horse some time.' Maddie seemed equally eager to match me up.

'My type? Well, they've got to be tall, good body, dark hair and blue eyes, preferably, great grooming regime, successful and professional.'

Liane snorted. 'So, your husband, basically. That didn't exactly work out, did it Smug? Come on, think outside the box.'

I didn't like the way this was going. I've only been in love once and got my heart broken. I'm not in any rush to get back on the market.

Back home, my phone beeped. Lauren.

127

'Hi, babes. I know you're feeling uncomfortable about online dating, but I might have spotted someone. Loads of people appeared at Christmas and there's a new family who kept coming. I know you've been too ill for church, but I noticed a new man. No wedding ring, forties, dad bod, smells nice, kind face, two kids. Want me to find out more? xx'

I didn't, really, but I am the soul of politeness. I replied that I was happy to have him pointed out to me on Sunday but that I was not ready to take it to the next level. I should have known that it wouldn't end there. **#dating #newman #notready**

Finally! After months of delay, my renovation has begun. The second floor is a rabbit warren of bedrooms, cupboards and scruffy bathrooms and is in desperate need of my incredible taste to transform it into a welcoming and contemporary space. I am turning two large bedrooms and the old bathroom into a self-contained flat. I will be letting it out in due course so it needs to be neutral and timeless.

After much consideration, I have chosen the everyday palette from Bitter and Twisted for the second-floor reno. The sitting room and kitchenette will be colour drenched in Loquacity and the bedroom and bathroom painted in Indolence. I've turned to the Hanoverian range with its thrillingly dark and exciting shades for the rest of the rooms on the second floor. The landing and common passages will be in Sugar Nib, the principal bedroom suite (double bedroom, fully fitted dressing room and en suite shower room) in Powdering Gown, Sophia Dorothea and Ansbach, the two small doubles in Rout Cake and Rogue Gene respectively, the Jack and Jill bathroom in Landgravine and my gorgeous new luxe five-piece family bathroom in Porphyria with a feature wall in Coburg. I don't suppose there are many women in this world who could take a shabby bathroom and transform it into a deliciously louche space with a huge freestanding roll-top claw-foot bath with floor-mounted taps, double width walk-in raindrop shower, marble countertop basin, oversized sculptural chandelier with cascading tiers, hand-scraped solid oak flooring and a restored open fireplace. Kevin and Dave, my marvellous builders, are scouring reclamation yards for just the right statement fireplace and overmantel. I'm fantasising about lying in a deep, bubbly, candlelit bath with the flames from the roaring fire reflecting off the intense dark-purple paintwork. Never let it be said that Issy Smugge is a slouch when it comes to on-trend interiors.

That said, I have ordered an oversized bath and there isn't enough of me to fill it up. It screams out for a partner to share it, and while once upon a time I would have only had to say the word to have an eager husband lowering himself into the fragrant waters with me, now I bathe alone. Which is fine. I am an independent career woman, after all. And I don't need a man.

Not a man like Johnnie, anyway.

I will have a look at this person of Lauren's at church on Sunday but I'm certainly not ready for a relationship.

Did I mention that Johnnie texted, suggesting it was time we formalised things and got a divorce?

And I am completely OK with that.

This June, it will be three years since I made the appalling discovery that my husband had been carrying on with my right-hand woman and au pair, Sofija, behind my back. At the time, I thought I would never forgive her or be able to see her again, and yet she is moving back in next month.

I have been getting on so much better with the children, and I even began to allow myself to think that I was learning to be a better and more connected parent. The days of me listening at their doors to find out what they're thinking are over and I haven't had a row with Finn for weeks. Milo safely in bed on Friday evening after a tiring week, I sat them down in the family room and told them that Sofija was moving back in with us. The joy on their faces was immediate.

'Really, Mummy? You're not joking? She's coming back forever and forever to look after us?'

Elsie was almost in tears and Finn was beaming while Chloë clasped her hands in delight.

'Well, not quite. She'll be living in Gandy's old room and she will help me with looking after you a little bit. But her new job is different. Are you happy, darlings?'

I appeared to have given them the best news possible. I love making my children happy, but this was bittersweet. I've only got myself to blame. For years I put all the hard parenting work on Sofija, and in the process she bonded with my children in a very special and unbreakable way. It hurt me terribly to see how much they'd missed her since I'd sacked her, but now, watching their faces irradiated with delight, I had to accept that by doing the right and adult thing, I was putting myself through yet another set of challenges.

It seemed that in the grip of my fever, I had texted Sofija begging her to come back, telling her how much I missed her. Who knows what the unconscious mind is capable of? I certainly found out when I was struggling out of the clutches of yet another sweaty fever dream and discovered her by my bedside with her cool hands and her delicious well-seasoned soup. She stayed long enough to tell me that her contract with the family in Ipswich was coming to an end and that she had decided to take on some agency work while she thought about what to do next. I was in no state to have a serious chat, so she left me with assurances that she would freeze and label the leftover soup and return in a couple of days to talk about the way forward.

With the benefit of hindsight, and knowing what I now know about my husband, I can see that I contributed to the whole painful situation. I loved Sofija and I trusted her, but equally, she was isolated and lonely and I didn't treat her with the respect she deserved. And the less said about Johnnie's behaviour, the better!

Sitting up in bed in a fresh pair of breathable linen pyjamas, we chatted about how the future might look. What I really need is someone who knows me, who doesn't have to be constantly briefed and who will help me to run the vast and successful machine that is Isabella M Smugge Inc. No more washing, drying and ironing, no more menial tasks. I know Sofija loves the children as much as they do her and of course she will want to help me with their everyday lives. But I don't need an au pair as much as I need an executive PA, a Ms Fixit, a supportive, understanding partner in my life's work.

We drew up a list of goals and visions for us both, agreed that she would work flexible hours and have every other weekend off and sealed the deal with a double-shot cappuccino, just like the old days.

She's back!

Now all I have to do is tell Johnnie.

Even though I am not interested in pursuing a romantic relationship at present, I dressed with extra care for church on Sunday morning. I pulled on a gorgeous cobalt blue pleated knit maxi-dress which clung to my curves in a most flattering way, teamed it with a trio of silver bangles, a chunky ring and a pair of hammered silver hoop earrings, put my hair up in a messy bun, did a light make-up and spritzed myself with perfume. The children dressed and breakfasted, I pulled on my go-to cream scarf coat and knee-length suede boots and opened the boot room door.

Walking in through the church porch, I was warmly welcomed by one of the many Sues and another smiling lady unfamiliar to me.

'This is Annette Dunning, Isabella. She's moved into the old school house in the village and she'll be joining your homegroup.'

I shook her warmly by the hand, noting as I did so that she clearly followed a regular skincare regime and had a good eye for colour. Lauren was at the front of the church chatting to Claire. Finn wandered off to talk to our youth worker, Ade, and the girls, Milo and I plonked ourselves down on a pew and took our coats off. I allowed my eyes to scan the congregation. There was no sign of a new man.

We were a few minutes early and the church was buzzing with conversation. In the background, grace-notes and arpeggios drifted from the organ loft where Bix Bloomfield, church organist, recovering addict and alcoholic and former pop star, was giving us a selection of warm-up music. There seemed to be more families than usual and I saw a few faces I vaguely recognised.

'Room for a small one, babes?' Lauren had joined me, her face aglow with excitement. 'OK, so the new man's called Robin Knight. He lost his wife five years ago. Two kids, Tallulah and Belle, one in Year Seven, one in Year Nine. Works for a big insurance company, moved from Leamington Spa with his parents and the girls a few months ago. They sold their houses, put the money together and they've bought that big old Victorian house behind the school. Claire says they came at Christmas to check us out and liked it so they're staying. You look nice. Is that a new dress?'

'This old thing? I just dug it out of the wardrobe at the last minute and threw it on. I'm a mess. Still feeling a bit rough, to be honest.'

This was a lie. I felt a bit bad about telling porkies in the house of the Lord, but I needed to change the subject. Lauren looked like a dog with two tails and I could tell that she was dying to matchmake. I shared the news about Sofija returning to the Old Rectory, which fortunately put all thoughts of connecting me with a complete stranger out of her mind.

At coffee time, I hung back while Lauren strode into the fray, elbows out. I sought the sanctuary of Claire's calming aura. I could be pretty sure that she at least wouldn't be playing matchmaker.

'Is it just my imagination or are there lots of new people here today?'

My friend beamed.

'There are! Several of the new families from the housing development came at Christmas and they've stayed. Ade has been doing a lot of work with the primary schools around here and it's bringing in younger families. Also, St Bartholomew's finally closed its doors just before Christmas. Such a shame, but its congregation was dwindling and it couldn't afford to keep the church running. So most of them came to us.'

That explained it. Now I looked more closely, I recognised several of the mums from the playground.

'Lauren mentioned a family called the Knights who bought that big house behind the school. Are they here today?'

Claire scanned the throng and identified said Knights, composed of a man of medium height and two girls.

'Over there, talking to Lauren. Would you like me to introduce you?'

And so it came to pass that I found myself shaking hands with a relatively decent-looking man with brown eyes and broad shoulders. His handshake was firm and he had a pleasant smile. That said, he could have done with a haircut and a closer shave and was wearing a shirt that did nothing for him. He was clearly a stranger to proper intense masculine grooming and was far too short. Lauren was hovering at his elbow, grinning from ear to ear and mouthing things at me. I obtained a cup of coffee and wheeled around to Claire to avoid her caperings.

'Isabella is very kindly hosting the new homegroup, Robin. We're so fortunate to have her in our congregation. She's got a wonderful spirit of generosity.'

I blushed slightly.

'Well, if you live in a massive Grade II listed Georgian rectory, you've got to fill it up with people. It's just me and the children rattling around in there at present.'

The words were out before I could stop myself and I felt my cheeks burning. What was I saying? For a start, the poor man could only afford a fairly bog standard mid-Victorian three-storey property which I was fairly sure wasn't listed, and also I was sounding desperate. 'Rattling around?' When has Isabella M Smugge ever rattled around anything?

'It's very kind of you to host, Mrs Smugge. My late wife and I ran our homegroup for years and I'm very much looking forward to joining this one.'

I bit the bullet and asked him about his work. I spent years pretending to be interested in Johnnie's hedge fund managing, so I've had plenty of practice.

'There's nothing duller than a man talking about what he does, especially when he works in period property insurance. I'd much rather hear about you. What do you do?'

I gave him an overview, majoring on the photography and charity work side to make myself sound less shallow. His elder daughter broke in.

'What, you're *the* Isabella M Smugge? I follow you on Insta and TikTok. You're well famous! She's like a proper celeb, Dad. You never said there was a celeb living here.'

I admitted that I *was* that Isabella M Smugge and graciously answered her questions. After some more desultory chit-chat and feeling Lauren's eyes boring into the back of my head, I made my excuses, pulled on my coat and departed.

'Where are you off to in such a hurry, babes? Got time for a coffee? Scott's got the girls so I'm a free agent.'

Back home, I fired up the coffee machine and got out some posh biscuits. I had never seen Lauren so excited or heard her so chatty.

'So, what do you think? He's nice, isn't he? Good firm handshake. I think he's mid-forties, so not too big an age gap. His girls are lovely. I know they're really missing their old school and their friends so we need to keep an eye on them. Finn's in Year Eight, isn't he? Which is a shame. Never mind. He might see them around school. It's a real pity he hasn't got younger kids so you could see him every day on the playground. Oh well, you can't have everything. He's not too tall either. I don't like a very tall man. You know his parents refuse to step inside a church since his wife died? They wouldn't even come at Christmas. They've stopped believing in God because everyone prayed so much that his wife wouldn't die, but she did, and they can't get over it. He's got a lovely way with him, don't you think? The parents do loads of the childcare so he'd have time to go out for a coffee if you wanted to get to know him a bit better. Claire says he's coming to your homegroup. That's lucky, isn't it? And he knows all about old posh houses because of his work so there's a bond already between you. So, what do you think?'

She'd barely paused for breath and I wasn't quite sure where to start. I admitted that he seemed nice enough.

'He's not tall enough for me, though. Johnnie was six foot three and I know looks don't matter in the grand scheme of things, but I prefer blue eyes and dark hair. He's a bit – I don't know – nondescript. He clearly doesn't go to the gym, which is a dealbreaker for me. But he does seem nice.'

Clearly I had not gone nearly far enough for Lauren.

'Nice? Do you know how rare it is to find a half-decent actual available man in a church? They're all taken, or single for a reason. You need to get in there quick before someone else snaps him up! You've got a massive advantage, having him in your homegroup. Now, what are you going to wear for the first one? No offence, babes, but you don't want to go too glam. You need to look approachable and – well, not available exactly, but not so fabulous that he thinks he's punching too far above his weight. Have you got any jeans? Want me to go through your wardrobe with you? I'd say jeans and a really nice top, not too much make-up and maybe just a pair of earrings. That'll do. You don't want to frighten him off. I think you need to…'

Fortunately, before she could give me any more advice, Elsie came out of the family room looking horrified and holding her nose.

'Mummy, Milo took his nappy off and he's done a huge poo on the carpet. It stinks!'

Never had I been so happy to hear that someone had lost control of their bowels in a principal reception room. I grabbed the wipes and went to assess the situation. Milo was standing there with his trousers around his ankles, looking delighted.

'I did big poo, Mummy!'

What is the etiquette exactly when one's child begins to explore unassisted toileting? Fortunately, Lauren is an experienced hands-on mother and immediately began praising my son for his sudden show of independence.

'What a clever boy, Milo! Did you do a lovely poo for Mummy? Shall we ask Mummy for your own special big boy potty so you can do it all by yourself?'

I have been wondering about potty training for a while. Milo won't be two until April, which does seem rather young, but of course he is incredibly intelligent and forward for his age. Finn had just begun to express an interest in shedding his nappies when I employed Sofija and she did most of the hard work. It's one thing to wipe your child's bottom while he is prone upon a changing mat, quite another to pick up a still-warm offering from your carpet and flush it down the loo (minus the wipe, obviously. We need to protect the environment).
#pottytraining #nextstage #poo

I am counting down the days to our holiday in Verbier when I can kick back, flood my feed with gorgeous shots of sparkling snow, pine trees and intense blue skies and fill my lungs with some pure Swiss air.

The smell in the back garden is getting worse. I must investigate. My to-do list is massive as always, but with Kitty doing so many of my images and the exciting yet terrifying prospect of Sofija returning as my executive assistant, I may not be quite so burdened come March.

On the advice of the school mums, I have sourced not one but four potties. The house is so large that I need to have them dotted about in case Milo goes rogue. In the last week, I have found offerings in:

1. The snug.

2. The cloakroom.

3. The pantry.

4. His bedroom.

What if he does a poo, or wees, and I don't know about it and one of the homegroup steps in it? I would have to change churches or leave the village. Also, the cat has been taken to being sick. So far only twice, but it is not pleasant to come down your gorgeous curving staircase in the morning and find a little steaming pile of straw-coloured vomit waiting for you. Lauren says it's furballs. I've had enough of unexpected emissions, thank you very much!

Isabella M Smugge's To-Do List

1. Confirm allergies and food needs for Mummy and Harry's party.

2. Find out what that weird smell in the garden is.

3. Book tickets for panto (just found out about this. Chloë forgot to tell me that her dance school is providing the backing dancers for said show. Have never been to one. What does it entail? Must ask Lauren).

4. Tell Johnnie about Sofija coming back.

5. Talk to Johnnie about Paige meeting the children.

6. Talk to Johnnie about getting a divorce. Why does he want one all of a sudden? Is he thinking of making an honest woman of Paige?

7. Start packing for Verbier.

8. Think about what refreshments to offer for homegroup.

9. Start toilet training Milo.

10. Confirm flooring for second floor reno.

11. Order lighting for second floor reno.

12. Clear out family room ahead of repaint.

13. Talk to Liane about what paint she wants.

14. Help to organise the Spring Disco.

15. Go to the spa with Mummy, Suze and Liane (this is supposed to be relaxing, but the thought of spending time in a steam room with my frenemy is stressing me. Also, what if Mummy embarrasses me? Which she undoubtedly will).

16. Draft new contract for Sofija.

There are about a million other things I should add, but it's just too ruinously depressing.

Amanda and Kitty are going back to Scotland at the end of March. I will miss them terribly. Kitty is doing well with Tony and she's going to continue her therapy via Zoom.

In other news, Charlene has invited me to join her and Liane at a craft event in April. It's a Johnnie weekend so I've said yes. Apparently one can expect high-quality handmade items, a good variety of homemade cakes and the opportunity to meet pleasant people. Issy Smugge says, yes please! **#craftcircuit #cakejoy**

March

Switzerland! Land of almost constant neutrality, cuckoo clocks, well-behaved cows and really good cheese. We had a blissful week, my little Milo went to the loo three times in his potty (it's a start) and played in the snow park. Conditions were perfect, the sun shone and we had a lovely time. Even Mimi is pleased with the content I produced. And without Johnnie there needling them to push themselves all the time, the children were relaxed and happy.

I have decided that I am going to agree to the divorce. We're never getting back together and it has to happen sometime. I'm not saying anything to the children for the time being. Time enough for that once they've met the mother of their future half-brother or sister. I have put a date in the diary for Paige and Johnnie to come over. I am providing a buffet lunch and have asked for prayer from all the top pray-ers of my acquaintance. Paige is still being sick sporadically, but is now on maternity leave which seems to have helped. Her due date is the 24th of this month. I had a difficult conversation with Johnnie when he dropped the children (minus Milo and his new toileting activities) back from a weekend away at the house.

'I don't like to say this, but the whole situation is on you, Iss. Poor Paige has only got a few weeks to go and she has to meet the kids when she's tired and suffering from swollen ankles and heartburn, and retaining water, and puking and I don't know what. If you'd listened to sense, we could have had all the kids in the house with us for a few weekends and she'd have got to know them before the baby arrived.'

I pointed out, in a rather acid tone, that an unexpected pregnancy and its unfortunate side-effects was hardly my fault, but as always, he refused to take any responsibility.

'She was so desperate that she came to meet you without telling me. As if she didn't have enough on her plate. And have you signed the divorce papers? I want to do the right thing and get married after the baby comes.'

I couldn't imagine that Paige would have the energy to organise a wedding straight after having a baby, but really it wasn't any of my business.

'I liked her, Johnnie. I'll be honest. She seems like a really upfront kind of girl. It was brave of her to come and meet me. You'd better treat her right.'

Surprisingly, I appeared to be developing a protective instinct towards the woman who would shortly be my children's stepmother. Which made her – what? My stepwife? Replacement? Successor? Was there even a word for our relationship?

'Treat her right? What do you mean, Iss? Of course I will. We're so in love. And once the baby comes, she'll be able to drink again and we can go out and have fun and I'm sure we can sort some kind of childcare.'

'Hmm. Is she giving up work, then?'

He looked a little uncomfortable.

'She says she's taking six months maternity leave then going back. She wants me to give up work and stay at home to look after the baby. I think she must have been joking, though. She hasn't been sleeping too well because of the heartburn and the night sweats, so she isn't quite herself, obviously. We'll get a nanny, or her mum can look after it.'

On the basis of our very brief acquaintance, Paige hadn't struck me as the kind of girl who made jokes about serious subjects such as work. I decided to 'stay in my adult', as Tony the counsellor would say, and hit my husband where it hurt, with the unpalatable truth. Because really, what was the worst that could happen?

'Most people your age *have* pulled back by now. They're all freelance consultants or running their own company. You've done pretty well to last as long as you have. All your colleagues are twenty years younger than you. Paige has got a point. And just think how marvellous it would be for you to really bond with your child. I think it's a great idea.'

I settled back on my gorgeous sofa and waited for the fallout. Which was a moment in coming as Johnnie appeared to have been struck dumb. After gasping like a recently landed sea bream for a minute or two, he recovered his speech.

'My age? I'm forty-one, Iss! Hardly old. I've got *years* left in me. There are a lot of youngsters at work but they don't have my experience and wisdom. And really? Me? Looking after a baby? That's like taking a million-pound racehorse and giving it a cart to pull. What a waste of my talents. I'll see it after work and at the weekends. Worked pretty well with our children.'

I wasn't letting him get away with that.

'And how is your hands-off parenting style going at the present time? I'd love to know.'

It's jolly hard to keep on being an adult when you're speaking to an entitled sexist moron. Within seconds, we'd returned to the more traditional separated couple slanging match, which went on for some time and only stopped when Milo came waddling into the room with his trousers around his ankles. I knew what *that* meant.

'Good boy, Milo! Did you do a wee for Mummy?'

'I done big poo, Mummy.'

He took my hand and pulled me towards the kitchen. Sure enough, a large and well-formed pile of faecal matter was sitting proudly on my gleaming floor. Never let it be said that Issy Smugge misses a golden opportunity when it presents itself. I called Johnnie through to the kitchen and pointed it out.

'Now's your big chance to bond with one of your children. I've got a call in five minutes so I'll leave you in charge. Johnnie, this is Milo, your youngest child. Milo, this is your father. See you shortly!'

I felt bad leaving a vulnerable and incontinent toddler in the care of a misogynistic narcissist, but, trying to ignore the angry yells coming from the kitchen, I walked through the boot room to the garden and slammed the door. Ha!

I love being able to switch off from domestic issues and snapping into my professional self. I also love that there's a lock on the door of my studio. Something told me that Johnnie wouldn't be able to cope, so I WhatsApped Amanda, busy doing coursework upstairs, to warn her that my husband was wrestling with the unexpected in the kitchen, and not to step in to help. Sure enough, halfway through my Zoom call, I saw him striding down the garden with a screaming Milo under his arm. I was in the middle of an important chat with one of my product placement partners and ignored him. After a few minutes of banging on the door, he gave up and marched back to the house. It's impossible to overexaggerate how happy this made me.

Call over, I returned to the house where I found Johnnie sulking in the family room while a half-naked Milo played with his bricks. I couldn't help smiling, which went down as well as you might expect.

'I don't know what you're laughing about, Iss! You're becoming a really irresponsible mother, do you know that? Leaving me to cope with – that!' He pointed a trembling finger at his son, who was now investigating his willy with great interest.

'I'm doing you a huge favour, Johnnie. In less than a month, it's all going to be broken nights and nappy rash and screaming, and you need to be prepared. You'll thank me when you're a full-time househusband.'

This led to another angry exchange. Milo got fed up and wandered off, probably to wee in the pantry. I was past caring.

'I've got something else to tell you. Sofija's coming back to work for me this month.'

He went pale and sank back into his chair.

'What? Are you actually trying to give me a cardiac arrest? I've read about this. Women go a bit wacko in their forties. They're not responsible for their actions. I suggest you go to the doctor, pronto, and get yourself medicated.'

I heard the sound of running water and footsteps on the stairs. Amanda called out.

'Isabella, I think Milo's weeing in the pantry. Do you want me to sort it out?'

'Would you mind? The wipes are on the island. He did a poo a few minutes ago, but Johnnie cleared it up.'

Johnnie dropped his voice.

'Seriously, though, Iss. Are you out of your mind getting that woman back in the house after what happened last time?'

'Err – just remind me what happened last time? You broke your wedding vows, went behind my back and slept with her! And then made out it was all my fault, you pathetic piece of...'

It was probably just as well that Amanda chose that moment to appear.

'Sorry to interrupt. All cleaned up. Hello, Johnnie, how are you?'

My husband stood up, his face overcast with rage.

'How do you *think* I am? How's Charlie, more to the point, abandoned on the other side of the world. You women! It's a conspiracy. I'll see you at our meeting, always assuming Paige hasn't gone into early labour because of all the stress!'

The front door banged and I heard him wheelspin on the gravel and head off down the drive. Good riddance. Amanda raised her eyebrows.

'There's a whole module's worth of bad parenting and repressed issues there.'

I love her! **#narcissist #baddad #girlpower**

Just before we flew out to Verbier, I hosted the first homegroup. The house was gleaming (I'm so happy Ali is back!), there were fresh flowers in every room and I had taken

Lauren's advice and worn a fairly simple outfit. Kick-off was at 7.30 and I served supper half an hour early to give myself plenty of time. However, everything, and I mean everything, was against me.

Both my daughters had come home in bad moods. Chloë had been overdoing the dance practice and was tired and grumpy. There had been some kind of friendship drama on the playground and my little Elsie was tearful and clingy. Milo had had a bad night's sleep and refused to have his nap and was therefore exhausted and overexcited. I'd gone for a quick supper, boiling wholegrain pasta and mixing it with a bright-red tomato and garlic sauce. Milo upended his bowl and the contents went all over the floor and splashed up the cupboard doors of the island. Just as I was clearing that up, Elsie and Chloë started having a row and the jug of organic tropical fruit juice was knocked over. A tide of sticky fluid went surging over my gorgeous rose quartz worktop and fell like a vitamin C-infused waterfall over the edge of the island. The splashes of red sauce had now been joined by an orange sea. Milo was yelling to be released from his highchair but had to be restrained as otherwise he would have tracked a sticky mess through the house. The cat was making odd noises in the family room but I had no time to attend to her.

Amanda and I mopped up the worst of the spillages and I served dessert. My freezer is full of frozen fruit from the summer, and I had elected for gooseberry crumble with custard. First of all, Elsie burned her mouth despite being told repeatedly to let it cool down, and burst into loud, uncontrollable tears. Chloë had been needling Finn ever since they got home from school about a girl on the bus who apparently likes him. Jake had let out something about it last time he was over and she simply cannot let it go. The Third World War was breaking out around my island. Kitty had already fled upstairs after eating a quarter of a bowl of plain pasta and was probably, even now, bringing it up in the family bathroom. I pride myself on my calm approach to parenting, but something broke inside me and I found myself with burning cheeks shouting at the top of my voice.

'Will you all be quiet? I can't hear myself *think*. I've got nine strangers and Sue Thompson coming in forty-five minutes and I need a clean, orderly house. I do everything for you and this is how you repay me!'

Whereupon *I* burst into tears. I was tempted to storm out and throw myself on my bed and let someone else deal with the whole hideous situation, but apart from the fact that my exit would have been impeded by the appalling sticky mess on the floor, I had people coming and had to appear gracious, calm and smiling. The only people not crying were Amanda and Finn, Chloë having joined in the sob fest.

My sister-in-law took charge.

'I think we're all a bit overwrought. Children, give Mummy a hug and tell her you love her. Isabella, I'll put Milo in the bath with your lavender and chamomile essence. That should knock him out. Take some deep breaths and ground yourself. Finn, get the mop out and give your mother a hand with the cleaning.'

Plucking a sticky, exhausted, screaming Milo from his chair, she stepped over the pools of sauce and juice and took him upstairs. I apologised for my outburst.

'I'm so sorry, darlings. Mummy had a very difficult conversation with Daddy the other day and I'm nervous about this meeting tonight.'

'Why?' Finn was assiduously mopping the floor. 'It's just like church, isn't it? You don't mind that.'

I considered. Why was I so on edge about what was, after all, just a gathering of people talking about holy things? I'd asked Ali to bake a batch of triple chocolate chunk biscuits and some of her renowned stem ginger shortbread, which I had laid out ready in the pantry. I took some deep breaths.

'You've got this, Isabella,' I told myself.

My little Elsie hugged me fiercely.

'I'm sorry I made you sad, Mummy. Will you put me to bed?'

'I can't, darling. Mummy has a meeting. But I promise I will tomorrow night. I love you. You didn't make me sad. It's silly grown-up stuff.'

Expressing a wish to join her little brother in the bath, she ran upstairs. The other two gave me cursory hugs and sloped off to do their homework. I was left alone in the kitchen with thirty-five minutes to go, dirty plates and cups everywhere, splashes of tomato sauce and juice up the drawers and sides of the island, and a dishwasher to load. All I had to do was clear up, feed the cat, put out the posh biscuits and refresh my make-up.

I had wiped over the island and half-filled the dishwasher when the front doorbell rang. Looking down at myself, I realised that there was tomato sauce down the front of my lovely cream cashmere jumper. My hair was coming down and I smelled faintly of cleaning fluid.

I opened the door and, to my absolute horror, saw Robin Knight standing there. His smile faded as he took in my shocked expression.

'It is tonight, isn't it? Am I early?'

I pasted on a welcoming smile.

'Not at all! Do come in. Please excuse the mess. We had a little bit of an incident over supper and I'm running a bit behind.'

My voice was at least an octave higher than usual. What was he doing here so early? There was no way I could put him in the beautifully dressed family room without him seeing the chaos in the kitchen.

'I'll just finish loading the dishwasher. Let me make you a coffee while I tidy up.'

'I wouldn't dream of it. Let me finish that for you. My wife was extremely particular about how the dishwasher was loaded. I pride myself on my skill!'

Ignoring my twittering protests, he filled my machine with glasses, cutlery and plates, put in the tablet, shut the door and turned it on in a most efficient fashion. I sprayed the drawers of the island with my floral-fragranced organic cleaner and began scrubbing at the remains of dinner. I was horribly aware of my flushed cheeks and stained top. What a disastrous start to the evening! Robin Knight was hovering, looking for more jobs to do. He seemed to be very keen to help (the opposite of Johnnie) so I sent him to the pantry to fetch the biscuits while I fired up the coffee machine. He came back a minute later looking puzzled.

'I'm terribly sorry. I can't see the plates you're talking about. There are some biscuits on the floor.'

My heart sank. I ran to the pantry and, to my horror, saw the remains of the beautiful homemade treats scattered on the floor along with convincing evidence that a short person had been consuming them. Milo! Of course! His behaviour at supper was the result of sleep deprivation and a sugar high. Why hadn't I left the biscuits on a high shelf? What on earth was I going to serve now? It was my understanding that no homegroup was complete without at least two kinds of refreshment. Robin came to the rescue.

'I'll text my mother, Isabella. We had our big shop delivered today and I'm sure we've got some biscuits knocking about. The girls get through packets of them.'

He seemed remarkably calm in the face of such a domestic catastrophe. Shop-bought biscuits! Mess everywhere! A designer top caked in tomato sauce! What else could possibly go wrong? I gave him an Americano with hot milk and showed him to the family room.

'Do you mind if I just run upstairs to check on the children?'

In my bedroom, I paced about taking deep breaths. I surveyed myself in the floor-length mirror. It was worse than I thought. My hair had escaped in wisps and was hanging around my flushed face, my eyeliner was smudged and I looked half-mad. I pulled off my jumper and selected a gorgeous square-necked, long-sleeved, black, skinny-rib top. Now my earrings were all wrong. I took them off and found some silver and crystal drops. I redid my hair, repaired my eye make-up, spritzed myself with perfume and added some deep-rose lipstick. My phone beeped.

'Hi, babes. Hope you don't mind, but I told Robin to get there half an hour early to give you a chance to chat to him. I know you'll have everything ready hours in advance. I said you always like people to come early ha ha. You can thank me tomorrow! xx'

Lauren (for it was she) had added a row of smiley face and heart emojis. I didn't have the heart to respond.

It never rains but it pours. Freshly lipsticked and free of encrusted food items, I ran back downstairs to find my guest looking helplessly around the kitchen.

'I think your cat has been a little unwell. I was just looking for a cloth and some anti-bac spray.'

My heart sank. Tabitha had deposited a lavish pile of cat sick on the carpet by the window seat. Great! I was spraying it and picking it up with a handful of extra-absorbent kitchen towel when the doorbell rang again. Robin answered it and came back with two packets of medium-quality biscuits. Then it rang again – Sue, efficient and smiling with a sheaf of notes under her arm and ten minutes early. To think that I, Isabella M Smugge, doyenne of lifestyle bloggers, author of *Issy Smugge Says: Let's Be Our Best Selves* and the woman to whom millions look for advice on gracious hostessing, interior design and hospitality, should be found by her guests kneeling on the floor scraping up cat vomit!

I could have cried. I contented myself with throwing the kitchen towel in the bin, washing my hands thoroughly, arranging the biscuits on my best plates and making Sue a decaf latte. Honestly! **#cringe #disaster #whyme**

As one of the UK's most beloved influencers, it's terribly hard for me *not* to take a picture and post it. So when I found myself at the local spa with Mummy and an extremely reluctant Liane Bloomfield (Suze had to cancel at the last minute), I had to have a stern talk with myself. Usually, I'd take some gorgeous, evocative images of luxury products, limpid plunge pools and my own beautifully pedicured toes on a lounger with a pile of glossy magazines. However, Liane looked as if it wouldn't take much for her to commit an act of violence in the steam room. I put my phone in the locker behind my clothes and tied the belt of my robe.

'Come along then, Liane, dear. So kind of you to join me. If you could just give me your arm – thank you.'

My mother has a habit of getting exactly what she wants. Unusually, however, she and Liane did not appear to be on the best of terms. I wished that Suze had been able to join us, but it hadn't been possible. We bobbed around in the plunge pool, Liane's head sticking grimly out of the steaming waters as she helped Mummy onto the jet bed. My attempts at light conversation were ignored. I took myself off to the sauna and arranged myself on the highest shelf to contemplate the rest of the day. Mummy had booked us all in for luxury pedicures before lunch. I didn't really need one as my nail woman comes every week, but I had agreed to a deep foot condition, soak and foot massage while Mummy and Liane had their toenails done.

I emerged and headed over to the drinks station. I selected a chilled glass from the fridge and poured myself a rosewater and sloe infused sparkling water (delicious!) and prepared to relax on a towel-covered lounger and read a magazine full of fascinating interior ideas and relationship advice. I stopped in my tracks as I heard raised voices around the corner where the loungers were.

'But I feel out of place, Mrs N! I don't belong here.'

'Nonsense! I need you. I can't expect Isabella to haul me in and out of pools. She isn't a professional. And anyway, I enjoy your company.'

'You should have told me, not tricked me into it. I feel stupid. Everyone's all posh and skinny and staring at me. I stick out like a sore thumb.'

'I asked you several times as a friend, Liane. You know I did. And you gave me a flat no every time. This was the only way I could get you here.'

I took a sip of my drink and wondered if I should intervene. I'd never heard Mummy and Liane disagree about anything, and there was nothing I could do to make it any better.

'Look, I don't like accepting charity. People giving me things or trying to be nice. I always pay my own way in life. I thought you understood that.'

Mummy sighed. 'I'm paying you as a carer today. You're acting in a professional capacity. But I also really want to spend some time with you and share my wedding present. I know you're a proud woman. So am I. Can you imagine how I felt when I had the stroke and I was suddenly dependent on my daughter, and had complete strangers washing me and dressing me? You were the only one I connected with. I really enjoy your company, Liane, and I wanted to say thank you to you for making a very difficult time less hard to bear. All right?'

Only Liane Bloomfield would continue arguing with my mother. Which she did, for a good five minutes more. The clock was ticking and our pedicures were nearly due. I took a deep breath and walked around the corner.

'Would you like a drink? This rosewater and sloe is absolutely delicious. So cleansing and hydrating.'

They both stared at me.

'I'm having a little bit of an issue with Liane. She's refusing to come and have her pedicure. I wonder if you can change her mind.'

I was sure I couldn't. But it seemed unlikely that my frenemy would walk out of a spa and leave a paying client helpless by the treatment rooms, so I took a deep breath and tried being brutally honest.

'Did I ever tell you how jealous I was of you when you first started caring for my mother, Liane?'

My gamble had paid off. Her jaw dropped.

'You two got on like a house on fire and I felt so left out. I could hear you laughing and joking together and I couldn't understand why someone who had just met my mother could "get" her so quickly. My mother doesn't like many people (sorry, Mummy, but you know it's true), and to see her bonding with you hurt me. I'm fine with it now, but I had to work really hard on myself to get over it. I'd like to be better friends with you. But I can't be if you keep pushing me away. And you're doing the same to Mummy. You need to get over yourself a bit.'

I waited for her to stand up and give me a punch on the jaw or start shouting abuse. Instead, Mummy piped up.

'I can't believe you're bringing this up again, you silly girl. I've always loved you. I thought you knew that. And I've explained to you why I like Liane so much. It's nothing to do with our relationship. But I have to agree with you. I spent most of my life shutting myself off and rejecting help and overtures of friendship, Liane. I'd hate to see you make the same mistake.'

There was a short silence while Liane gazed at her feet. When she spoke, there was a quaver in her voice I'd never heard before.

'It's how I get through life, all right? If you expect the worst, you won't be disappointed. Sorry I made you jealous, Smug.'

She looked sideways at Mummy and gave her a reluctant smile.

'Come on, then. Those toenails aren't going to paint themselves.'

This spa is quite a find! The three of us sat laughing and chatting, our feet soaking in large beaten copper bowls (so now) while tinkly music played and enticing fragrances drifted up from the warm water. I never thought I'd be sharing a spa experience with Liane Bloomfield, who, of course, turned out to be distantly related to two of the therapists. I'd expected awkward silences, but in fact I could barely get a word in edgeways.

'How's your mum, Els? Did she have it out in the end?'

'Yeah, but she was in the hospital for weeks. Size of a grapefruit, apparently. Just take your foot out and I'll exfoliate. I can see you spend a lot of your time standing up! Mate, chuck me the Extra Strong Oatmeal and Grapefruit Foot Scrub. I'll need a couple of applications on these hooves!'

I waited for a row to break out, but blood is thicker than water. Liane turned to her third cousin once removed (I think I got that right).

'Are you still on the dating app? I've tried out a few blokes, but they've been rubbish. Loz and I saw Aidan Ling on there the other day pretending to be single.'

'I wouldn't trust him as far as I could throw him. Yeah, I found someone. He's OK.'

She began filing Mummy's toenails enthusiastically.

'He's not the best-looking, but he's a nice guy and he didn't send me any pictures of his...' At this point, she coughed and glanced at Mummy, who was drinking in the gossip eagerly. 'Anyway, we've been out a few times and I could do worse. How's your mum, Liane? Who's she seeing at the moment?'

Liane sighed. 'Still with Dodgy Gary from the depot. He's such a perv. I won't let him in the house.'

They continued in this vein for some time, and I found out more about village life in an hour than I had in three and a half years. Relaxed and with immaculate toenails, we headed off for a light lunch, and such had been the impact of our morning together that Liane accepted Mummy's offer of a rainforest facial without any argument at all. Result! **#spaday #bonding**

Only my husband could get two women pregnant by mistake with such appalling timing that their progeny could very well share a birthday. My little Milo was born in early April and Paige's due date is 24th March. If she goes over (and I understand they usually let you go for two weeks before you're induced), her baby could be born on the same day as its half-brother!

In other news, the second floor reno has begun! I have had to host homegroup in the drawing room, which doesn't get used much in the winter. Fortunately, it has a magnificent marble fireplace with an open fire, the original wood panelling, sash windows and window seats. When we moved in, I decorated in Belle Peinture's Huntsman Green, which has stood the test of time and fits in well with my delightful Georgian interiors. I've moved the furniture from the family room in there for now and may, in fact, keep it as the homegroup room.

After my first disastrous week, things settled down a bit. I am struggling to remember everyone's names, but have made a list and copious notes about their appearance, dress sense and social background.

Robin Knight (he was wearing a much nicer shirt this week and insisted on bringing in all the coffee for me on my second-best silver tray) is proving to be quite interesting, although he is just not my type. And I'm not ready to dip my toe into the turbulent waters of post-separation dating, either, whatever Lauren says. And she says an awful lot!

His elder daughter is a super-fan of Issy Smugge, which has given him many brownie points with her. It was a difficult decision to leave their home in Leamington Spa and move to Suffolk, but finding out that the UK's most beloved mumfluencer and lifestyle blogger lives there too has softened the blow considerably.

Sue Thompson is our leader, and a splendid one she is too. We spent our first two sessions getting to know each other and there was no praying at all, freestyle or otherwise. On week three, she asked for a volunteer to kick things off and concluded conversation with the Almighty with a rousing 'Amen!' which left no room for confusion. I confined myself to some light murmuring and nodding.

Annette Dunning and her husband, Richard, are perfectly pleasant. Mid-sixties; enjoy walking, birdwatching and golf.

Typical empty nesters. I, on the other hand, have a nest that is full to bursting. What with me, Amanda, Sofija, Kitty and my four children, plus the staff, there is never a dull moment. (Note to self. Is a full nester a thing?)

Trisha Dyne, a small, enthusiastic woman with a great fondness for leopard skin, lives on the high street and only became religious last year. She is full of questions, which is a huge relief to me as I don't have to ask them. She is pleasingly impressed with my interiors and has asked for my advice on her own redecoration project. Only the front room and downstairs loo, but Isabella Smugge is a woman of the people!

Elsie's friend Poppy is a very sweet child and has been over for playdates several time. Both her mother and her aunt, Gillian and Jen Smale, are part of our group. Gillian is a Pink Lady like Liane and Jen works at the local care home where their mother, a retired nurse, now lives. There was a surprisingly emotional moment as we introduced ourselves on week one.

'She devoted all her working life to helping others.' Jen's eyes were full of tears. 'The dementia's pretty bad now, but she's still so kind. She often bandages up the other residents at the home. She's got such gentle little hands. They let her do it because it calms her down and she thinks she's back at the hospital.'

There was a tactful pause while Jen blew her nose and wiped her eyes. I have had no experience of demented relatives, but going round the room, it seems that few families are untouched by this horrible disease.

The Conklins (Kaitlin and Jason) are a recently married couple who commute to town every day and are thus frequently late to group. They seem very nice.

Our final member is a lady called Anna Cornwall who is a sister at the local hospital and a dementia specialist. Should Mummy or Harry ever exhibit signs of confusion, I shall know where to go! **#newfriends #drawingroom**

A miracle has occurred! I have managed to get through a whole week without anyone annoying me, being sick or pooing on the floor! To think that my life has come to this. The cat is keeping her stomach contents to herself and Milo seems to have grasped the notion that toileting in the correct place can be fun. The entire family bellow, 'Good boy, Milo!' every time he manages to do one in the loo, and I have invested in a travel potty. It seems that he is incredibly young to be self-toileting (however erratically), and the girls on the playground are terribly impressed.

It's just as well, as I am bracing myself for the Official Visit. Paige and Johnnie, plus bump, are joining us for luncheon and a chat on Saturday. Sofija has taken the weekend off and is visiting her friend Mari Luz in London. Amanda and Kitty are shopping in Ipswich. Mummy offered to come and mediate, but I have declined. I need to put on my big girl pants and be there for my children, who are exhibiting mild signs of anxiety.

Thank goodness, then, for the panto, for which I have tickets. I booked a much-needed Mums' Summit at the café on Wednesday morning. Liane had been invited, but was working.

'Thanks for asking, though, Smug. Next time, maybe.'

As she marched off the playground, roll-up in hand, Lauren turned to me, open-mouthed.

'Did she just say thank you? What have you done to her?'

It seems that the conversation at the spa, sticky although it was, has had a real effect on my frenemy.

I promised a full rundown in due course and checked my phone. Johnnie had promised to let me know if Paige went into labour. Nothing as yet.

Many of my friends find redecorating a huge pain. My new homegroup friend Trisha, for example. I popped round to her house for coffee (reasonably good quality) to assess the situation. She lives in an old cottage with beams and low ceilings. The whole place was painted in a rather dreary dark-pinkish shade and her furniture was in desperate need of an upgrade. However, it's amazing what the right throws and cushions can do. I promised a trip to a homeware shop and suggested that I give her the remains of my Bitter and Twisted Loquacity for the walls. Perhaps I should start an interior design consultancy.

As we were discussing accent colours, there was a knock at the door, which opens straight on to the high street. Eighteenth-century cottages are charming, in their own way, but I personally couldn't live my life with brick floors, low beams and a distinct lack of hallway space. An elderly gentleman in a suit and well-polished shoes was standing on the doorstep. He raised his hat and smiled.

'Good morning. I've come to see how Mrs Edcock is feeling today. May I come in?'

Trisha sighed. 'Hello, Frank. Pat doesn't live here any more. Do you remember? She moved away ten years ago.'

The old man frowned. 'But my secretary assured me that she was the first visit on my rounds today. She was a little anaemic, which is only to be expected. May I see her, please?'

Trisha grabbed her coat from the peg and took her visitor's arm.

'Come on. Let's get you back home. Back in a minute, Isabella.'

I was bemused. The man looked vaguely familiar, but then lots of people do. It's a fairly large village and even someone as well connected as me can't expect to know everyone. Ten minutes later, Trisha returned.

'Sorry about that. Dear old Frank. His dementia's got much worse. He was the local GP here for years, then did locum work when he retired. I'll just text his daughter-in-law and let her know that he's been wandering again.'

I must do some research on the correct way to avoid degenerative conditions of the brain. I know you're meant to do crosswords and take up new hobbies in your declining years. I am very much in my prime, but I trust will never let myself get in the kind of state where I have to be taken home by a kindly neighbour.

Trisha and I concluded our business and I returned to my lovely home, grateful for my own good health and excellent genes. Not everyone is so fortunate.

My house was sparkling, every room filled with fresh flowers, the children beautifully dressed and the garden as pretty as it could be in March. Ted had filled the hanging baskets and containers around the front door with winter pansies and green foliage and the drive was freshly raked. I spent the morning with the children, trying to answer their questions honestly.

Bang on midday, the front doorbell rang. Dressed gorgeously in a mint-green midi skirt, ivory cami with slinky cardigan over my shoulders and a pair of statement slip-on platforms, I opened the door to see my husband looking just as suave and handsome as ever and poor Paige pallid and fit to drop. I had lit a fire as it was cold and wet, and had a scrummy lunch ready to serve. I had avoided cured meats, unpasteurised cheeses and seafood and gone for a lovely East Anglian cheeseboard with artisan crackers and homemade chutney, plus grapes, a platter of hams with vine tomatoes and capers, marinated salmon, warmed breads and butter, dips and fresh fruit. Buffet-style is always best in such a situation.

Conversation was stilted. Paige has finally stopped being sick but is sleep-deprived and uncomfortable. Johnnie chatted easily about himself and work and referred several times to how wonderful it would be after the baby was born and his partner was 'back to her old self' (his words). Finn resolutely raised the subject of football, which got us on to the London team Paige and her family support. I know nothing of the beautiful game and am not in the least interested in it, but Finn is an enthusiast and managed a few minutes of lively conversation. I tried drawing Paige out about her family. She's an only child who was brought up on a rough estate in East London (her words, not mine) by a single mother. She was brilliant at maths at school and saw it as her escape. And so it has proved.

When I told Mummy that Johnnie was seeing a young girl from work, her response was typical.

'Some giggling blonde typist, I suppose. It's such a cliché. They see an older man and want someone to buy them things and make them feel special. Honestly, darling!'

Paige, in fact, is climbing rapidly to the top of the tree and has no need of Johnnie's money. At our first meeting, when I mentioned the fiendishly expensive *Huit Heures de Mademoiselle* lipstick that had been left behind at the chalet in Verbier and which I assumed Johnnie had bought, she got quite offended.

'I don't need a man to buy me stuff. I run my own show.'

She started off at the firm as a risk analyst and is now the youngest manager they've ever had. By the time she's thirty, she'll probably be holding down a senior position and will be able to take her pick of jobs. I know from living with Johnnie that being a success in that industry means working long hours, travelling a lot, being put under huge pressure to meet targets and improving oneself constantly. We've only met twice, and one of those times she was being sick in a bowl, but I could see the steely determination and fiercely ambitious brain beneath the young, unlined face.

Over lunch, I asked her about her plans.

'Six months maternity leave, then back to work. Johnnie's going to do consultancy work from home and be the main carer. My mum will fill in where she's needed.'

I glanced at my husband, who was wearing the indulgent smile I've come to loathe.

'Come on now, Paige, we haven't nailed that down yet, have we? Can you really see me at home looking after a baby?'

She shot him a filthy look and for a minute it was like having Mummy in the room.

'Err – yeah, we have and yes, I can. There is no actual way I'm staying at home with a baby. I've got my career to think of. I'll love it and that, but you've already had four and you know what you're doing. And you're old, mate. The glory days are long gone. You know it and I know it. Take the offer and bow out gracefully.'

It was all I could do not to leap to my feet and burst into loud applause. It seemed that Johnnie had found the only woman in the world who would stand up to him and refuse to play his controlling games. This was someone I could work with. Suddenly, being in a blended family with Paige didn't seem quite so challenging.

By coffee time, the children had departed and a sulky Johnnie pretended to have an important call to make, stalking off to his car for privacy and leaving the woman he used to love and the one he is now starting a family with alone.

'Listen, this is weird and I can't believe I'm saying it, but I really like you, Isabella. After all the stuff Johnnie said, I was expecting someone massively up her own backside, but you're not like that at all. I'll be honest. I never planned to have a baby. I don't even like them. And Johnnie was only ever supposed to be a bit of fun. I meant what I said, though. No way I'm giving up my career.'

'And why should you? I only managed to keep mine going because my au pair Sofija did so much for me. I never had to change nappies or do all the boring mum stuff because she was always there. It'll be a shock for Johnnie, but he's just going to have to face up to it. Do you want to swap numbers? We're going to be in each other's lives and I'm here if you ever want a chat or some advice.'

'I'd like that.' She smiled at me and we sat in companionable silence as the dishwasher whooshed away to itself and the birds sang outside. Perhaps, then, with all the buds swelling and the grass growing and the spring bulbs pushing the first green shoots up through the fertile soil, it was inevitable that another new life would begin to make itself felt. Paige suddenly gasped, clutched at her stomach and looked down at the carpet, where a small puddle was rapidly getting larger.

'My waters have gone! What do I do?'

I assured her that everything would be fine and ascertained that she was booked into an exclusive private hospital in London. Her bag, already packed with all the necessaries, was in the boot of the car. I told Johnnie, who typically made it all about himself.

'But we had plans tomorrow! What if all that – stuff – ruins my car seat? Iss, get me some towels, quick.'

I assured Paige that if she wanted to have the baby at Ipswich Hospital, a mere twenty-minute drive away, that would be absolutely fine.

'What? Go on the NHS? Are you mad, Iss? I can have her at the hospital in under two hours. It won't come before that, will it?'

Paige staggered to her feet and screamed in Johnnie's face.

'I don't care where I have it! Get me in that car and start driving, or I won't be responsible for my actions. Isabella, thanks for lunch. Your kids are great. I'll text, all right?'

With a bang of the front door and a screech of tyres on the gravel, they were off. What a day. I shall have to have my sofa professionally cleaned. **#labour #newbaby #newstart**

April

I need a break! I know I had one just a month ago, but I am ready for another one. We're off skiing again in Verbier for Easter. I decided to extend an olive branch to Silvia, although I knew she'd be spending at least three weeks with Johnnie, Paige and the new baby. I dropped her a text the minute I decided on my impromptu holiday, which was about fifteen minutes after my guests' abrupt departure.

'Hi, Silvia. How are you? Just decided to fly off to Verbier over Easter. Would you like to come with us? xx'

Back came her reply.

'Isabella, my angel! What a treat. I haven't heard from you for ages. I would so love to but Johnnie has just telephoned to say that the baby's on the way. They're going to need me to help with those first few weeks. I'd love to join you another time. Lots of kisses to the children xx'

I was jubilant. I'd done my duty and invited her on a holiday I knew she couldn't possibly say yes to. Which got her off my back for a month or two. I'm going to ask Mummy and Harry to come instead. I was assailed by a slight pang of conscience as I realised I'd done what I'd sworn to stop doing, namely making plans without consulting Sofija. I texted her to ask if she'd mind being home alone for a week or two, running the show. Apparently, she doesn't. But that's a warning for the future. I must think of her feelings ahead of my own as we restart our relationship.

Paige was in labour for eighteen hours and had a pretty rough birth. I know this because Johnnie insisted on texting me constantly throughout the whole sorry business. The baby is a boy weighing 6lb 11oz. Paige wants to call him Axl, after a person rejoicing in the name Axl Rose, who I am given to understand is the lead singer of a heavy metal band called Guns N' Roses. I mentioned this on the playground.

'Axl? He's my hero. Love that band!'

Liane Bloomfield is a huge heavy metal and rock fan and went on to tell us that she'd wanted to call her youngest son (Zach) Axl, but had contented herself with it as his middle name instead. Apparently Axl's bandmate is called Slash. I can only hope that Paige is keeping a stern eye on contraception methods. Slash Smugge. It does have a certain ring to it.

'What does Johnnie think of the name?'

Naturally, my husband wasn't having any of it. He was keen to call his new son Henry or Arthur, both of which Paige hated. So the baby is currently nameless and being fussed over by its paternal grandmother. I texted Paige to offer her my congratulations and received a reply in the middle of the night saying that she couldn't wait to get back to work.

'I hurt all over. My boobs are huge and they're agony. The baby won't stop crying. Johnnie's really getting on my nerves. I can't believe I'm telling you this.'

I sent back a kindly and sympathetic response and packaged up some gorgeous sustainable baby clothes and various maternity creams and lotions which helped me when I delivered Milo in the traditional way. Poor Paige. And I never thought I'd be saying that.

In other news, Issy Smugge can now add 'have been to see a pantomime' to her list of achievements. It was actually rather fun. Lauren, Scott and her girls were at the same performance as us and she had given me a rundown on the playground that afternoon of what to expect.

'Wait till you see the dame! He's a local legend. He's an HGV driver, about six foot four, built like a brick convenience, really rocks the frock and tights combo. Funny thing is, he's always loved dressing up as a woman. His wife doesn't mind and the other drivers accept it. He's been the dame for as long as I can remember.'

The pantomime is performed at the village hall and I felt an unexpected rush of excitement as we took our seats and gazed up at the curtained stage. I was just settling myself in my seat when Lauren dug me violently in the ribs.

'Isabella!' she hissed in my ear. 'Over there. I told you! I said you had to snap him up quick before someone else did, and now look!'

I'd never heard my friend speak so angrily. She was scowling in the general direction of Robin Knight, who was holding hands with a pleasant-looking middle-aged woman I vaguely recognised from church.

I shrugged. 'So? Why shouldn't he go out with someone? I told you, he's not my type. He's boring and he's too short. I'm holding out for a hero.'

I was half-joking, but to my surprise Lauren's eyes filled with angry tears.

'This kind of opportunity doesn't come along every day! A nice man who goes to church and doesn't have any weird habits as far as we know. And now that Sallie-Ann's bagged him. She only started coming to our church a few months ago. I was all ready to matchmake and you're spoiling it.'

I was mystified.

'Why are you getting so upset? Plenty more fish in the sea.'

Lauren tutted loudly. 'But there aren't! That's the point. Do you really want to be scraping the barrel with Derek from Great Yarmouth and all those other weirdos? You can't keep on comparing everyone to Johnnie.'

I could see that my friend was really upset and decided to use humour to diffuse the situation.

'I'll get Liane to swipe right on Derek for me and make Robin jealous. We can have a date in the café and I'll hold his hand and gaze into his eyes till Robin dumps Sallie-Ann (although they make a lovely couple) and then I'll run off with him. Will that make you happy?'

Lauren let out a reluctant chuckle just as the lights dimmed and the curtain went up. Show time!

During the interval, restored to partial good humour but still shooting angry looks at Robin and Sallie-Ann, Lauren asked me if I was enjoying the panto. To my surprise, I was. The dame, resplendent in a satin sheath frock with full-length gloves and tufts of hair peeking out of his armpits, was a remarkably good actor. Or possibly actress. Were I a man playing a lady, I would probably shave my legs, but the stubble poking through his fishnets added to the lure of the piece. As did his thick Suffolk accent.

Chloë danced beautifully, of course. Gazing up at her on the stage, I could see that she had found her niche. I will fight hard to make sure she gets to where she needs to be in life, whatever Johnnie says.

Robin's girlfriend clung to his arm and was whispering in his ear throughout the whole second half. They left early, arms around each other's waists. Which is fine. It's nothing to me. **#dontcare**

Thank heavens for Verbier! Sitting on our balcony gazing out over the valley with the lights twinkling and the piste-makers gliding up and down and Robin Knight's middle-aged squeeze just a memory, I savoured my glass of dry and fruity Chasselas Blanc (I had no idea that Swiss wines could be so delicious). I could feel the stress of the last few weeks dropping away and as I breathed in the crisp, fresh mountain air and smelled the enticing fragrance of raclette drifting through from the kitchen, all felt right with my world.

It turns out that Harry is a pretty decent cook. He and I have been sharing kitchen duties and tonight he's giving us that Swiss favourite of melted cheese and mountain meats.

I had a bit of a moment today. I'd come down a red run with the children and left them at the restaurant having hot chocolates while I went up one more time. I've been feeling sluggish and – dare I say it – a little bit middle-aged of late, and pushing myself to the limit on a tricky run is just what the doctor ordered. Soaring over the sparkling snowscape in the chair lift, I let my mind drift. Suddenly, I heard a voice.

'I want you to spend more time with Me, Isabella.'

I was fairly sure that the mysterious voice belonged to God. Either that, or I was losing my mind. It seemed only polite to reply.

'Hello. Is that You? I can certainly schedule more blocks of quality time if that's what's required.'

'I want you to really know Me,' replied the voice.

Many of the homegroup speak about the good Lord as if He is a personal friend. I feel that I have a fairly healthy relationship with Him, bearing in mind He's invisible and I don't really know what I'm doing. However, it was obviously time to take it to the next level, as in all thriving relationships.

'All right, then. Thank You very much. And thank You for this lovely holiday and the chalet and Sofija coming back. I am trying hard to do the right thing and be a better person, as You know.'

'I don't want you to try. I want you to spend time with Me.'

I have always been a Type A overachiever, very much a tryer and a self-improver. As I pushed up the bar on my seat and braced myself to slide off the lift and down the run, I considered the option of just being. It sounded like a bit of a challenge. The obvious thing to do was to text Claire and ask her advice. I shot down the mountain in record time and, as I arrived at the restaurant where the children were finishing their hot chocolates, I was more than ready for a hearty lunch.
#switzerland #ontheslopes #friendofgod

Back at the chalet, I texted Claire.

'I think God has been speaking to me. How do you know it's definitely Him? It might have been my imagination. How's Easter going? xx'

After a while (Easter is a very busy time in the Church of England, it seems), she replied.

'Everyone hears Him differently. What did He say? Busy, but good thanks. Are you having fun? xx'

I passed on the gist of the conversation. Claire is an expert on such things and explained that while doing good deeds is important, it's more about spending time with God and developing one's relationship. He wants us to be close to Him, it appears, and not just importune Him when we want something. I am rather prone to doing this, although I always make sure that I pass on my thanks when He does what I ask.

'Why don't you ask your homegroup for some thoughts? Have you set up a WhatsApp group? I'm on ours all the time! Happy skiing. Had coffee with Sofija yesterday, btw. I'm so glad she's back xx'

I pondered. I am starting to get to know the homegroup, but we're not friends, exactly. I expect that will come. I filed the whole business away under 'to be considered' and rose gracefully to my feet to join the rest of the family around the dinner table.

A well-planned skiing holiday is a delight. One rises and has a hearty breakfast, then skis all morning. Lunchtime is an opportunity to take a breather and enjoy the scenery and the company of one's family, then one skis vigorously all afternoon to deal with the many calories taken on board, has a long hot restorative shower, a preprandial drink or two and a lovely dinner. What could be more fun?

After a few animated card games and some Scrabble (a Smugge family favourite), the girls went off to bed and Finn sat playing on his phone. All was quiet and serene until Mummy's phone beeped.

'Good heavens! Randy Rupert's dead!'

This was big news. The said Rupert, father of Lavinia and husband of Audrey, was not a popular or a pleasant man, but just the same, it's always a shock to hear of the sudden demise of someone you sort of know.

'Apparently he was at the London flat with a companion having dinner. Halfway through the starter, he choked on an oyster and that was that! Well. A companion. We all know what *that* means. Poor Audrey. I'd better text her. Or is it too soon?'

'Are you saying he was having an affair?'

Mummy tutted and took a large mouthful of wine.

'Of course! He was never faithful to Audrey. There was always someone in the background. It was kept very discreet and the women were always from a good family. I will say that.'

Poor Lavinia. I debated whether to send her a text of condolence. With my recent exchange with the good Lord very much on my mind, I reached out.

'Hello, it's me. Can I ask Your advice? Should I text Lavinia about her father? All advice gratefully received. With many thanks.'

I waited but heard nothing. I expect He was busy.

'Poor Audrey will be lost without him. She needs someone she can rely on, a good friend who's always there. We're back on speaking terms, but I think she's still a bit cross with me. I'll organise some flowers and send her a message in a couple of days.'

I thought about my old enemy's face, tear-streaked and vulnerable as she shared painful childhood memories. Suddenly, I knew the answer to my question.

'Hi, Lavinia. I've just heard about your father. I am so sorry. Please message me if there's anything I can do to help. I know how it feels.'

Now that Mummy has mastered modern technology (more or less), she is rarely seen without her phone. It was going mad with notifications the day after the shocking news of Randy Rupert's death broke. While the children put on their ski suits and suncream, Mummy filled me in.

'He'd gone off-piste with this one, darling. A much younger woman, Australian if you please! I must text Audrey. It'll look odd if I don't.'

So much for a peaceful holiday!

In other news, my husband has also been texting non-stop. He has persuaded Paige to move to the house in the Colne Valley for the first few weeks of their son's life (still no name) and will finish at work on 1st May. Paige is making 'unreasonable demands', it seems. These are (in no particular order):

1. Asking him to change the baby's nappies.

2. Sending him out to the shops for maternity products.

3. Making up the night feeds and administering them.

4. Carrying out household tasks.

5. Cooking meals.

'I mean, why doesn't she ask my mother? That's why she's here, to help out. I'm exhausted and I'm struggling with the whole business of setting up the consultancy work and calling it a day at the office. Paige doesn't seem to understand. Could you speak to her, Iss? She likes you and it might come better from a woman. I can't go on like this.'

I paced around, clenching and unclenching my fists. Paige had been in touch, as had Silvia, but I had no intention of helping Johnnie to be any more of a rubbish partner and father than he already was. I decided to ignore his message and smiled wryly at the thought of my husband being a hands-on parent.

Lavinia texted me back.

'Thanks. I appreciate it. All a bit of a shock. Ma holding up very well, considering. Funeral in three weeks.'

I replied at once, taking advantage of the new channels of communication opening up between us.

'It must be so hard for you. I am sorry. Mummy sends her love too and she's been texting your mother. Hope the funeral goes well.'

There was a short silence and then she replied.

'Appreciate it. People keep trying to console me and saying how upset I must be feeling. I'm not going to lie, I don't really feel anything. It's just a lot of admin for me (although I've got my PA doing most of it) while my brothers lie around and try to second-guess the will. Not going to pretend to be sad when I'm not.'

On our last day, Mummy sat sipping her coffee and gazing out at the sparkling slopes and blue skies.

'Audrey's coping incredibly well. Of course, there's still the reading of the will and, knowing Rupert, he's probably done something massively inappropriate like leaving his mother's jewels to this Australian person. But Audrey will be very comfortably off. They've got that big house and estate (although of course the eldest son inherits), the London flat and lots of stocks and shares.'

I returned home, lightly tanned and feeling like a new woman, to find the family room redecorated and all the partitioning and plastering on the second floor finished. Sofija has been a marvel, of course, running the show, managing all the trades and keeping Mimi happy. I braced myself for the meeting with my agent.

'Sweetie! You took your little nanny back. We chatted while you were away and she's completely on side with Brand Smugge. Now, where are we at with the divorce? We're going to have to think how to break that news to your followers. You've established yourself as an independent single parent going it alone while staying gorgeous and on trend, and your stats are good. I've had any number of offers for new paid partnerships since you hopped into bed with Bitter and Twisted. When can

Mimi expect to see some lovely pictures of your second floor, darling?'

I shared the news that I had my decree nisi and that Johnnie and I were doing our best to expedite the decree absolute.

'We can make some capital out of this for you. You're not the first family-friendly influencer to be cheated on, betrayed and dumped, and you won't be the last. Now, *Ascendancy* magazine wants to come and do the interview this month and take some pictures. They've promised me a four-page spread, and last time they did that it was for Michelle Obama. So you're in good company, sweetie!'

She laughed, raspingly, and lit a new cigarette from the stub of the old one. I shudder to think what state her lungs must be in.

'So the piece is all about your climb to the top, your invention of influencing as a profession and the impact you're having on the up-and-coming stars. You'll reach a whole new audience.'

Sometimes it's best to agree with Mimi and make it easy on myself. So I did.

It was good to be back on the playground. Liane came over to the Year Three line of her own accord to share news of her Easter decorating frenzy.

'I tried that colour drenching, Smug. Did the whole front room in that purple paint you gave me. Looks well classy. Ceiling's in the same colour.'

With an effort, I managed to conjure up an enthusiastic smile. Colour drenching, as you will know, dictates that one paints the walls, skirting boards, radiators and even the ceiling in one shade, thus increasing the illusion of space in small or awkwardly shaped areas and turning larger rooms into cosy cocoons with darker hues. Porphyria is a very strong colour, and in my large, light-filled bathroom with a feature wall to break it up, it was going to look amazing. In a smallish front room with poor lighting (I had never actually been to Liane's house, but I couldn't imagine she was an interior design expert), such a treatment would make it feel dark and closed in. My heart sank. My kind impulse to help a fellow parent had backfired horribly. Lauren joined us.

'Tell Smug what you think of my front room, Loz.'

My friend was enthusiastic.

'It looks amazing, babes! Well nice. We went up Cheap and Cheerful and got a new lamp and some curtains in the sale. I remembered what you said that time we all went with your mum and talked Liane into getting a new light as well. She went for this big old chandelier – it's gorgeous.'

I waited for an invitation to view said room, but none came. However, I wanted to encourage the new, slightly warmer relationship with my frenemy.

'I'm so pleased! I'm nowhere near finishing the work at my house, although the family room's done.'

'Tell you what, Smug, if you've got any more leftover paint, send it my way. I've got the decorating bug! Now I've painted the front room, it's made everything else look shabby. I'm still on the list for a new house on the development, and tarting my place up a bit's helping take my mind off it.'

Seize the day and all that. I invited her back for a coffee. It was a golden opportunity to bestow some subtle decorating advice. Claire appeared.

'Hello, everyone. How were the holidays? Isabella, you've got a lovely colour.'

It's been ages since we had a proper chat and I wanted to ask her advice about the whole being chums with God thing.

'Liane, do you mind if Claire joins us? Milo's spending the morning with my mother and her husband so we've got the house to ourselves. Well, apart from all the workmen on the second floor. I can go through paint colours with you.'

Liane indicated that this was acceptable and we headed home.

'How are things going with the move? Where are you on the list?'

I don't know how Claire finds the time to keep up with everyone on the playground. To my shame, I realised that I had been so busy silently judging the use of Porphyria for colour drenching that I'd forgotten to ask Liane how her potential move was going.

'Rubbish. I was number fourteen last time I called them up. I meet all the criteria. Village born and bred, five kids, single mum and my girl's got asthma. The damp doesn't help at all. The only good thing about my house is the garden. It's huge, but I can't keep up with it all now I'm doing so many nights. Uncle Bix comes and mows it for me and keeps on top of the weeds.'

I was confused.

'Uncle Bix? What – you mean Bix Bloomfield? The church organist?'

'Duh! Where have you been, Smug? Obviously!'

Of course! There was no apparent physical resemblance between the woman clad in tight jeans, black leather jacket, band shirt and spike-heeled boots striding along beside me and the nervous, hermit-like, eccentrically dressed former pop star who entertained the congregation with variations on Beach Boys and Rolling Stones hits before the service, and who last week (if I was not very much mistaken) had played us in with some late Hendrix. The former keyboard player with the Do Wells, a mid-sixties pop sensation, Bix Bloomfield had crashed and burned after a painful band split, a chequered solo career and a catastrophic fondness for hard drugs and alcohol.

'So, he's your uncle? I had no idea.'

'He's my dad's second cousin, but close enough. He's always been plain old Uncle Bix to me.'

Back at the Old Rectory, I fired up the coffee machine and served homemade granola bars studded with cranberries and orange peel. We sat cosily around the island chatting about paint colours. I have been itching to get my hands on the vicarage interiors (uniformly drab and scruffy, it pains me to say), and this appeared to be the ideal opportunity to share my munificence with a wider audience. Coffee drunk and refreshments consumed, I led my visitors to the cart lodge where the Bitter and Twisted paint cans were stored.

'I've got a couple of big tins of Pretension and Irony left over from the family room. Claire, if you want some for the vicarage, you're very welcome.'

I could see she was thinking about it.

'I'd love a refresh in the front room. It gets used so much and it's looking really dingy. If Tom's OK with it, then I'd love to accept your kind offer. What a treat! We've talked about it, but we feel bad repainting when the church did it all when we first moved in.'

That left all the Hanoverian colours, some more suited to a damp, elderly council house than others.

'I'm going to do the hall and stairs next. Got any more of that purple spare, Smug?'

I told a little white lie and waved my hand invitingly at the tins of Ansbach and Powdering Gown.

'Either of those would be perfect for a hallway. They reflect light, which is what you want when you come into a house. And I've taken out the old lamp shades from the second floor which are only just over three years old. You're more than welcome to have a look through and see if you fancy any of them. They'll only be sitting up there gathering dust otherwise.'

I could see Liane wrestling with this. The last thing she needed was me breathing down her neck, so I directed her and Claire up the stairs to the boarded first floor and went back to the house to make more coffee.

Five minutes later they were back. Liane stood outside the boot room dragging enthusiastically on a roll-up so I seized the chance to talk to Claire about holy matters. It seems that religious people who are doing it all properly read their Bibles every day and engage in something called devotionals too. I can see that I will have to get up ten minutes earlier every morning to build this new activity into my day.

'What brand would you recommend for a beginner like me? I've got my old school Bible but I don't get on too well with it, to be honest.'

Claire smiled and took a sip of her latte.

'I'd say go for *The Message* translation. That's the one Tom uses at church. It's written in everyday language so it's much more accessible. I'll look out some reading notes for you. It's good to find a bit of time every day to spend with God.'

I made a note on my calendar to repeat daily at 06.30 hours. 'Talk to God.' That should do it.

Liane returned and the conversation reverted to interiors. I convinced her to take the Ansbach, Powdering Gown and a pair of rather gorgeous teal and copper lampshades. Result!

Claire gathered up her keys and phone.

'Thanks for the coffee and the paint, Isabella. That's so kind of you. Liane, would you like me and Tom to pray about you getting a house on the new development?'

Liane looked a bit stumped.

'Err – yeah, OK. If you like. Thanks, Claire. Appreciate it. Bye, Smug! Cheers for the paint.'

And they were gone, leaving me with a warm sense of satisfaction and a to-do list as long as my perfectly toned arm. **#busymum #paintjob #reno**

We celebrated Milo's second birthday in Switzerland so I swerved a full-on party at home this year. Johnnie texted to change access arrangements.

'Look, Iss, I can't have the kids for a while until Paige has got her head around the whole baby thing. I'll make it up to them in the hols. I could take them all to Dubai with me when I fly out to see Charlie. Paige and the baby might stay here, although I said we could book nannies. Hope Milo liked the cuddly toy.'

My husband's idea of the perfect present for his two-year-old son was a vast stuffed polar bear sporting a red bow tie. It was propped in Milo's room near his cot, but brought on screaming nightmares. And who wouldn't be scared to wake up in the night and see the world's largest carnivorous land mammal looming menacingly over one's bed? I put it in Elsie's room but she objected to it, so it's now lying on its side in the drawing room behind a sofa, a massive trip hazard. I shall have to see if Rebecca Bennet will accept it as a raffle prize for our next school event.

Silvia has been texting regularly and sending pictures of the new baby. According to her, the latest name to be mooted is Hudson Henry Smugge, which I think sounds like a firm of solicitors.

On Monday, I got her latest update.

'Hello, darling, how are you and the children? All going very well here. Johnnie simply adores the baby, as you would expect, and he is a dear little thing. They've changed their minds about the name. Now the frontrunner is Henry Arthur – a nice traditional choice and goes so well with his surname, don't you think? Paige is doing very well and is a natural mother, just like you, my angel. Sending love, see you soon xx'

Hard on the heels of this optimistic bulletin from the front, Johnnie texted, giving me a completely different picture of life *chez* Smugge.

'I don't know how much longer I can stand this, Iss. I'm exhausted. Paige is being very difficult about the baby's name. She likes Hudson Axl, which sounds very common, don't you think? She stays in bed most of the day and leaves me to do all the hard work. Her mother isn't a fan of me, for some reason, so what with yours and now hers, I'm feeling very unloved! Thank God for Ma. Have you thought about coming down and getting on side with Paige?'

Paige WhatsApped to thank me for the baby gifts.

'I love the clothes. My mum came up for a couple of days. She's not a fan of Johnnie or Silvia. How did you cope with her being your mother-in-law? She's so pass agg. Driving me crazy. Baby is called Hudson and I'm compromising with Henry as a middle name as long as I can add in Albert

after my granddad. Hudson Smugge. What do you reckon? I'm worn out with all the broken nights. Sorry to keep messaging, but you're the only one in this crazy family who talks any sense.'

Interesting times.

I have agreed to accompany Charlene and Liane to a craft fair this weekend. Tony the counsellor has worked such wonders that although Charlene's still anxious and has the odd panic attack, she is pushing doors that once remained firmly shut and padlocked.

'I'll take the girls if it helps, babes. We can go to the park and have a runaround. Would your mum have Milo?'

I thanked Lauren and wondered what to do about Finn. Charlene piped up.

'Jake's coming along to help me set up. If Finn wants to come too, they're old enough to wander around town by themselves. We can give them some money for lunch and they can come and help us pack the car.'

I ran the idea past Finn, who was surprisingly amenable.

Bright and early on Saturday morning, we set off, my boot packed with boxes full of handmade textiles and my seats occupied by two teenage boys, Charlene and Liane. Charlene had promised homemade cakes, good coffee and a range of high-quality crafts. My standards are so high, however, that I was bracing myself for disappointment.

I needn't have worried. We were greeted by an efficient-looking woman with a clipboard who ticked Charlene's name off a list and directed her to a table by the refreshments and next to the raffle.

'Here's your token for a free tea or coffee. I was baking till three this morning. Give me a shout if you need any help.' She trotted off to talk to another batch of stallholders and I surveyed the scene.

Tables were laid out attractively and there was a mouth-watering display of baked goods on the bar at the end of the room. I wandered over to have a look. Victoria sponge, cheese straws, sausage rolls, brownies, chocolate cake, flapjacks and cheese scones were reposing on the counter presided over by a smiling woman in a crisp pinny. I handed over Charlene's donation to the raffle (some colourful bunting) and eyed up the cakes.

'Pull your finger out, Smug! We've got work to do.'

Liane Bloomfield was helping Charlene to unload her boxes. I arranged a selection of deep wicker baskets tied with gingham ribbon along the front of the stall and filled them with gorgeous handmade items, while Charlene and Liane laid out the cushions. I had to move a few things around when they'd finished and change up some of the key items; ignoring their twitterings, I got the stall looking incredibly professional. As we sipped our coffee (surprisingly good, real depth of flavour), I interrogated Charlene to see if she was ready to face the masses.

'How many followers have you got on Insta? Have you been posting regularly?'

Charlene looked confused.

'I haven't got an account. I set up a little website and I'm on Facebook, but that's it.'

Honestly! How do people think they're going to prosper in business if they don't have a social media and marketing strategy nailed down? Leaving them to fiddle about with lavender bags, I took some fantastic shots of the products, the stall, the interior and exterior of the hall plus some images of the row of Tudor houses opposite, and set up an Insta account. I gave Charlene an impromptu tutorial on the merits of stories, posts and reels and WhatsApped her a list of suitable hashtags.

'Now, get a notebook and let's go and introduce ourselves to everyone else. You need to follow them on Insta and get them to follow you back. Tag everyone and post regularly today. I'll show you the kinds of photos that really work with textiles. You'll soon get the hang of it.'

I marched her briskly round the hall which was now full of artisan makers. We had, in no particular order:

1. A woman who makes her own lampshades using vintage fabric (I took her card for Mummy who is in dire need. Harry's wife clearly had no taste).

2. A pet portrait artist.

3. A soap maker (her products smelled heavenly).

4. Two friendly ladies who make colourful fused glass.

5. A husband-and-wife team who make their own wooden gift items.

6. A local brewer.

7. A very well-presented woman with an impressive range of hand-poured scented candles.

8. An artisan gin maker (ideal for Mummy's birthday present).

9. Someone who makes their own crystal jewellery.

10. Various ladies selling cakes, biscuits and scones.

11. A cornucopia of hand-knitted jumpers.

With the exception of the latter two ('Oh no, dear, I don't hold with that social media'), everyone was happy to follow Charlene. By the time the doors opened, she had thirteen followers and had posted a story and a reel with my assistance.

Everyone has their own sales techniques, and sometimes, just sometimes, what they call a dream team is born. Charlene, nervous and unsure of her own talent, needed both me and Liane Bloomfield by her side. The doors opened at ten and I eyeballed a group of middle-aged ladies heading our way. They clearly needed more cushions and bunting in their lives.

'These are made with the highest quality fabrics, all hand sewn. Any room can be refreshed inexpensively with the right cushions. I always advise my followers to switch up their accessories in spring.'

I smiled engagingly. One of them took the bait.

'Followers? What do you do?'

I explained.

'You're Isabella M Smugge? Oh, my goodness, I thought I recognised you but I didn't expect to see you somewhere like this! I've got all your books. And you say these are hand sewn? I was thinking about redoing my lounge, actually, and I could do with some new bits and bobs.'

Ker-ching! Five minutes later, we'd sold six cushions and some bunting and Charlene was in profit. The lampshade lady was doing brisk business and I scented the possibility of a collaboration. Leaving Liane to apply her own special sales technique to the hapless members of the public, I wandered over for a chat. Sure enough, she was happy to direct her customers to Charlene's stall and I promised to reciprocate. By the time I got back, Liane was haranguing a nervous-looking woman who was dithering about buying a patchwork quilt for her granddaughter.

'You won't see anything better than that in a fancy shop. All handmade by my friend. She's a single mother. That quilt's the difference between a good night's sleep and her tossing and turning worrying about paying the bills. Do you really want that on your conscience?'

Fortunately, Charlene was getting in another round of coffees and therefore missing Liane's unorthodox sales technique. I swung into action.

'This is a legacy purchase, madam. Your granddaughter will treasure it and hand it on to her children. Imagine that – your generosity today influencing future generations.'

Darn, I'm good! The woman coughed up and bought four lavender bags into the bargain. **#teamwork #selling #handmade**

The day wore on. I made a number of gorgeous purchases, Liane won a raffle prize and I bonded with several of the stallholders. It was jolly good fun. I may bring Mummy next time. Johnnie texted me three times but I ignored him. Isabella M Smugge is now the Craft Fair Queen and has no time for sleep-deprived narcissists! What a great way to finish the month. Roll on May! **#saleslady #ontheroad #dreamteam**

May

The countdown is on for the post-wedding party at the Old Rectory! Out of politeness, Mummy sent an invitation to the recently widowed Audrey Harcourt ('She won't come, darling') and received an acceptance by return of post. I shall make sure to monitor her alcohol intake.

Johnnie's self-pitying messages keep coming. The latest news is that Paige wants him to have a vasectomy. I love my children more than life itself, but my husband has more than done his bit on that score. I have decided to ignore his communications, then answer them all in one go in the evenings. I don't need him living rent-free in my head, thank you very much.

I love May. The skies are blue, the clouds are fluffy, and nature is doing its very best to assist Issy Smugge with her content. Frothy pink cherry blossom, the trees mantled in fresh green, and melodious birdsong. I couldn't have planned it better myself. The new development is nearly finished and we expect some new families on the playground. Liane has moved up to number ten on the waiting list for a house but is still convinced she won't get one. We'll see.

I was waiting for my copy of *Ascendancy* magazine to hit the mat. A four-page full-colour spread about Isabella M Smugge and all her works would normally incite Lavinia Harcourt to spitting rage and result in a vitriolic attack in her gossip column, but of late, all she'd levelled at me were a few half-hearted digs.

Pottering around in the kitchen, I was surprised to hear a knock on the boot room door. Most people just walk straight in. I opened the door to see Frank, the retired doctor who had made such an unexpected appearance at Trisha's house. As before, he was smartly dressed and raised his hat to me.

'Good morning, my dear. I've come to call on Lady Hamilton. Shall I go straight up?'

We bought the Old Rectory from Lady Hamilton's estate (probate is a bit of a nightmare but it was all worth it) and moved in nearly four years ago. How did I tell this elderly gentleman that his patient had been dead for five years?

'May I offer you a coffee, doctor? Her Ladyship is asleep at the moment.'

This was clearly the right thing to do. He walked in and took a seat at my island.

'I don't think I've seen you before. What's happened to Peggy?'

I carried on with the deception while making him a coffee.

'She's visiting her mother. I'm helping out while she's away.'

I WhatsApped Trisha.

Help. Frank the retired doctor is here. What do I do? x'

I kept Frank talking ('What has her ladyship done to the kitchen? It looks different') and gave fake bulletins on Peggy's mother's health until there was another knock at the boot room door. A flustered-looking woman was standing there.

'I am so sorry! Frank, come on, I need to get you home.'

She looked on the verge of tears. In the spirit of neighbourliness, I invited her in and offered her a coffee.

'Oh no, I couldn't possibly intrude on you any further. I'm Julie Shemming, Frank's daughter-in-law. His Alzheimer's has got much worse this year, I'm afraid. He's still living independently, but I don't know how much longer that can go on.'

She was clearly in no mood for a chat. She gave me her number ('Please text me if Frank appears and thanks for being so understanding') and led her father-in-law out. How awful. I hope I never get like that.

Being an adult is jolly hard. I made the decision to invite Sofija back into my life while wracked with fever, but even when I recovered from my illness, I was glad I did it. It doesn't mean it's easy, though. I wonder how long it will be before I can look at her and not see her holding hands with my husband and gazing adoringly into his eyes, the way they did when I uncovered their affair three years ago. I don't love Johnnie any more and I can see him for what he is. But just the same, living in close proximity to the woman I used to trust implicitly and who shattered that trust is hard. I don't know if we will ever get back to the way we were – is that even possible? – but we're both working hard on our relationship.

Do I regret reaching out to her? No. Can I see a time when the awkwardness that still exists between us is gone? Possibly.

Putting my emotions to one side (and it's generally a good idea in business), inviting her back into our lives has made my children very happy and has transformed my work–life balance.

If only she hadn't slept with my husband behind my back.

Oh well.

Had I not become the UK's most beloved Instamum, I could very easily have been a designer. There's nothing I love more than planning out a room, thinking about paint colours and lighting, then choosing just the right statement furniture. I spent a happy morning with the wonderful carpet man from Woodbridge talking about my carpets and floor coverings. What a delight to be in the hands of an expert! **#flooringluxury**

Mindful of my trip to Cheap and Cheerful with the girls last year, when I helped Lauren upgrade her front room, I have toned down my interior design blogs. Very few people are fortunate enough to have unlimited funds, and I enjoy sharing tips and tricks to help my followers achieve a stunning new look on a very small budget. I've been on *Morning, You!* (Britain's flagship breakfast show) several times, talking about this very subject. Sitting in my studio with a steaming mug of peppermint tea by my side (so refreshing!), I penned my latest article.

Designer Know-How at a Fraction of the Price: Issy Smugge Tells You How It's Done

There's nothing worse than living with outdated, shabby rooms and feeling powerless to change them. I'm here to tell you that you can – and at a fraction of the price charged by top designers. Here are my never-fail hacks for achieving a flawless finish for a swoon-worthy interior.

1. Invest in just one statement piece per room and watch the pennies on the rest. If you're doing up your living room, spend as much as you can on a really good sofa and then accessorise with low-cost cushions (keep an eye out for sales) and curtains. If you have a friend who's handy with a needle, why not come to an arrangement? Commission a pair of floor-length curtains in an end-of-line fabric (so much cheaper) and pay your friend in babysitting or cooking. Buy some cheap picture frames for family photos or wall art and customise them yourself. Decorative blankets, throws, footstools, candles and vases can be sourced cheaply at most homeware stores, or online.

2. Think about your lighting. If you can, find an extra-luxurious chandelier or lantern. Then accessorise with some low-cost table lamps. That one statement piece of lighting will be the focus point of your room and it will last for years, especially if you pick a neutral colour that won't date.

3. The bathroom is the ideal place for a super-quick and easy makeover. If you can't afford new tiles, invest in tile paint. You'll need to thoroughly clean and prep the surface and apply a few coats, but put in your EarPods and your favourite podcast and the time will fly. With new, smart tiling, you can afford to splash out on high-quality towels. Egyptian cotton is best, but there are lots of options out there. Pile them high on a unit (source a cheap one and zhuzh it up with some paint and new knobs), then scour your local charity shops and markets for cute glass containers or vintage jars to hold toothbrushes and toothpaste.

4. We spend around one-third of our lives in bed, so why skimp on your bedroom? I love to turn in early with a good book and drift off to sleep in a super-comfy bed dressed with luxe sheets and fluffy pillows. If you've got the money, splash the cash on a new bed. If not, why not get a new mattress and memory foam mattress topper, then invest in some cheap cushions and throws to dress your bed gorgeously? Search out the sales in home décor shops and find yourself a roll of end-of-line wallpaper for a feature wall. Hang a mirror to make your room look bigger and see how good you feel at bedtime. If you've got the space, search out a vintage armchair. It makes any bedroom look more like a boudoir!

5. Mix and match. Be bold! There are no rules in interior design that can't be broken. If you love it and you want to live with it, snap it up! China can be mismatched, important pieces reclaimed or upcycled, and it's amazing what you can do with some furniture paint and a coat of wax.

Issy Smugge is the friend of the people!

On Friday, Mummy and I had a much-needed catch-up at the café. Walking down the hill, I remembered that I am meant to be spending more time with God. Oops. I sent up a quick apology and asked Him to put Liane's name on top of the list for a new house.

The café was nearly full. Two tables of builders from the new development, various people in matching, trendy clothes with loud voices, who I took to be tourists, and a scattering of locals. Mummy was bursting with news.

'Audrey Harcourt's a dark horse. She's hardly buried Rupert and rumours are reaching me of a new relationship! She's selling the London flat and buying herself a little bolthole. Goodness knows what she's going to be getting up to!'

I counteracted with news of Johnnie's proposed vasectomy. Mummy snorted.

'About time! I'd do it myself if I could get him to hold still. Wretched little man. So you met his fancy piece? What did you think of her?'

Only my mother could describe Johnnie's Gen Z girlfriend and mother of his fifth child as a fancy piece.

'I really like her. Brainy, tough and she's certainly got Johnnie's number. He keeps sending me whiny texts about how hard his life is. He's left work and spends most of his days trying to avoid feeds and nappy changes. He's pushing for the decree absolute so he can get married again, but I don't think Paige is up for it.'

Our lunches arrived, and between bites of tuna salad, Mummy filled me in on yet more exciting news.

'I've been asked to be a judge at the Village Show! I wonder if I could persuade Harry to move here. There's so much going on. Although I don't suppose Karen would stand for it.'

I don't suppose she would, which is a pity. I never thought I'd hear myself say it, but I actually wouldn't mind having Mummy living nearby. **#familyties #judging**

The piece in *Ascendency* magazine ('Isabella M Smugge: The Influencer's Influencer') has had quite an impact. Mimi is delighted.

'You did so well talking about your marital woes, darling. You come across as patient and forbearing but feisty. Let me know how the divorce is proceeding and I'll spin it to make you look even better.'

Not quite what I had in mind when I exchanged my vows with Johnnie, but that's the way of the world.

Closer to home, the new development is almost finished and there is excitement on the playground. The school is always chronically short of money and the latest donations from the PTA have been very gratefully received.

'I've heard there's at least six new families coming, babes. It's great news for the school!'

I was confused.

'Why?'

'Because every time a new child registers, the school gets money for them. We've just got to hope they all come here and don't go to Allonsfield. It's teeny with a rubbish playground, but some of the snobby parents send their kids there because of the class sizes. What we want is a couple of families with about six children each who don't drive – that means they have to come here.'

In the distance, I could see Liane Bloomfield, who appeared to be running – not an activity in which I've ever seen her engage. Panting and breathless, she screeched to a halt and threw her arms around Lauren.

'We're in, Loz! I got it! Four bedroomed, all brand new. I should be in by the end of next month.'

Was this the moment, finally, when Liane and I would embrace and admit that we quite liked each other? It seemed not. She released Lauren from a bear hug and gave me an awkward pat on the shoulder.

'All right, Smug? How about that, then? Big posh house, just like yours. I'd better get a cleaner!'

She laughed raucously, attracting the attention of Hayley Robinson who was scuttling past.

'Heard the latest, Robinson? I've bagged myself a brand-new house on the estate. We'll be neighbours!'

From the expression on Hayley's face, this did not appear to be good news.

'No, we won't. Chris and I are thinking of moving. All that digging and the building work has disrupted our family life, and now the view's ruined by those horrible new houses. How come you get it all handed to you on a plate and we have to work hard for every penny?'

On another day, there would have been a massive punch-up. However, today was not that day. Liane rolled her eyes at Hayley Robinson.

'You've got a face like a trod-on chip and you're a complete waste of space, but I love everyone today. Even you, you loser!'

Off she skipped, leaving me and Hayley standing awkwardly together. Thank heavens, Claire, the social glue of any social situation, was suddenly at my elbow. I passed on Liane's news.

'What an answer to prayer! That's wonderful. Tom and I are so looking forward to welcoming all the new families to the village. We're going to go round to each house with a little care package and a card. That's what we always did in our old church. The PCC have finally agreed. We haven't really got the money, but God will provide.'

I did a tiny eye roll. God is very good and all that, but Claire never seems to learn. He has put an extremely well-heeled influencer in her life for a reason. In a matter of minutes, a sum had been mentioned and I had transferred it to the church account. A great day for answered prayer!

The whole business of prayer, answered and otherwise, came up at homegroup this week. I am getting into the groove of this whole meeting together and talking about holy things. Just as Claire predicted, we are all opening up to each other and starting to dig a bit deeper. As I passed round the dark chocolate and mint Ottolenghi fridge cake nibbles (delicious!), Trisha asked the Big One.

'See, this is what I don't get. How come if God is so good and all that, people still get ill and sometimes don't make it?'

There was a long discussion, much of which went over my head. Richard Dunning seems to know the answers to everything and has an encyclopaedic knowledge of the Good Book, from which he quotes constantly. If I were on a TV quiz show with him and the subject came up, we'd win for sure. However, lovely Sue has a way of putting things that even entry-level religious people like me and Trisha can understand. The fridge cake had all gone by the time Robin got a word in edgeways.

'I don't know the answer. I wish I did. Everyone at church prayed so hard for healing, we laid hands on Rosie, she went away to a prayer retreat but she still died.'

'But how come you still believed in God after that? I'd be furious with Him.' Trisha was asking the questions I wanted to but was too nervous to voice.

'He was always there, day and night. He never left me. I shouted at Him, I cried, I made bargains with Him, and even though I lost my Rosie, He was so loving and kind to me. My parents just couldn't get over it. They used to come to church with Rosie and me and the girls from time to time, and they simply adored her. When she died, they turned their backs on it all forever. It makes me so sad.'

He looked down at his hands and his voice wobbled. I felt a stab of sympathy for him. I still don't fancy him, though. Not that I should be thinking about such things at homegroup. Obviously.

When it came time to pray, I took a deep breath and leapt in. My words weren't polished or well thought out and I gabbled a bit, but I must have been doing something right as everyone was doing the murmuring and 'Yes, Lord!' thing.

I hope you won't judge me for this, but I've always felt a little smug that while my husband has many failings, he has at least always taken his children two weekends out of four and never quibbled about paying for anything. Liane and Charlene have ex-partners who are strangers to the concept of collaborative parenting, and who seem perfectly happy to splash the cash on their new girlfriends and their children but conveniently forget the ones they left behind. It seems I too have now joined the ranks of the forgotten women.

Johnnie hasn't had the children since before Hudson was born, and every time I mention it, he tries to make me feel guilty.

'As if I haven't got enough going on, Iss! I've told you, come down here with the kids if you want. Hudson screams constantly and he only sleeps for about an hour at a time. It's killing me. I can't make Elsie's party. Buy something from me and I'll pay you back.'

Surely, I am married to the Father of the Year.

I've retained the wonderful Alison Whitfield, who did one of Chloë's birthday parties a few years ago. Elsie is having all the girls in her class over for a cake-making and decorating event. I am resigned to my immaculate kitchen disappearing under a layer of icing sugar and fondant.

As the girls put on their aprons, Lauren and I sat down for a much-needed coffee. Children's parties are exhausting! Thank heavens for Alison, who could probably run a small country unaided while whipping up a batch of butterfly cakes.

'I think there's trouble in paradise. I saw Robin and Sallie-Ann having words at the bus stop yesterday. This is your big chance.'

Lauren gave me a sly sideways glance and grinned.

I tied on a ruffled apron and pulled my hair up into a scrunchie.

'I don't know what you mean. He's very nice, always helps me with the coffee, talks about his wife and his girls a lot.'

My friend clearly wasn't buying it.

'You *so* know what I mean! And even if you don't feel that spark right away, you could go out for a bit and see if something happens. People have arranged marriages and they end up falling in love. Think about it. If you got married, he could move in here with the girls. You've got enough bedrooms. And you could turn your shed thing into a granny annexe for his mum and dad.'

I held up my hands. 'You're jumping the gun a bit! We don't even know if he's still in a relationship. And what about the children? How would they feel if I started going out with someone?'

'Hmm.' Lauren seemed sceptical. 'And where exactly is the father of your children today? I bet Robin would never miss a party, whatever was going on in his life.'

She had a point.

The front doorbell rang. Probably a delivery. I wiped my sticky hands on my jeans and got up to answer it.

Issy Smugge is known for her effortless hostessing and she always knows what nibbles to serve at every occasion. I'd made a double batch of the fridge cake, and when homegroup came to an end, I gave the leftovers to Robin for his girls. Being the diligent chap he is, he'd washed up the dish and brought it back. It would have been the height of discourtesy not to invite him in.

Even with the efficient Alison keeping ten overexcited Year Threes busy rolling out icing, my kitchen was utter chaos. Walking back down the hall, I caught sight of myself in the mirror. Great! I had a smudge of icing sugar on my nose and my hair was escaping from its unstructured messy bun. Just once, could I not be immaculate and perfectly put together when interacting with this man? Not that I cared what he thought of me.

I shot him into the family room and left him with Lauren while I made him a latte. A situation seemed to be brewing. Rebecca Bennet's second daughter, Charlotte, was pointing at her fondant icing flowers and mocking Elsie's friend Poppy.

'Your flowers are rubbish! They look like dog poo! Mine are miles better, aren't they, Elsie?'

I have brought my children up to be strong and resilient (and goodness knows, they've needed to be), but she was putting my little girl in an awkward position. I stepped in.

'That's not very kind, is it, Charlotte? Everyone's flowers look beautiful and it's not a competition.'

She stared straight back at me, rather cheekily, I thought.

'My dad says if you don't come first, you're a loser. My flowers *are* the best. I'm really good at making things.'

Poppy's eyes were filling with tears. This was not the way I'd envisaged the party going. I heard footsteps behind me and there was Robin Knight.

'Is there any spare icing? Maybe you could show me how to make the flowers, Charlotte.'

Rebecca Bennet is an excellent chair and a very efficient woman. However, just occasionally of late, I've noticed that she can be a touch pushy. She's always right, always carries her point and all her children seem to be the best at everything. Chloë is devoted to her eldest daughter, Liza, but I'm not quite sure about the dynamic. Claire's daughter Hannah is spending less and less time with Chloë and I'm not very happy about that. I must speak to Claire about it.

I handed out the coffees and observed proceedings. Robin was making a complete hash of his flowers, skilfully drawing Charlotte's attention from the other girls. I met Alison's gaze over their heads and rolled my eyes. Honestly!

What do you say when a child has behaved appallingly and their mother asks the inevitable question?

'Has she been a good girl?'

The truthful answer was, 'No, actually. She's been a right royal pain in the backside and if she was mine, I'd be asking myself some serious parenting questions.'

But mummy etiquette forbade me from saying this, and I smiled and assured Rebecca Bennet that her daughter had been a delight. Robin was bustling about and helping Alison put everything away. I could feel Lauren's eyes boring into the back of my head and felt strangely awkward. Poppy was still tearful and her mum was late, so I gave her a cuddle and praised her cupcakes extravagantly. Walking to the cloakroom to wash my hands, I was followed by an eager Lauren.

'This is your chance! He looked over at you when you were scraping the icing off the floor and I could have sworn it was one of *those* looks. And how adorable was he with Poppy? Nothing more attractive than a man who knows how to parent and who offers to do the washing-up. He and Sallie-Ann might well be on the rocks. Why don't you ask him to the café? I'll hold the fort here.'

I could feel myself blushing again like a Regency heroine.

'I can't do that! He'd think I was coming on to him.'

'You *should* be coming on to him, babes! Otherwise he won't know you like him and he won't dump his girlfriend. Tell you what, *I'll* ask him out for a coffee then it'd be rude to leave you behind and we'll just take the kids with us.'

I hated to upset my friend, but she was going too far.

'Look, Lauren, I really appreciate that you want to find me a lovely man, but I don't think Robin is it. He's too short, he's a bit boring really and I can't feel any spark at all. Let's just leave it, OK?'

She stared at me.

'Are you actually doing this? I can't believe you! I'm off.'

And with that, she turned on her heel and banged her way out of the boot room without even saying goodbye to Robin or Alison. I was left standing, cheeks hot, heart banging (note to self – could this be an early menopause or just emotional distress?), wondering what on earth I'd done to upset my friend so much.

Once all the guests and Robin had finally gone, I sat at my sticky kitchen island with my phone in my hand, wondering what on earth to do. Liane is Lauren's closest friend, but I didn't really fancy texting her and asking why it mattered so much that I gave Robin Knight a whirl on the romantic merry-go-round.

I decided to text Charlene, who is also close to Lauren.

'Hope you don't mind me asking, and tell me if I'm poking my nose in, but is Lauren OK? She's just got really upset because I don't want to go out with this man from church x'

Back came the answer in seconds.

'Yeah, she's pretty stressy at the moment. Her mum dumped her partner and he was the only one Lauren ever really got on with. She's now with one of the Roziers and Lauren doesn't like him or the family. I reckon she's trying to plan out a happy-ever-after for you to help her not think about what her mum's up to. Tony says it's displacement. You know, you can't change or control other people's actions, so you throw yourself into something else to try to forget. She'll be OK. Could you maybe try one date with this bloke and see how it goes? X'

I wasn't sure how to respond. I feel so bad for poor Lauren, but I can't go out with a man I don't feel any attraction towards just to make her feel better.

Can I?

Thank heavens half term is finally here! There were ructions after Elsie's party. I was called in by her teacher to discuss an unpleasant situation. Charlotte Bennet, it seems, is trying to break up her other friendships and keep my little girl all to herself. Gentle questioning led to a storm of tears. My poor little Elsie has been keeping it all in.

'Becky is my best friend, but Charlotte keeps being mean to her and telling her I've said horrible stuff. I want to be friends with everyone but Charlotte says I'm only allowed to be hers. I don't like her any more, Mummy. I don't want to sit next to her at school. But you're friends with her mummy and I don't want you to get into trouble.'

My maternal heart swelled with indignation. Rebecca Bennet and her grumpy-looking husband may be wealthy, influential and have a great eye for a house, but they clearly have some parenting issues going on. I assured Elsie that her happiness was paramount and braced myself for some difficult conversations when school restarts.

The merry month of May will be crowned with a beautifully planned party at the Old Rectory to celebrate Mummy and Harry's union. These days, one wedding reception just isn't enough. I'm so glad I agreed to host as it's taking my mind off my worries about Elsie, and Johnnie's constant texting. We're currently working out who gets what. I am buying him out so that the house will be in my name and we're splitting everything else straight down the middle. Including the children. Not that they will remember they have a father if young Hudson doesn't start sleeping through the night pretty soon.

The smell in the garden is still there, but I'm going to wait until after the party to investigate. The basin in the downstairs cloakroom isn't draining properly either, but again, that can go on the back burner. The tipi people are coming on Wednesday, the caterers are poised, firepits ordered, playlist done, and all I have to do is act as the gracious hostess. What could possibly go wrong? **#weddingblessing #party #hostess**

June

Sometimes, lying in bed with the cat sprawled across my legs, I think back on my life and carry out one of those evaluations that only occurs in the middle of the night when you can't sleep. Am I better off living minus a husband in a beautiful house in a thriving country village, or was it all a lot better when I was in my comfort zone back in town? The pros of being a Suffolk resident are:

1. I have lots of real friends who would never betray me, who like me for myself and who wish me well.

2. The air is fresh and almost entirely devoid of pollutants.

3. The girls can walk to school.

4. There is much less crime (unless you count oil theft and pig rustling).

5. There are hardly any traffic jams.

6. It's commutable (not that I really go into town very much).

7. I don't have to think about what Johnnie wants all the time and repress my own feelings (ha!).

8. There is absolutely no danger of Mimi dropping in unannounced.

9. I can see the stars at night.

All good, solid reasons which reassure me that I did the right thing by leaving my easy, comfortable life behind.

However, we also have the cons, namely:

1. You cannot shake a stick around here without everyone knowing about it and importuning you in the street and/or WhatsApping you to fire off impertinent questions about your personal life in a never-ending stream.

2. Nothing is private. Ever. At all. See above.

3. Things that normal people take for granted (being connected to the mains sewage system and not having to worry about flushing the loo or scraping unmentionable substances off your lawn) are not a given around these parts. More of that later.

I have finally given in to Johnnie's pleadings and scheduled a weekend at his house, with Paige and Hudson and all our children. I was going to hold out, but then I found Chloë crying in her room and yet more awful toxic stuff came bubbling out.

'Are we ever going to see Dad ever again? Now he's got a new baby, he might forget about us. And Liza is being really mean to Hannah and I don't know what to do.'

I had been feeling fairly satisfied with the way I was steering the family ship through the turbulent waves of life, but I have to confess, recent revelations have been like walls of icy water crashing over my decks. When Sofija was my au pair, we never sat and had a drink together, but once the children were in bed, I poured us both a glass of fruity Merlot and broached the subject of the Bennet girls.

'I can't believe that such young children could be so manipulative and unkind. I'm having a meeting with Elsie and Chloë's teachers when they go back to school and I'll have to mention it to Rebecca. What do you think?'

It pains me to admit that in the old days, I spent so much time loading jobs on to Sofija that I never really took the time to get to know the real her. I wonder how I would have acted had I been in her shoes.

'My mother used to tell me, "Sofija, you don't have to take on all the sadness of others." These poor girls are behaving like this because they are unhappy. This must come from the parents. We give Elsie and Chloë lots of love and encouragement and work out strategies to deal with this. Is best, I think, Isabella.'

We chatted late into the evening and the owl was hooting in the oak tree outside my bedroom by the time I collapsed into my wickedly comfy bed. Neither of us has yet mentioned Johnnie, the shared mistake that holds us together and keeps us apart.

In my time, I've written acres of prose on how to plan and execute the perfect party. Whether it's choosing exactly the right centrepieces, matching up linen and chair covers, pairing canapés and reception drinks or making the difficult decision between a tipi or a sailcloth tent, Issy Smugge always has the answer. At no point in my long career, however, have I ever been faced with the hideous emergency that arose on Friday morning, the day before Mummy and Harry's glamorous post-wedding party celebration.

We'd had a lovely half term. I took Sofija's advice and showered my girls with love and attention. We went to the beach, the forest, the cinema; I hosted playdates and sleepovers without complaint and was the soul of hospitality. I gave Sofija a few days off and she went to London. I missed her professional support, but I welcomed the chance to have my house back to myself. Will I ever truly forgive her? I just don't know. I lay awake for an hour on Thursday night, fretting about my feelings towards her, before falling into an exhausted stupor.

You have to believe me when I tell you that a voice roused me from sleep. Early dawn light was filtering through my curtains and birdsong rang out melodiously. I was suddenly, instantly, completely awake. Who had called out my name? The baby monitor was silent. I checked on the children, all of whom were peacefully asleep – and quite right too, as it was only five o'clock in the morning. I went back to bed and lay there for some time, trying to get back to sleep and failing. I bowed to the inevitable, rolled out of bed, pulled on my dressing gown and slippers and padded downstairs. I opened the back door and breathed in the crisp morning air. The bad smell had intensified somewhat and, as I peered down the back garden where the tipi was up, I noticed what looked like pieces of white paper scattered around the lawn. Strange. I walked down to investigate and suddenly realised what I was looking at. I froze. Effluent was spattered up the side of the tipi, and the stench was almost unbearable. My stomach dropped and I had a flashback of the estate agent who sold us the house reminding us about the need to keep the septic tank maintained.

With all the things that had happened since we moved in, I had completely forgotten that we even had one. And now it had apparently exploded, all over my beautifully manicured lawn just thirty-two hours before 150 guests arrived expecting perfection.

If ever there was a time to seek divine intervention, this was it. I sent up an urgent request for assistance. Almost immediately, I thought of Lauren. Then I thought again. Could I really contact her after she'd been so cross with me? But this was an emergency.

I pulled my phone out of my pocket. A miracle! She was online. I WhatsApped.

'So sorry to message this early. Disaster. There are – things – all over my lawn. Bad things. The septic tank has exploded. What can I do? xx'

Whether metaphorical or actual, Lauren always knows how to deal with the faecal matter in my life. Back she came, God bless her.

'Liane's dad's cousin's husband might help. He runs the company that pumps them out. They're usually booked weeks in advance, but I'll see if I can sort something xx'

Thank God! I WhatsApped back.

'Listen, so sorry I annoyed you the other day. I know you're just trying to set me up with a nice man. I promise I'll think about it properly and not dismiss it. Is he still with Sallie-Ann, do you think? xx'

She replied immediately.

'Not sure. She works at the primary in Allonsfield and they're due an Ofsted inspection, so she's probably pretty busy. Haven't seen her recently. But I'll keep my ear to the ground xx'

I returned to the kitchen and paced anxiously. Never, in all of my influencing life, would I have thought that I would be searching the county for a man with a tanker to empty a vast underground container filled with waste matter. What was I going to do about the tipi? A quick spray of anti-bac and a wipe around wasn't going to touch it. My phone beeped.

'Liane's calling him. He owes her a favour. Be back to you shortly xx'

Lauren is the best friend a girl could have. I replied, *'What are you doing up so early, anyway? I thought it was only me who got woken up at the crack of dawn xx'*

A brief pause and she responded, *'Weird. Who woke you up? I swear, I was in the deepest sleep and then it was like someone touched my arm and I was awake. Good thing, though! lol xx'*

Not for the first time, I realised that I was in daily communion with Someone who was even more organised and all-seeing than the UK's most beloved mumfluencer. Darn, He's good! I sent up a prayer of thanks and poured myself a glass of refreshing rhubarb and orange pressé. I really fancied a comforting hot chocolate, but under the circs, it seemed inappropriate. **#disaster #explosion #oopsie**

I don't care what Lauren says (in the nicest possible way). Liane Bloomfield has saved my bacon and I am going to buy her something gorgeous to say thank you. At 7.30am, just as I was considering cancelling the party, a huge tanker drew up on the drive of the Old Rectory and a cheerful man in a boiler suit jumped out.

'Morning! Mrs Smug is it? I hear you've got a bit of a problem with your tank.'

For a man who spends his professional life up close and personal with the things other people try to flush away, he was very jolly. He made no move to shake my hand, although bearing in mind his profession, this was probably just as well. Bright May sunshine was flooding my lovely garden and exposing the full horror of the situation. My voice shook slightly.

'Can you help me? I've got a big party for my mother and her husband tomorrow and I don't know how I'm going to clear all this up. I feel so stupid. I forgot that we had a septic tank.'

He smiled reassuringly. 'Don't you worry, Mrs Smug. Tanks are our business. All this rain we've been having has probably filled it up, and if you haven't had it pumped out for a year or two, it will have backed up. I'll get the tanker hooked up and we'll have it emptied in no time. I'll do my best to clean up the grass too.'

I made him a large Americano with hot milk. As I shut the front door, the reassuring but slightly disgusting sound of both solid and liquid matter shooting up a hose reached my grateful ears. I texted Liane.

'Listen, thank you so, so much for speaking to your dad's cousin's husband. I appreciate it more than I can say. Is there anything I can do for you to say thank you? x'

I waited for ten minutes, pacing around the kitchen (windows firmly closed) until she replied.

'Don't need anything, thanks, Smug. If this had happened any other day, he wouldn't have been able to fit you in. His first job of the day cancelled last night. Bet your garden doesn't smell too sweet! lol.'

Miracles do happen, it seems.

My septic tank has been drained to the disgusting dregs. My life makes sense again.

In spite of Liane's refusal of a thank-you gift, I couldn't rest easy. Flowers wouldn't do it, nor chocolates, but I did wonder if an offer to send some of my workmen over, loaded up with Bitter and Twisted paint, when she moved into her new house might be an acceptable thank you. I ran it past Lauren.

'She does love that purple paint you gave her, babes. Worth a try. Wait till she's moved in and then offer when I'm there.'

Once my lawn had been thoroughly cleansed, I briefed Ted Ling, my monosyllabic gardener, to mow it vigorously to ensure that no faecal fragments remained. I pulled on a pair of rubber gloves and set to scrubbing the tipi and trying to remove the smell. After half an hour, I admitted defeat. Thinking outside the box, I ran upstairs to my dressing room where some boxes of product were stored. As you'll probably remember, I used to be the face of *Influencée Pour Femme*, an enticing fragrance with grassy notes and a floral finish. It was extremely high quality and lingered long on the skin after application. My thinking was that if I treated the affected area with the contents of several bottles, its heady aroma would mask the less-pleasant scents clinging to the tipi. I knelt on the grass, spraying furiously, while Ted powered grimly up and down on the ride-on mower. ('This won't do the lawn any good at all, missus. I only cut it last week.') If that doesn't do it, nothing will. **#lastditchattempt #perfume #smells**

After the stress of scrubbing tipis and meeting men in boiler suits at dawn, the party was quite relaxing. Naturally, to Mummy's annoyance, Veronica Madingley didn't turn up ('Honestly, darling! That woman! If I didn't know for sure that she existed, I'd think she was a figment of my imagination!'), but everyone else did and it was jolly good fun. I noticed miserable Karen standing in the corner of the tipi, sniffing the wall.

The caterers were their usual fabulous selves. They produced a delicious range of nibbles to go with the signature reception cocktails (Apple Martinis, Limoncello Spritz and Carajillo), and we sat down to spinach roulade with smoked salmon and cream cheese; locally sourced fillet of beef with potatoes dauphinoise, griddled asparagus, baby carrots with citrus butter and steamed baby broad beans; and finished with individual Eton Mess. I've built my career on making everything look perfect and if you were to gaze upon me, sitting at the top table in a gorgeous mint-green sheer gauze skirt with snakeskin flats and a crisp white shirt with the sleeves rolled up and lots of funky silver jewellery, you'd think that I'd never had to scrub wee off a tipi in my life.

Dessert finished and, with everyone chatting happily, I slipped away to commune with the caterers. Mummy had finally agreed to go with at least one trend and have street food for the evening. I walked into the boot room and heard the team chatting in the kitchen.

'I've never been in such a fabulous place. She must be loaded. What does she do?'

'She's a really famous influencer on Insta. She writes blogs and tells you how to dress and stuff like that.'

'Wow. Lucky her. She seems really nice, but I feel really sad sometimes when I see these huge houses and perfect gardens. I work so hard, but it's never my party and it's never my beautiful house.'

I felt a stab of pain on the speaker's behalf. I've never had to worry about money, but there's plenty in my life that I'd change if I could. I resolved to give the caterers a vast tip. Goodness knows they've earned it.

In other news, Audrey Harcourt turned up at the party with a man! Gone was the shy, dowdy mouse I'd met at Freudian Sip and in her place was a tanned, well-dressed woman clutching the hand of a silver-haired Lothario (Mummy's words, not mine).

We convened by the taco truck.

'Audrey hasn't wasted any time! They've been in Antigua for two weeks soaking up the sun, and Rupert hardly cold in his grave.'

I pointed out that the poor woman had had a pretty rubbish life up to now and that it was a bit rich for Mummy to begrudge her this new-found happiness.

'I suppose so. I just hope she hasn't been taken in by some shyster who's after her money. She's sold the flat, you know, and cashed in some of the shares.'

Seize the day, I say, and watch this space.

Back at school, things in the playground were distinctly awkward. I'd emailed Rebecca Bennet over half term, saying that we needed to chat. Her demeanour was frosty in the extreme. I hadn't realised that she was one of those women who refuse to believe that her children are capable of bad behaviour. The girls reported increased meanness and disruption in the classroom. There was only one thing to do. I approached Rebecca on the playground at drop-off, my heart beating and my palms sweaty.

'Hi. Can we have a chat? There seem to be some issues between the girls. They always got on so well before and I'm sure we can sort it out.'

The woman with the lowered eyes and the folded arms was no longer the friendly, smiling, proactive PTA chair I thought I knew. To my horror, I realised that she had turned into an enemy.

'I hope *you* can sort it out. My half term's been ruined. Liza is beside herself and my poor little Charlotte just doesn't know what she's done wrong. Your daughters have got a lot to answer for. Mr Bennet is very upset.'

The playground wasn't the place for such a conversation. I invited her back to the Old Rectory for coffee.

'Some of us have to work. I've got a big consultation to finish. I could fit you in on Friday at 1.00 for half an hour. Come to mine. And tell your girls to think about the consequences of their actions, if you'd be so kind.'

Well! I was speechless. As she walked away, Chris and Hayley Robinson fell into step with her and they walked off the playground, heads together. I didn't like the look of that at all.

I was still gazing after them when Lauren appeared at my elbow.

'All right, babes? That looked a bit heavy.'

I brought her up to speed. She chewed her lip and looked shifty.

'What? Tell me.'

'Look, I never said anything before because you seemed to be getting on so well, and Liza and Chloë are such good friends. But I don't like her. I never have. She's a manipulator.'

I was rather taken aback. I thought I'd got better at reading people.

'Really? I've never seen that side of her before today.'

My friend frowned. 'She's only interested in people who can be useful to her. Her girls blank mine, and unless I make a point of saying hi, she ignores me. I'm not rich or posh and I don't live in a big house. No offence.'

We exited stage left, joined by Liane Bloomfield.

'All right, Smug? You look as if you lost a tenner and found a pound.'

Lauren filled her in.

'That Bennet woman's showing her true colours. She was horrible to Isabella just now.'

Liane snorted. 'She would be. Stuck-up madam. I've noticed the Robinsons are all over her like a rash. You watch yourself, Smug. I know her sort.'

With great difficulty, I lured both of them back to the Old Rectory. Liane has been in my house many times, but rarely on a social footing. I made her a coffee before she could change her mind, and got out some pistachio and coconut biscotti. Chewy though they were, they couldn't compare to the dense and complex nature of our conversation.

'But she always seemed so nice. She did loads of playdates, shared dance drop-offs and pick-ups, helped me with parties – I thought we were friends.'

'Think about it, babes. Have you ever challenged her before or called her kids out on their behaviour?'

I pondered. Now I came to think about it, I hadn't loved the way Liza spoke to Chloë sometimes, or appreciated her apparent need for exclusive friendship. Hannah had been my daughter's closest friend, but these days we saw much less of her. My little Elsie is best friends with Becky and gets on very well with everyone in her class. But Charlotte Bennet has been coming up in conversation a lot, as have the many friendship dramas in Year Three. Could it be a coincidence?

'So what do I do? I'm going to hers on Friday to talk about it. If it were me, I wouldn't get all offended and huffy. I'd try to work through it.'

'Yeah, but she's not you, is she, Smug? You might be posh and rich, but I will say this for you. You don't look down your nose at people. Well, not any more. Tell her to sort her kids out or you'll go up the school about it.'

I felt sad and crushed, which is not like me. Lauren gave my arm a comforting squeeze.

'Cheer up! We've got your back.'

I felt suddenly tearful, and under cover of pretending that I needed the loo, I hid in the cloakroom for a few minutes and took deep breaths. All of a sudden, everything seemed too much. Friendship issues with two of my children, both emanating from the same family. Me having to share the same playground twice daily with a woman who seemed to dislike me and yet had, until very recently, been someone I thought was a friend. My divorce coming ever closer. Constant draining texts from Johnnie. I needed something to take my mind off it – not work, not a new paid partnership, not a long hot luxurious bubble bath in a candlelit bathroom. Something else. But I couldn't tell you what.

I returned to the kitchen to hear Liane and Lauren making arrangements.

'Scott says he'll drive so we can have a drink. What about the drum kit? Is he using the house one?'

I offered them another coffee and asked what was going on.

'Nothing you'd be interested in, Smug. My boy's got a gig on Friday night. They're headlining for the first time. I'm pumped.'

Maybe this is what Issy Smugge needed. The chance to dress up as a rock chick (as I believe women who enjoy loud music are called), to dance, to drink, to forget herself for a few blissful hours. My voice came out higher and more eager than I'd planned.

'Can I come? Please? I haven't been out to hear live music for so long. Johnnie didn't like it, you see. I'd be happy to pay for a taxi for us all.'

There was an awkward pause, broken by Lauren.

'I don't know if it's your kind of thing, babes. It's a small place, it gets really crowded and it's very loud.'

There was that eager voice again.

'I don't care about any of that. I used to love live music and dancing and I never get a chance to go to anything.'

Liane seemed to be experiencing a painful internal struggle.

'You can't embarrass me. Don't wear fancy clothes. Jeans, boots and a plain top. Don't talk to me unless I talk to you. All right?'

It wasn't the most gracious of invitations, but it was good enough, particularly as I was driving my children down to Essex to stay for two days and a night *chez* Johnnie and Paige on Saturday morning and I was not looking forward to it one bit. I booked Mummy and Harry to babysit (Sofija's seeing friends) and ran upstairs to search for a suitable outfit. **#rockchick #livemusic #rockandroll**

The people in my homegroup are fast becoming friends. I've stopped aiming for perfection and if the children are still milling around or there's a mess in the kitchen, that's just too bad.

I haven't completely let my standards slip, however. I always choose a lovely outfit and take care with my hair and make-up. Just because I'm a busy working mum doesn't mean I have to let myself go.

It was such a beautiful evening that I suggested we all sat outside. The mood was different – freer somehow. The birds were singing joyfully as they flew home and the sky was streaked with golden bars of light streaming through the clouds. Of all the group, the one I have bonded with least is Richard Dunning, and yet it was he who asked me if I was all right.

'You don't quite look yourself this evening, if you don't mind me saying so.'

I could have lied and said everything was fine, but instead found myself spilling my guts about the whole Rebecca Bennet situation, my worries about the girls and my apprehension about spending much of the weekend with Johnnie and Paige. And young Hudson, of course, who is currently suffering from acid reflux.

We sat and talked until the birds were asleep and the sky was darkening. We always finish with prayer requests for each other, and tonight there were tears in my eyes as everyone prayed for me. Even Trisha, who struggles with praying out loud, asked for peace and reconciliation for the situations I found myself in.

Sitting in my beautiful garden, with the fragrance of roses on the soft summer breeze, surrounded by people who cared about me, I felt something I've never felt before. I couldn't quite describe it to you. It was as if a warm blanket was gently thrown over me as they spoke and as if a barrier, erected many years ago, was breached. I felt tears spill from my eyes and stream down my cheeks, but I didn't feel sad. It was a very odd feeling. I sat and cried quietly, without shame or fear, until everyone finished praying. No one except Trisha seemed surprised. Tissues were produced and hugs given. Sue said something about the Holy Spirit which I banked for later. I need to ask Claire about some of the things we've been talking about in homegroup.

Robin was the last to leave, walking out behind the Conklins. He looked over his shoulder, giving me a serious, thoughtful look. Usually, I'd smile or say something to break the mood, but I didn't. I simply gazed back until the door gently closed behind him.

I had a summit with Lauren and was totally honest about my feelings. We had a really good chat and she revealed all kinds of terrible painful things she has been carrying, all around her parents' acrimonious split when she was a child and her mother's apparent inability to remember that she has a daughter who might actually have some needs of her own. It moved me to tears and I found myself hugging her and apologising.

'I wish I could feel something for Robin. I can see that he's a good man. I did catch him looking at me in homegroup and he hasn't mentioned Sallie-Ann at all.'

Lauren gave me a squeeze and disengaged herself.

'They called it a day. It's all amicable. Lou's cousin works at Allonsfield primary and Sallie-Ann told her. They had a few dates but she never met the kids. Just went out for coffee and dinner a few times. She's OK about it. Now would be the time to start flirting a tiny bit with him if you wanted to, babes, but I get you don't feel that spark. I just think – well, what if you tried and you had things in common and stuff kind of developed from there? I've seen how unhappy Johnnie made you and I'd love to see you find someone lovely to look after you, like I did with Scott.'

I conceded that she had a point. Arranged marriages often seem to work and they're based on practical stuff like shared interests and goals. Robin Knight is clearly a good parent and a hard-working person with no apparent frightful qualities or vices. I could do a lot worse. **#notsure #newman #dating**

Rebecca Bennet has definitely been talking to the Robinsons about me. They now all stand together and her husband was on the playground on Thursday morning – unheard of. They stared at me as I walked past. I smiled but may as well have been invisible for all the response I got. More painfully, one of the new PTA members, a lovely girl called Natalie Gee, was also being far less friendly than usual. I don't know her very well, but I really like her. She's a wheelchair user (a 'wheelie', as she calls herself) and has quite a story. Seeing me approaching, she abruptly performed a three-point turn and zoomed off towards the veranda.

I went and stood with Claire, who never changes and who is a true friend in the storms of life. I shared the latest on the Bennets.

'Oh dear. Sorry to hear that. She says hello to me, but I've noticed a drop in the temperature this week.'

I got straight to the point.

'Listen, some stuff happened at homegroup last night. I felt like something touched me and then I started crying, but it wasn't because I was sad. I still feel bad about this whole situation, but not like I did before.'

Claire explained that one of the many benefits of being a person of faith is that you have an extra dimension upon which to rely. Things that seem impossible are suddenly achieved. Gordian knots are cut. Paths appear in the wilderness. You can pray for this kind of thing, apparently, and ask for the Holy Spirit to come and help. I was a bit hazy as to what this might mean, but more than happy to accept any assistance I could get.

'When I find myself in a tough situation, I always say, "Go ahead of me." It never fails. Try it when you see Rebecca and anyone who's being funny with you. I'll be praying for you too.'

I love Claire. I gave her a big hug and booked her in for coffee at mine on Monday. My weekend is starting to look like a metaphorical sandwich. Two lovely crusty slices of seeded wholemeal bread (the gig on Friday and coffee with Claire on Monday) and a filling of the utmost yukkiness (time spent with Johnnie, his girlfriend and sleepless baby). Swings and roundabouts. The good and the bad. **#funtimes**

I have been to the Bennets' house many times, always welcomed in as a favoured guest. Today was different. I knocked on the door and stood waiting on the doorstep. After several minutes, Rebecca opened it and motioned me in. She marched into her sitting room, where her saturnine husband was arranged in a chair, like a brooding black beetle.

'We thought it best that we both dealt with this situation. Coffee?'

I declined.

'We've spoken to the girls at length. Liza adores Chloë and she would never try to push any of her other friends away. If anything, Chloë's the one who's been smothering Liza. We've told her to start cultivating other friendships. It's healthier for her. And as for your allegations about Charlotte, we are very hurt. We've raised all our daughters to be their very best selves (*you* of all people should appreciate that), and if you can really accuse a little girl of trying to spoil a party by innocently boasting about her handiwork, then you're not the person I thought you were.'

I remembered Charlene's advice. I took a breath, put my head on one side and murmured, 'Interesting.'

There was a short pause. Mr Bennet leaned forward.

'I don't get involved in playground spats. I leave all that to my wife. But I won't have my daughters accused of things they haven't done. You can consider the friendships at an end.'

This was undoubtedly an awkward situation. I had two children in the same classes as these people's daughters, and also in the same dance classes, and we served on the same PTA committee. I drew deeply on the feeling of peace which had descended upon me in my garden on Wednesday evening.

'I'm sorry you feel that way. I believe what my girls have told me, and the evidence of my own eyes. My children aren't perfect, but I do know that they're good and loyal friends. Have a think about what's happened and know that my door is always open if you want to chat.'

And that was that. Without further ado I was escorted out and the door shut firmly behind me. Great. I can't wait for our next PTA meeting! **#awks #drama**

I felt ludicrously excited on Friday night. I selected a pair of straight-leg light-wash jeans, chic navy-blue mid-heel ankle boots (so now!), a Breton-style cotton jumper, a trio of silver bangles and a chunky ring. I put on hoop earrings, applied a smoky eye and put my hair up in a half tail. A quick spritz of perfume (not *Influencée Pour Femme*, which I will never wear again as long as I live) and I was ready to roll. My offer of paying for a nine-seater to the venue and back again had been accepted, and I found myself Ipswich-bound with Lauren, her husband, Scott, Liane and her boys. Plus a drum kit. Every so often, we'd turn a corner or go round a roundabout and there would be a clash of cymbals from the back. It was quite exciting.

Lauren hadn't been exaggerating. The venue consisted of a small, dark lobby plastered with pictures of other bands, a bar (mercifully light and with seating), a large courtyard next to an Indian restaurant and a room with a stage. A lavishly tattooed man with long hair wearing black was sitting behind a sound desk fiddling with buttons and leads. There seemed to be nothing for me to do, and since we had two hours before any music started (there was a sound check to be done, the drum kit to be set up, band merch to be displayed and tickets to be sold, it seemed), I took Liane's advice and pushed off to the pub over the road where I caught up on some emails and notifications. I also took the opportunity to enjoy three vodka and oranges and a small bag of salted peanuts. Because why not? Rock and roll!

Pleasantly relaxed, I returned to the venue two hours later as requested. The atmosphere had changed completely. The courtyard was full of young people, many wearing exotic costumes. Leather and fishnets featured heavily. I began to regret playing it safe. Issy Smugge has never owned a leather jacket, but perhaps it's time she invested in one. I found Lauren and Scott at the bar.

'First band's on in a minute, babes. All girl heavy metal. Drink?'

The bar offered only cider and beer, so I accepted a pint of something local which tasted pleasantly of apples, and prepared to plunge myself into the local music scene.

We were meant to leave for Johnnie's at ten, but I didn't wake up until nine and even then felt rather fragile. Mummy brought me tea and toast in bed, with a side of painkillers. I think I may be suffering from a hangover, but it was all worth it. The cider was so delicious, and so easy to drink, and I got very thirsty because I was dancing and singing along. I had such a good time!

Liane's son's band were amazing! I would never have thought that being crammed into a tiny room with around eighty sweaty, drunk music fans could be so much fun. The throbbing bass lines, the drum solos, the singing, the shouting, the moshing, as I believe it's called – all of it worked together to drive all thoughts of Johnnie and Rebecca Bennet and PTA drama completely out of my head. Liane Bloomfield's face, lit by the glow of the stage lights, wore an expression of love and pride I'd never seen before as she gazed at her son, his red curls freed from his man bun and tumbling down his back. He certainly was an excellent drummer.

I rolled home sometime after midnight and went straight to bed, a huge grin on my face. I think I should do this kind of thing more often. **#holyspirit #livemusic #rockchick**

July

At church on Sunday, Tom talked about promises. There is so much I've got to learn. I try to read my on-trend version of the Bible every day but often fail. Lauren assures me this is normal.

'Honestly, I start every month with such good intentions. But then I oversleep, or the kids want something, or Scott needs help and I don't do it. Claire says it's OK. God understands.'

My little Milo was happily playing in the crèche (newly set up as we have so many families joining us), and I was free to sit and gaze at Tom with his handsome features and his lovely curly hair and blue eyes as he told us comforting things. Lauren was away with her in-laws that weekend. I got to church early and sat in my usual pew, where I was joined, unexpectedly, by Robin and his daughters. I was thinking of nipping to the loo and texting Lauren, but was prevented by the worship band firing up some guitar-based background music and Tom launching into his talk.

'God never goes back on His promises. Even if you can't see how on earth they can be fulfilled, He already knows. Claire and I often remind ourselves of what He's promised when times are hard. He says, "Strength! Courage! Don't be timid; don't get discouraged. GOD, your God, is with you every step you take." When you're feeling that life is too much, speak out these words.'

I liked the sound of that and made a note on my phone. Tom continued.

'This is one of my favourite pieces of Scripture. I've got it framed in my study and I read it every day. When I was preparing my talk, I felt very strongly that someone here today needs to hear it and really allow it to sink into their heart: "Don't fret or worry. Instead of worrying, pray. Let petitions and praises shape your worries into prayers, letting God know your concerns. Before you know it, a sense of God's wholeness, everything coming together for good, will come and settle you down. It's wonderful what happens when Christ displaces worry at the centre of your life."'

I must confess that I was on automatic pilot after that. 'Shape your worries into prayers.' I liked that. I had enough worries to keep me praying for the rest of my life! But suddenly, it felt as if a bright light had illuminated the dark corners of my mind, where no one else sees and where all the fears and terrors and bad things lurk like skeletons in a fully fitted built-in closet. I usually head straight for coffee once the service is over, but instead found myself sitting in the crèche, chatting with Robin, who had no business to be there while Milo played happily.

'I've got so much on my mind at the moment and I haven't been sleeping too well. Those words really helped, though. Isn't that weird?'

Robin appeared not to find it weird at all. 'I've clung to so many Bible verses over the years, never more so than when Rosie was ill. That was meant for you, you know. As a comfort. So what's going on in your life to keep you awake at night?'

When I was still a happily married woman with three children and thought my life was perfect in every way, if you'd told me I'd be sitting on a tiny orange plastic chair in a draughty hall at the back of a Suffolk church talking to a mid-height widower with a dad bod about my innermost feelings, I would have laughed in your face. Robin is such a good listener, however, that I poured out all my sadness and anxiety about the Rebecca Bennet situation and even touched on my weekend with Johnnie.

'That must be so hard for you. I can't even imagine handing my girls over to someone like that. How did you cope?'

It had not been easy. For a start, we were two hours late owing to my overindulgence the night before. Milo was unsettled and grizzly and wet himself on the way. I caved and put his pull-up back on. Because, really, who cares? The children were quiet and on edge. My head was killing me.

We arrived at the house, inside which I could hear a baby screaming. I knocked and Paige appeared with the baby over her shoulder, stains on her top and a wild look in her eye.

'Isabella! You're here. I thought you'd changed your mind. I wouldn't have blamed you. Come on in.'

It was the most bizarre situation. My soon to be ex-husband was slumped at the kitchen table in the light-filled glass extension at the back of the house, coffee mug in hand.

'Hi, Iss. Hi, kids. Good to see you. Sorry about Hudson. He hasn't stopped yelling since he woke up.'

Now, I have not always been the most hands-on mother. But from the way the baby was drawing his legs up, I suspected a bad case of trapped wind.

'May I?'

Paige was only too happy to hand her first-born over. Casting my mind back to a trick Sofija used to have with Elsie, I put him gently on my knee, face down, and began rubbing his back in a circular motion. As I had suspected, just like his father, he was full of hot air. Fully burped, I restored him to an upright position on my knee and looked into his face. There was no resemblance to Johnnie whatsoever. What hair he did have was blond and his eyes were exactly the same shape and colour as his mother's.

It was a pretty good start to our relationship. He seemed happy to stay on my knee, gazing at me with that unnerving baby stare while the children rushed out into the garden to play. Paige announced a late lunch in due course and Johnnie perked up.

'About time! I'm starving. Well done, Iss. You'll have to show Paige what to do before you leave. She can't seem to stop him crying.'

After we had dined, I suggested a walk. The countryside around the house is beautiful and I felt that I needed some fresh air after my late night. Paige put Hudson into a sling and strapped him to her front, where he immediately fell fast asleep. Johnnie went for a lie-down and the two of us, plus children, went forth.

My concerns about co-parenting and interacting with Paige were completely unfounded. She is refreshingly direct.

'He's useless. What did you do to get him to help with the kids when you were together?'

To my shame, I had to admit that I put it all on Sofija and let Johnnie have his own way in everything.

'Now I've met his mother, I can see how he got like that. I can't wait to get back to work. I love Hudson, but I need Johnnie to step up. And if he doesn't, I can't see a future for us.'

I assured Paige of my support and we walked on through the beautiful Essex countryside, the children running ahead and little Hudson snoozing peacefully on his mother, quite unaware of what his future held.

Back home, safe in the knowledge that I could start sending the children down to Johnnie and Paige's one weekend in four (they've really taken to her and the house is fully baby-proofed, with the exception of one giant hazard in the shape of my husband), I continued to work through the various challenges facing me. Not least of which was the upcoming school fête, run by the PTA. We had mini-meetings galore, uncomfortable in the extreme since Chris Robinson is now BFFs with Rebecca, and Natalie is barely speaking to me.

Before each one, I muttered, 'Go ahead of me. Strength! Courage!' and it did seem to help. A tiny bit. Whatever I might think of Rebecca's personality and parenting, she is a remarkably dynamic organiser. She has organised an arena with a packed timetable of singing, dancing, majorettes, close-up magic, belly dancing and other delights, and whipped the WI into shape to organise the tea and cakes tent. My mother has joined and will be manning the urn, not a sight I thought I'd ever see. We'll have all the usual face-painting and tombolas and an ice-cream van and suchlike. Chris Robinson is still firing off pass agg comments on the PTA WhatsApp group but Rebecca is no longer slapping him down.

I am rising above it all. I am also allowing myself a large glass of wine every night as soon as the children are in bed, which is helping no end. It's also helping me to forget my mixed emotions around Sofija, but only between the hours of 9pm and 12am.

Looking on the bright side, my second-floor renovation is complete! I am sublimating my feelings of rage and anxiety around Rebecca Bennet and her entire family into blogs, posts and articles about how to transform one's house. The self-contained flat is wonderful! Mindful of current trends, I designed the kitchen with a peninsula rather than an island, and added in a built-in vintage record player and a rack of vinyl for a playful design feature. It's got soft lighting, terrazzo countertops and a general mid-century vibe. Jess and Andy, the lovely people who look after babies and young mums in Kenya, are coming over in October and I have given them full use for the entire month. I will start listing it for rent in August and give all the proceeds to Jess and Andy's work.

Johnnie is furious and doesn't want me 'letting goodness knows who into the family home' (his words), but I couldn't care less what he thinks. My gorgeous luxe Edwardian-style bathroom looks fabulous painted in Porphyria and I have enjoyed a few relaxing candlelit soaks in it of late. The bathroom in the flat is very nice, but I needed a truly luxurious sanctuary for myself on the second floor. Up there, I now have an en-suite principal bedroom with dressing room and two more doubles with a Jack and Jill bathroom, plus a four-piece family bathroom and storage on the second floor. Mimi is delighted and I'm getting a huge amount of traction on the socials. I'm pleased, but my mind is elsewhere at the moment. Somewhere that has nothing to do with how many people share my posts or tag me. It's more about likes.

But we won't worry about that for now.

The new development is finished and Liane Bloomfield has moved into her new house. Something has changed in her, or perhaps it's me. Ever since I saw her at the gig, beaming with pride and hugging her son and his bandmates as they came off stage, I've seen a new, softer side of her. On the playground, she was uncharacteristically cheerful.

'Honestly, I don't know myself! No damp, loads of built-in storage, Zach doesn't have to share with both his brothers any more, the girls have got a lovely big walk-in wardrobe in their room and the garden isn't overlooked. Uncle Bix came over at the weekend and planted up loads of bulbs for me and did the hanging baskets. It's all white, but I'm saving up to get some new paint and I'll soon change that.'

There was my cue. Lauren and I were ready.

'Babes, how are you getting on with your paint problem?'

I put on a fake sad face. 'I'm really struggling, to be honest. The workmen overestimated massively on it. I don't know where I'm going to store it all. I might have to take it to the tip.'

I saw Liane's eyes flicker. I am expanding my horizons and now is the time to do it, as the school has seen an influx of new children and parents since the housing development was finished. It couldn't have come at a better time. Chloë and Elsie are making new friends and trying to pull away from Liza and Charlotte Bennet. A family called Whiting has moved in, distant relations of Lauren's (she did explain how, but I confess I tuned out), and their daughter Georgie has enrolled at dance, putting Liza's nose out of joint.

'Georgie is really kind, Mum. She says that I'd be great at ballet because I'm so bendy and I've got good balance. Can I give up acro and tap and start doing ballet with her, please? She's much better at modern than Liza. Miss Eleanor says she's a natural and Liza got really upset and shouted things. Miss Eleanor told her that real dancers don't sulk and that we all need to support each other and work as a team. Liza says she might go to the dance school in Woodbridge because her mum says Miss Eleanor doesn't recognise talent when she sees it.'

I was delighted to hear this. Georgie Whiting's younger sister, Aimee, is in Elsie's year and is a very sweet child. I've had both the girls over for a playdate and they seem charming.

Sofija, God bless her, has been chatting to the girls about their friendship issues and supporting me with all the playground drama. Thank heavens she has offered to take Chloë to dance so that I can swerve at least one awkward interaction with the Bennets, who continue to be cold, aloof and downright unpleasant. Every day there's a toxic huddle on the playground comprising Rebecca, Mr Bennet, the Robinsons, Natalie and now Oliver Whitmore's mother, Sally. That's six people who are anti-Issy Smugge and who are causing her to have bad dreams and panic attacks. I have found myself doubled over in the kitchen, struggling to breathe, on five separate occasions this month. That said, the warm feeling which I experienced at homegroup hasn't gone away, which is a relief. I used to love walking down the hill towards school with my girls, but even the beautiful summer weather, fragrant flowers and the cheerful greetings of other parents cannot distract me from the poisonous knot of anti-Smugge-ers by the veranda. Only a few weeks until we break up for summer, but I have to get through the fête first. **#enemies #meangirls**

Mummy's stepdaughter, Karen, is still the worm in the apple in an otherwise blissful married life. I receive regular updates and bulletins. The mock orange trained over the new wrought-iron arch over the front path is 'common'. The entrance hallway, stairs and landing colour-drenched in dark grey with accents picked out in dull gold is 'depressing'. Mummy has joined the WI and the gardening club and she and Harry are spending a lot of time in the village. As I would if Karen were on my case.

One morning, I'd just returned from school when my phone rang. Mummy.

'Isabella! Something terrible has happened. Harry fell down the stairs. I'm in the ambulance with him going to the hospital. There's blood everywhere!'

She burst into uncharacteristic sobs.

I had a full morning planned but, alerting Sofija, I dropped everything and drove at top speed down the A12 to the hospital. I arrived in A&E to find the two of them in a curtained-off side room. My poor stepfather was white as a sheet and covered in blood. A very rough estimate of his injuries appeared to be a broken nose, a broken leg and possibly a fractured wrist.

'What happened?'

Mummy blew her nose.

'We'd had breakfast in bed and he was taking the tray down. He must have slipped. How on earth are we going to cope? He can't drive and I've lost my licence. We'll have to rely on public transport! Can you imagine?'

I reassured her that it wouldn't come to that and waited with them until he was admitted. With great difficulty, I persuaded Mummy to return to the Old Rectory with me and promised to drive her to the hospital that evening to visit.

It never rains but it pours. Mummy safely installed in the new double room on the second floor, I got a phone call from the school. There had been a fight at lunchtime between Chloë and Liza Bennet. Could I please come in to chat to the Year Five teacher and the other parents. Sighing heavily, I left Mummy propped up on the sofa in the family room with a coffee and a smoked salmon and cream cheese bagel, and trotted off to school.

Our world needs lawyers. I know that. However, it's a great pity that one of their number, Rebecca Bennet, decided to move to our village. We shuffled awkwardly into a dingy room with mismatched furniture and a dismal painting of drooping blooms on the wall where the Year Five teacher was awaiting us. I sat down while the Bennets glared at me.

Weeks of tension and unhappiness had culminated in a full-on fight between my daughter and her former friend at lunchtime.

'We can't have this kind of thing happening at our school. I appreciate that Chloë and Liza have been struggling with friendship issues. They need to talk this out, and as parents, I'd like you to facilitate that.'

There was a snort from Rebecca. 'This all started because *she* made some ridiculous accusation against Charlotte over a child's party. My husband and I have found out all kinds of alarming things about the way she's bribed the school with money and equipment. Our treasurer has alerted to me to some possible breaches of policy.'

I wasn't having that.

'You know that's not true. We talked about it. You said that Chris was a weaselly little toerag with the personality of a decaffeinated teabag.'

'I most certainly did not!'

'You did!'

'Did not!'

'Did too!'

'Prove it!'

'All right, I will. You just say the word and I'll prove you said those things.'

The teacher intervened.

'Mrs Smugge. Mrs Bennet. This is getting us nowhere. We are going to have an assembly about conflict and how to resolve it, but in the meantime, I must ask that you model adult behaviour to your children. We have absorbed a number of new pupils from the housing development and we don't want their experience of our school to be negative.'

Great. Isabella M Smugge, the doyenne of lifestyle bloggers, being told off by a primary school teacher. I can see that the Bennets and their clique are going to be causing me and my family any amount of issues. **#playgrounddrama**

I normally love the summer months, but there is a dark cloud of anxiety hanging over me. The cat did a dirty protest in the downstairs cloakroom this morning, Milo has started pooing all over the house again (I trust temporarily) and Harry is going to be out of action for weeks. We set up a camp bed in the office downstairs at his house, but he's not sleeping properly and looks awful. Mummy and I left Karen fussing over him and went out to sit in the garden, still relatively barren and badly laid out, but improved by some flowering shrubs and roses put in by its new owner.

'Isabella, I'm going to ask you a question and I want you to answer me honestly.'

Mummy fixed me with a beady eye. I wondered what was coming. Was she going to ask me if I knew any reliable assassins? Was she breaking up with Harry again?

'This isn't going to work. I can't have my husband on a camp bed downstairs while I sleep alone. How am I supposed to get to my WI meetings and the gardening club and all the Village Show planning meetings? Can we please move back in with you just until Harry gets a bit better?'

In principle, this seemed an excellent idea, but there was the problem of my curving Georgian staircase. Mummy waved her hand impatiently.

'I've thought of that. We could sleep on the sofa bed in the family room. He doesn't have to climb the stairs then, and we're close to the cloakroom and the kitchen. I don't want to impose on you, darling, but I can't see any other way.'

I had to confess that neither did I.

'You're both very welcome, but I'm not telling Karen!'

I can just imagine how that's going to go.

As ice-cold sparkling spring water dilutes the alcoholic punch of an Aperol Spritz, so my lovely friends are acting as both antidote and diluent on the playground. Lauren and her girls wait for me outside the gates, and Claire, Tom, Lovely Lou, Kate and Maddie are always ready to spring into action if need be. The other day, I disgraced myself. I'd had a panic attack when I woke up and was feeling shaky and miserable. The sheer injustice of it all had hit home and I'm not ashamed to say that I had a little cry in the shower. An on-trend pair of oversized double-bridge sunglasses in crush blue have become a vital part of my look. I know I'm a coward, but I feel safe hiding behind them. Standing waving to the girls, I heard sniggers. Rebecca was staring at me and I watched as Hayley Robinson bent down to whisper something in Natalie Gee's ear.

I don't care that Hayley and Chris hate me. I really don't. And the Bennets are clearly two-faced and not worth my attention. However, Natalie and I were getting on really well. We'd had some lovely chats, she'd opened up to me about how she feels about being a wheelchair user and I thought we were becoming friends. To my horror, I felt my eyes fill with tears. I certainly wasn't going to give *them* the satisfaction of seeing they'd got to me.

Liane came striding over. Once upon a time, I would have done nearly anything rather than let her see me in a state. But our relationship has been changing, slowly, subtly, and I found that I didn't mind one bit.

'What's up, Smug? Tell me who did what and I'll give them a smack.'

For a moment, I was sorely tempted to take her up on her offer. What joy there would be in watching the village's most terrifying inhabitant inflict violence on my enemies. I explained. Liane frowned.

'I'd expect that from the rest of them, but I thought that wheelchair woman was all right. Let's get this sorted.'

Natalie had her phone out and the Bennets were slithering off the playground. Liane marched over to her and started jabbing a finger in her face. Natalie is not a woman who takes criticism well, it seems, and raised her voice. Fragments of conversation drifted across the playground.

'... what you're playing at, you loser!'

'He said... not how she appears... mean things.'

'Shut it, you complete... can't trust a word... half a brain.'

'Used to that kind of thing, but... seemed different... stop yelling at me.'

It was time to intervene. I walked over, accompanied by Claire.

'Shall we go to the café? I can see a teacher glaring out of the window at us.'

Looking back over my life, it seems that lies and deceit have followed me around like a couple of creepy stalkers (although are there any other kinds?). My father had an affair with my mother's best friend behind her back, I fell passionately in love with my sister's boyfriend and stole him from under her nose, my husband cheated on me with Sofija. And now, lies are being told about me in the playground. It seems that Chris and Hayley told Natalie that I'd been bad-mouthing her and her son. I have been doing no such thing.

'Hayley told me you said that there are too many new kids coming to the school and it's affecting the ones who were here first. You seemed so nice, but then Rebecca had me over and showed me your Insta and said did I really think that someone like you who makes her living from showing off would care about ordinary people? I suppose I felt a bit insecure about knowing someone so famous, so I believed her. She was ever so convincing.'

Liane scowled at Natalie. 'Smug would never say anything like that. She's a bit of a show-off but there are worse things to be. Do you know that Hayley took money from a woman to sell stories about Smug's personal life? That's how she built that kitchen. Been in there, have you? Blood money, through and

225

through. Why didn't you ask Smug if she said that stuff before believing every word you were told? Are you thick or what?'

Natalie looked abashed. 'I haven't been here long, and I had such a rubbish time at the last school that I was grateful when people wanted to be friends with me. Sorry, Isabella. I did like you, but they had this way of saying things that made me believe them. Hayley told me you got her kicked off the PTA. Is that true?'

I put her straight and invited her over to the Old Rectory for coffee whenever she fancied it.

I returned from school on Wednesday morning to find a pile of post on the kitchen island. Sipping the double-strength cappuccino made for me by Mummy (it's nice to have her home again), I opened it and there was my decree absolute, the final proof that I married a man who didn't love me enough to be faithful and who spent all of our relationship trying to control me. What an odd mix of joy and grief. I don't quite know how I feel.

Natalie is now being nice to me again and has been shunned by Rebecca and her crew as a result.

Karen is ringing Harry every day to try to persuade him to 'see sense' (her words) and come home.

Being a Wednesday, the boot room door opened at 7 pm and Robin walked in. I'm not sure who was more surprised, him to see a well-preserved mature lady clutching a large G&T, or Mummy to see a strange man walking into her daughter's kitchen. I introduced them and saw her give him an appraising look, which was nothing compared to the look of surprise on Robin's face when he met Harry, now sporting two black eyes and a crooked nose.

We sat out in the garden again. Sallie-Ann's shadow stood between us, but I could hardly say, 'Sorry to hear you broke up, fancy a coffee?' Not that I want to go out with him. Although his eyes are actually rather nice when you get up close.

I launched into the whole frightful Bennet imbroglio.

'I wish I could go back to last year and meet Rebecca again but not make friends with her. I was so taken in. I'm dreading our next PTA meeting.'

Robin looked at me.

'Why don't you leave? Get this fête out of the way and step down. You've done three years and you don't owe them anything.'

I had a little ponder while Sue went through the study notes. The Bennets and the Robinsons would talk about me behind my back and accuse me of running away. But did I really want to keep on jumping through hoops to make other people happy? Relaxing in my well-upholstered garden chair, I had the sudden and unexpected realisation that what I would really like more than anything else was to go out for dinner with Robin Knight and see what happened. My 'phone beeped. A text from Johnnie.

'Our decree absolute's come through, Iss. End of an era. I'm going to ask Paige this weekend to marry me. Give the kids my love.'

The end of an era indeed. **#itsover #goodbyejohnnie #newissy**

August

Issy Smugge is nailing it!

1. School fête and awkward meetings with enemies – done!

2. Resignation from PTA – done!

3. Difficult discussion with Karen – done!

4. Chat with Paige (at her request) regarding her putative marriage and my ex-husband's second – done!

5. Full potty training of final child – done!

6. First rental of the self-contained second floor flat – done!

7. The whole of Liane Bloomfield's house painted in Bitter and Twisted – done!

Even Hayley Robinson couldn't find anything to carp about on Fête Day. I was on site at 8am, fifteen minutes ahead of our esteemed chair, clipboard in hand ready to micro-manage a hugely successful event.

The WI ladies, including Mummy, had set up shop in an enormous old-fashioned marquee loaned by the church. Urns were steaming and plates of homemade cakes and scones being laid out. Harry was parked under the cherry tree in a comfy chair clutching a sausage roll, and Sofija was in charge of the children. Milo is warming to her, although he is, and I trust always will be, a mummy's boy. I had worked hard to bring in gorgeous prizes for our raffle and contacted some of the stallholders I'd met at Charlene's events. At £20 a pop for a stall, booking up ten of them made good fiscal sense, whatever Chris Robinson had to say.

'I think what our secretary fails to understand is that this is a local fête for local people.'

(Cue barely contained sniggers from myself, Natalie and Mrs Tennant.)

'Do we really want to set a precedent for traders from further afield to come and take over our events? I've never heard of any of them. And will our families really want to buy lampshades and wax melts and quilts? I say we major on cheap attractions like the tombola.'

Mrs Tennant appears to know everything about everything that goes on at school. I'd said nothing to her about the current unpleasantness, but she had intercepted me on the way to the staff room and asked after my health in a most kindly fashion. Now, she replied to Chris' ludicrous statement.

'We're all about community at the school. Reaching out and offering new and exciting products makes our events look more attractive. I will certainly be visiting those stalls, and let's remember that Isabella has brought in £200 with these bookings. They bring their own tables and chairs and we simply rent our space. I think it's an excellent fundraising model.'

That shut the treasurer up. Rebecca shot me a dirty look and began speaking about signage and toilet provision, the less glamorous side of PTA work. Under Any Other Business, I announced my resignation, which was accepted with no questions asked. Mrs Tennant looked surprised and disappointed.

'I'm sure everyone would like to join me in a vote of thanks for our outgoing secretary. You have been an incredibly supportive member of the committee and I for one will be very sorry to see you go.'

Our esteemed chair appeared to be sucking on a lemon, but forced out a few ungracious words. Chris Robinson leapt in again.

'My wife, Hayley, who many of you know used to be the secretary before our current incumbent came to the village, is prepared to step back into the role.'

The plot thickens! I departed and texted Kate.

The dark side is taking over xx'

#shenanigans #drama #coup

At a stroke, I am no longer married to Johnnie and I am free of PTA drama. Hooray! My departure made no difference to the situation on the playground. I was still being shunned by the poisonous Rebecca and her cronies. However, as the summer term drew to a close, I felt a real sense of progress in other areas of my life.

Mummy is hatching a daring plan. She's never liked Harry's house and has come up with a way of offloading it.

'I don't think Harry wants to live in that place any more than I do. It all centres on Karen. It's a lot to ask, but would you be prepared to have her over here for supper? I can swallow my pride and pretend to be interested in her boring stories, and if you can serve her favourite foods, I think we might be able to soften her up a bit. I'm working on Harry. The WI chair has a little house on the high street up for rent. She says she'll give me first refusal. It's got a downstairs bedroom with wet room. Ideal for now until we can sell and find somewhere permanent.'

I was all for it. Harry rang up his daughter and lured her over with the promise of a cosy chat. I felt a fleeting sense of compassion for her, which was quickly dispelled when she arrived. Karen's face is set in lines of anger and disappointment and her voice is unattractively whiny. Not the ideal supper guest, but catering to her love of simple food, I produced lasagne with a green salad and followed it with tiramisu. She consumed vast amounts and softened enough to say a few nice things to Mummy about the garden.

After supper, we went and sat outside. Mummy and I had agreed to continue buttering her up, so we listened to an endless recitation of how useless the trainee teachers she mentored were, what was wrong with the state school system and how she would change it for the better, given half a chance.

Harry broached the subject of the move. I watched as Karen's face turned white and, in an instant, I realised that what we were dealing with here was a frightened child.

'But you can't leave the house! You promised Mum. She'd hate it.'

Harry took his daughter's hand and looked lovingly into her face.

'Mum would want me to be happy. I'm not getting any younger and the house is too much for me. I'll be able to give you and the boys a lump sum from the sale and you can come and stay with us in the village. I can walk everywhere and it's such a supportive community.'

Karen began sobbing and dashed to the cloakroom. Leaving Mummy to console Harry, I followed her and lurked outside. When she finally emerged, looking more frightful than ever with tear tracks down her pasty face, I diverted her to the snug.

'Look, Karen. I understand how you're feeling. I was so upset when our parents got together. It took me ages to accept Harry. But I have. Will you have a think about what's being suggested? Honestly, I think it would be better for both of them.'

If my life was a book being dramatised for the television, at this point, soupy music would have begun playing and we would have had a tearful chat about love. But Karen blew her nose loudly and repeated her assertion that her mother would not have approved of anything currently going on. Which was exceptionally unhelpful. Laying my hand on her arm, I looked into her puffy eyes and assured her that I would work with her to make sure our respective parents were well looked after. She appeared unconvinced, but it's a start.

Hard on the heels of one honest chat came another. As the serial monogamist that he is, my ex-husband has indeed proposed to the mother of his child. More and more, I wonder what goes through his brain. Does he truly believe that he's such a catch that he only has to ask and the answer will be 'Yes'? From Paige's recount, this does seem to be the case. Over Zoom (and what a great invention that is), she shared her feelings.

'So he can't even change a nappy without the Third World War breaking out, but he somehow manages to bribe his mother to come and stay, she takes over with Hudson and he orders in a three-course romantic dinner. Did he ever cook when you were together?'

I admitted that he hadn't. He was an enthusiastic consumer of food, but a stranger to the intricacies of its preparation.

'So I've just got Hudson settled and Silvia grabs me and says, "Paige, darling, how about you find a lovely clean outfit? A woman needs to make that extra effort in a relationship when a baby comes along." I'm so gobsmacked that I stick on a clean top and brush my hair. She's a funny one, isn't she? Anyway, down I go and he's hovering about in the kitchen with a huge bunch of flowers, gazing at me with puppy-dog eyes. I've been living on toasties and chocolate, but suddenly I'm eating prawns with some fancy French name and he's staring into my eyes and telling me I'm the love of his life.'

I assured her that Johnnie had an apparently inexhaustible capacity for identifying women who would swallow this kind of schtick.

'I could feel what was coming. Sure enough, he produces this huge diamond engagement ring after the pud and goes down on one knee.'

I was intrigued. 'What did you say?'

She laughed. 'No, of course. I don't want to get married. Never have. I'm a career girl. With a lot of training, he might be OK as a dad, but he's not husband material. Sorry. No offence.'

I assured her that none was taken.

'I'm back at work at the beginning of September and I'm not living out here in the country. I've told him it's London or nothing. I'll come back for weekends when your kids visit. That's fine. But we're going back to the flat and he and my mum are doing the childcare. And I'm not letting him stick a plaster on our issues with a big posh engagement ring and a fancy wedding.'

I really, really like Paige. Which is weird, but strangely satisfying. I'm ignoring Johnnie's increasingly peevish texts. I can't believe that once I thought he was the perfect man. **#changes #newstart**

Never have I been happier that school has broken up. No more donning my sunglasses and muttering, 'Go ahead of me,' as I walk on to the playground, no more knots of fear in my stomach, no more wincing as I feel the daggers of spite being hurled at me. The other day, in the café with Lauren, the whole lot of them came in and sat whispering and sniggering, darting malevolent glances at me. Is nowhere safe?

Harry is getting better, but slowly. It's lovely having him and Mummy back. They're going to move into her friend's cottage at the end of August for three months to see how they get on. Karen is still not at all happy.

Frank Shemming appeared unexpectedly at our last homegroup. I was so touched to see the kindness and compassion with which he was treated. Robin took his arm and gently guided him to a chair, and he sat and sipped a cup of tea, looking round the garden with clouded and troubled eyes. I have befriended his daughter-in-law, Julie, a charming woman who is wrestling with some unpalatable truths.

'Frank was always so independent. He did all the cooking and cleaning when Margie was ill and he kept the cottage spotless. These days, it's all at sixes and sevens. I just don't know where to turn.'

Fortunately, I had the answer.

'I'd get in touch with Caring Touch. You know, the Pink Ladies. They were marvellous when my mother had her stroke.'

To my relief, she's taken me up on my suggestion. I've grown fond of Frank, and his decline into confusion and frailty tears at my heart. I don't like to think that one day we all come to this, but seeing Harry hobbling around the Old Rectory and even Mummy not quite as vital as once she was, the fragility of life hits me right between the eyes.

Not that I've got much time for philosophical musings! Having four children at home for six weeks is keeping me very busy. To Mimi's horror, I've pulled back on my family-based posts, with hardly any images of the little Smugges and not much bragging either. I read a book about how technology and social media has changed our lives, and it was a wake-up call. Without asking their permission, I compromised my children's privacy for my own ends and I'm not doing it any more. I've always wanted to make others' lives better and I'm tending towards doing it with acts of kindness rather than banging on about how marvellous I am at parenting or dressing beds or whatever. My posts about mental health and teenage health issues have got loads of traction and I've been invited on to several podcasts to discuss my views. Mimi is not impressed.

'Sweetie, it's not broken so why fix it? You were doing so well with all your lovely posts about paint and luxe bathrooms and reclaimed fireplaces. That's what your followers want, not all this goody two shoes nonsense about helping people. Sincerity isn't hot right now.'

I may have to start thinking seriously about how my relationship with Mimi plays out. Note to self. Is there such a thing as a trial separation from one's agent? **#kindness #sincerity #movingon**

When I first moved to the village, I saw only what was on the surface. Half-timbered houses clustering around the square, the eighteenth-century pub with its swinging sign, the Victorian school surrounded by trees, the pond, the narrow streets. And, of course, my own gracious residence at the top of the hill by the church. Four years on, I'm a wiser and perhaps slightly sadder woman. Nothing is quite as it appears. Friends betray you, husbands show their true colours, loneliness is everywhere, even in a crowd.

And nowhere was this more evident than at the Village Show, held annually in the village hall and with which my own mother has become involved. I was rather looking forward to it. With its quaint traditions of home crafts, vegetables, artistic works and homemade products, it promised to be a most enjoyable experience.

Mummy had scuttled up to the hall early as she had two hours of hard judging ahead of her. Over a glass of chilled New Zealand Sauvignon Blanc the evening before, she waved away the delicious small plates of nibbles I had prepared.

'I've got to save myself, darling. I'm judging the home-baking class. I'm going to start with the homemade fruit liqueurs then taste the breads, cakes and scones, take five minutes then do chutneys, jams, jellies and marmalades. I'm fasting tonight so as to be completely ready. Oh, goodness, now what?'

Her phone beeped. Ever since she'd moved back in, the Village Show WhatsApp group had taken over her life. An unpleasantness about raffle prizes, tension over the question of whether a Suffolk Rusk qualified as a bread (it doesn't – somewhere between a biscuit and a scone, apparently), attempts to nobble the judges with lavish gifts and fallings-out over vegetable categories had played out in what I had thought was a quiet and community-minded village.

Judges had to sign a waiver agreeing that they would not accept presents of any kind before the show, that they would judge without any bias and comport themselves in a manner befitting their status. It all sounded like hard work to me.

'Several of the WI aren't speaking, darling. Our last meeting was most uncomfortable. The flower-arranging category causes ructions every year. And they've changed the rules on the vegetable class so that people living 1.5 miles outside the village boundary can enter. That means Allonsfield Gardening Club, and they're extremely competitive. If one of them wins the Vegetable Cup, it's war!'

At twelve noon prompt, we joined a long line of people outside the hall waiting to go in. I found Mummy sitting on a chair with her eyes closed and her hand to her head.

'Oh, my goodness. I'm never eating again as long as I live. Seven chocolate cakes! Nine gingerbreads! Any amount of bread. And starting with the liqueurs was a mistake.'

The Vegetable Cup stayed in the village, thank heavens, but Allonsfield swept the board in the shallots section, longest bean and trimmed carrots. My own gardener, Ted Ling, staggered home with an armful of prizes, including the hotly contested Bloomfield Challenge Shield. Two ladies fell out over their entries in the Floral Art class, with one accusing the other of interfering with her dahlias. All in all, it was a lively day full of drama. **#villageshow #undercurrents**

Harpreet has taken over the job of keeping my brand engaging and relatable during August. I'd worked super hard writing all my blogs and content in the previous two months and was devoting August to the family. Suze, Jeremy and Lily are spending a fortnight with us (bliss!), and I love having a houseful again. I am allowing Karen to come and visit as often as she likes and modelling relentless positivity in an attempt to improve her frightful personality. It's rather wearing.

I've grown closer to Charlene as we have attended craft fairs together and it's been wonderful to see her grow in confidence. I included her in the invitation to a big day out to the beach on a particularly sublime summer day. I woke early, pulled on some jeans and a structured vest, ran a comb through my hair and went out for a little walk. It was just after 6.30 and everyone in the house was asleep. I walked up our lane, breathing in deep, invigorating breaths and glorying in the beauty all around me. How fortunate I am to live here! I'd never go back to the way my life used to be.

I turned around after a good twenty-minute tramp and began to make my way down the lane between the rolling fields back to the Old Rectory. In the distance, I saw a figure making its way towards me. Closer inspection revealed it to be Frank Shemming, clad in a tweed dressing gown and slippers and carrying a small suitcase. He was swinging his arms and whistling cheerfully. I've learned that it's best to take a view on his mental state and act accordingly, so sending a quick text to his daughter-in-law *('Hi, Julie, sorry it's so early, Frank's walking up my lane x')*, I hailed him.

'Morning Frank! How are you?'

He gazed at me as if trying to remember something lost long ago.

'Good morning, my dear. Now – I am sorry – I don't seem to be able to place you.'

I made a split-second decision to be myself rather than Peggy the imaginary housekeeper.

'I'm Isabella. I live in the Old Rectory with my family.'

He frowned. 'Lady Hamilton lives there, my dear. I think you must be getting a little mixed up.'

I thought quickly. 'We're staying with her. Would you like to come back with me for a cup of tea? It's very early.'

He patted my arm in a fatherly fashion. 'How kind. But will you forgive me? I'm in rather a hurry as I am on my way to meet my fiancée. We're catching the boat train. Good day to you.'

He raised an imaginary hat and began walking up the lane towards the farm with me trotting along at his heels. I was at a bit of a loss. Julie had responded to my message but still had to get dressed and out of the door.

'I'd be happy to give you a lift to the station. Why not come home with me and have a little breakfast?'

He shook his head. 'I couldn't possibly impose on your kindness. The boat train leaves at nine. This is our engagement holiday. Nothing untoward, you understand. Separate bedrooms.'

We seemed to have reached a stalemate, but at that moment I heard footsteps. Julie, looking incredibly flustered and with a coat thrown over her pyjamas, ran up behind us.

'Frank! What on earth are you doing out? Don't you know what time it is?'

She took his arm and tried to turn him around, to his distress.

'Madam, please! I don't believe we've met but I don't have time to talk now. My fiancée is waiting and we have a train to catch.'

Julie's eyes filled with tears. 'Frank, you're not going anywhere. Margie died five years ago. Don't you remember?'

To my horror, the old man's face crumpled and he began sobbing heartbrokenly, like a child.

'Not my Margie! We were going to be married. What happened to her? Can you tell me?'

I felt terrible. There's something about the tears of a very old person that wrenches at my heart. I took his hand and looked into his face.

'Why don't you come back to my house and we'll have a nice cup of tea?'

With his head bowed and his shoulders shuddering with wracking sobs, the old man allowed himself to be led into my house. I settled them both on the sofa in the family room and brewed up a pot of tea and made some toast. By the time I served it, Frank had completely forgotten our previous conversation.

'Lady Hamilton must have been decorating. Are you her housekeeper, my dear?'

I tried to explain that I was the owner of the Old Rectory. He seemed to accept this.

'And what does your husband do? I trust we're not disturbing him, barging into his house like this.'

It would take more than an elderly retired doctor with dementia and his distraught daughter-in-law to disturb Johnnie, presumably taking his nightly rest in Essex while Paige did all the work. I decided to play along.

'He's not here at present. I do the work – I write and take photographs.'

Frank looked surprised.

'You work? Well, I never. How very modern! And you have children? Your husband must be a very understanding man.'

That was one way of putting it, but I certainly wasn't going to shatter my new friend's illusions.

Frank had perked up and was clearly enjoying his tea.

'I saved up for a year and bought my Margie an engagement ring. We're to be married in May. Her parents don't approve of her throwing herself away on a poor medical student, but I've assured them that it will be my life's work to make her happy.'

I glanced over at Julie and saw that her eyes were full of tears. Something told me to reach out to Frank in the place where he thought he was.

'She's a lucky girl to have you, Frank.' I smiled at him and was rewarded by the sight of his wrinkled old face lighting up.

'I do hope so. We won't have much money to start with, but I qualify this year and I'll be starting off at a local practice. This is a lovely place to bring up a family, should we be blessed with one.'

I watched as he shuffled back to his house, holding Julie's arm and raising his imaginary hat to me. It was absolutely heart-breaking. If I ever develop dementia, I shall instruct the children to play along with anything I say and remind themselves of the good times. Although I am only forty-two and I hope to have a long way to go yet!

In a case of life imitating art, Issy Smugge was at the beach with her family, surrounded by hashtaggable moments (**#livingmybestlife #beachlife #suffolkinfluencer #makingmemories**) and ignoring each and every one of them. My phone was in my pocket on silent and it was jolly well staying there, thank you very much.

It was glorious weather so I hired a couple of beach huts and invited the Knights, Charlene and Jake, Lauren and her family and Suze, Jeremy and Lily to join me, Sofija and the children at the beach for a day of outdoor fun. Maybe it was something to do with the salty sea breezes and the huge Suffolk sky, but the little nagging pain in my heart that stabs at me every time I think of Sofija and Johnnie together was stilled, albeit temporarily.

My entire glittering career has been an exercise in putting a spin on things, but there was no need to exaggerate anything on this beautiful August day. The sun was glinting on the waves, seagulls cried and swooped overhead and the beach was full of happy families building sandcastles and enjoying themselves. By twelve, everyone was starving, so Robin and I took food orders and began strolling up the promenade towards the fish and chip shop.

I feel much more comfortable around him now I've got to know him better, and the fact that I was out and about with windblown hair, virtually no make-up and wearing last season's clothes bothered me not one jot. Johnnie would have made lots of little comments, but Robin didn't seem to mind what I looked like.

It was strangely relaxing, actually.

Maybe Lauren's right. I fell passionately in love at first sight with Johnnie, allegedly my soulmate and the love of my life, and look how that turned out. Perhaps I should forget about a thunderbolt from above and try to get to know Robin a little bit better and see where it goes.

I invited everyone back to the house for a scratch supper. Finn was already going to Jake's for a sleepover and Lauren and Scott had plans, so it was a small but happy party who congregated around the dining room table for cold salmon and chicken, salads and a couple of Ali's amazing cheesecakes. Thank heavens for the Georgians who built their rooms to accommodate large and extended families. The children had run off into the garden and we were having coffee. I glanced at my phone for the first time since I'd had my lunch and saw five missed calls and any number of texts from Johnnie. The last one read:

'Iss. Where are you? Why aren't you answering your phone? Don't play hard to get. You haven't said no, so I'll see you very soon x please remember all the good times we had. I miss you x'

I let out an involuntary yelp and pushed my chair back. The text had been sent fifty minutes ago so he could be here any minute. I called him but it went to answerphone. I texted back.

'I don't know why you want to see me, but I don't want to see you. Turn around and go back home. We're divorced, or had you forgotten?'

The texts told the usual self-absorbed story. In spite of knowing how tired he was and how busy setting up his consultancy, Paige was being unreasonable and her mother was being unpleasant to Silvia. A huge row had blown up (started by Paige, obviously) and she'd told him to go back to London and think about their future.

I filled in my friends, family and whatever Robin is.

'That wretched little man! If I was his mother, I'd be ashamed. Do you want me to deal with him, darling?'

I love my mother. I gave her a hug and assured her I could face him.

The sound of children's laughter floated through the French windows as we sat in silence and listened for the crunch of tyres on the gravel.

Within minutes, I heard the sound of his car and his footsteps walking impatiently along the York stone path that leads past the dining room. He stood at the French doors, looking in at the group of people staring back at him. I took a deep breath.

'Hello, Johnnie.' **#hesback #summerfun #movingon**

September

I had the most wonderful summer. I feel like a new woman. As does my ex-husband, but that's another story.

Mummy and Harry have moved into the little cottage on the high street. Karen is over constantly but it's a small price to pay for them having their own space where they can start to write their own story together. She's still difficult, interfering and negative, but I suppose not that many leopards truly change their spots.

I have been inside Liane Bloomfield's house! Walking back from the shop, I ran into Claire and Bix Bloomfield walking towards the new development. I'm used to rubbing perfectly toned shoulders with the stars, but the stooped, grey-haired man in old dungarees and a patched linen shirt with love beads around his scraggy neck looked nothing like the handsome, smiling sixties pop star he had once been. But then I suppose we all change, some of us more overtly than others.

'We're popping over to Liane's. Bix is cutting her lawn and doing a bit of planting. Do you want to come along?'

I took a huge risk and said yes. When we arrived, she looked surprised but invited us in. The hall, painted in Ansbach and Powdering Gown, was light and welcoming and I noted glimpses of Porphyria, Sophia Dorothea and Rogue Gene in other rooms as she led us to the garden. Never did I think I would find myself sitting in a deckchair in Liane Bloomfield's back garden sipping own-brand lemonade from a plastic glass watching the former keyboard player of the Do Wells mowing the lawn. I'd go so far as to say that I would now count her as a friend (although I'd never tell her, obvs).

'Thanks for the praying and that, Claire. No offence, but I don't really believe in any of that stuff. Appreciate you having a word, though.'

Claire smiled and reminded her that I had also importuned the Almighty.

'Trust you to have a hotline to the man upstairs, Smug. And listen, thanks for the paint. I love it. My room's that dark-purple colour and Charl ran me up some black curtains. Well classy.'

Each to their own, I suppose.

Claire shared her own news.

'We've had a breakthrough with Joel. The school has managed to get some support for him and we're hoping that we can keep him in mainstream education. Please do keep praying.'

I asked her back to the Old Rectory for coffee, which turned into lunch. We sat on my terrace, looking out over the pond and the towering trees at the end of my garden. There was a lot to catch up on.

'I'm dying to hear the whole story. What happened? Does Johnnie understand that you can never take him back?'

I took a bite of my cave-aged mature cheddar and apple and real ale chutney sandwich (delicious!) and filled her in.

I suppose it was sheer bad luck that Paige finally snapped on the day I had the whole family over. My ex-husband's face was a study as he gazed at his former girlfriend (my sister), his former wife (me) and the woman he cheated on me with (my executive assistant and former au pair). Plus, of course, his former mother-in-law who loathes him, his former girlfriend's current husband and his former wife's church mate and sort of friend. Who does definitely like her if the looks he was shooting her over coffee were anything to go by. As webs go, it was remarkably tangled.

Issy Smugge has written enough books around interior design and party etiquette and living a gorgeous, well-polished life to know that there are rules around social introductions.

That said, I don't suppose Jane Austen ever had to wrestle with a situation like this. As the highest-ranking woman, Mummy, the daughter of a viscount, was technically honour-bound to introduce Robin to Johnnie. However, she was too busy glaring at him to do anything of the kind, so it fell to me, as the hostess, albeit in a slightly quavering voice.

'Do come in. I think you know nearly everyone. This is Robin Knight. Robin, this is Johnnie Smugge, my ex-husband.'

I watched as Robin rose from his seat and extended a hand. Seeing them standing together, something clicked in my mind and I felt a tiny throb of excitement in my heart. Johnnie, tall, handsome and beautifully dressed, certainly looked pretty good on the outside. But Robin, I realised, with his kind face, rumpled hair, off-the-peg clothes and dad bod, was a far better bet.

'This has the potential to be a bit awkward, Iss. I didn't realise you were entertaining. Can we go somewhere private and chat?'

The old Issy would have scuttled out of the room, heart beating at double speed, and let him sit and talk wherever he chose. The new one offered him a seat at the dining table in full view of her – friend, let's say – and a bunch of people who had no reason to love him. He squirmed.

'This is extremely inappropriate, Iss. You must see that. You're embarrassing your guests.'

Was he always this thick-skinned?

'No, Johnnie. You are. What have you got to say?'

Looking back over my marriage, I can see all the red flags. Just because I was wealthy and successful and lived in a big house didn't mean my life was perfect. I don't know where the next year will take me, but I wonder if I will be spending it alone – or is there the faintest of chances that I might find some kind of happiness again? A different kind, with less expensive aftershave and designer shirts and more listening and empathy.

Looking back, it was a miracle Johnnie got out alive. With unbelievable cheek, he told the assembled masses how he now realised he might have made a life-changing mistake by leaving me. I noticed at least 50 per cent of the said assembled masses noting that word 'might'.

'You are saying I am mistake, Johnnie?'

My executive assistant spoke up and was rewarded by a squeeze of the hand from Suze.

'Yes. You were. You led me on and I should never have let myself drift away from Isabella. My *wife*.'

Mummy glared at him. 'Ex-wife, you miserable snake. One of the best things that's ever happened to me is you leaving my family, you dreadful little man. My daughters both deserve better. And don't you dare speak to Sofija like that. What a pack of lies!'

Most men would have called it a day there, but I suppose you don't make it far in the cut-throat world of international finance without having virtually no shame. Johnnie ploughed on.

'We've got four children together, Iss. Or have you forgotten? The minute the divorce came through, I realised I'd probably made a mistake. I still love you, Isabella.'

I'd had enough.

'You don't know what love is, Johnnie. You nearly ruined my relationship with Suze forever, you cheated on me with Sofija, even though you knew how much she meant to me, you've been a rubbish father and now you're messing up two more lives. If there's a shred of decency in you, you'll get in your car and drive back home and make it up with Paige. She deserves better than you, but hopefully she'll give you another chance, for Hudson's sake.'

Suze got up and stood next to me.

'You cheated on all of us, Johnnie. But you're the loser.'

With a final look back at me, he obliged, slithering out of the French doors and crunching back to his car (convertible and red – such a cliché).

And if a confrontation like that didn't warrant the opening of not one but two of my best bottles of champagne, I don't know what did! **#goodbye #itsover #familylove**

I went out for a coffee with Robin. There were a couple of awkward silences and we ran out of things to say a few times. But maybe, just maybe, there is something worth pursuing. I expect I'll find out when we go out for dinner next week. Mummy and Harry are babysitting.

Sitting in my lovely garden, watching the birds flap lazily home across the sky, I let out a sigh and relaxed back in my ludicrously comfortable and on-trend modern rustic recliner in gorgeous charcoal grey. Lounging in its twin next to me, Mummy took a swig of her post-supper gin and tonic and sighed too.

'Well, it doesn't get much better than this, does it, darling? I have to say, I like that young man of yours. He beats Johnnie into a cocked hat, not that that's too difficult.'

I could have argued with her and said that Robin wasn't my young man, but gazing up into the sky and inhaling the fragrance of my late-flowering roses, the thought that he might be felt rather good.

Issy Smugge says, here's to a new adventure. **#yearfour #dating #freshstart**

Author's note

Jess and Andy are based on my dear friends Alan and Jane Hutt who really did leave a comfortable life in Suffolk to found a loving home for young mothers and their babies in Kenya. They rescue and restore girls who find themselves pregnant through no fault of their own, help to get them back into education and to find vocational work. If you want to find out more about them, you can visit their website: www.beehiveafrica.org

Acknowledgements

Writing this book felt like re-entering a familiar world and finding out what the characters had been up to while I had been away. I returned to the Old Rectory supported, as always, by my amazing family who are 100 per cent behind me as I disappear into the studio and forget my own name during the writing process.

I met Elaine Kasket at Primadonna Festival last year and read her book, *Reboot* (London: Elliott and Thompson, 2023), which taught me so much about the way social media has changed our society and informed Issy's changing world view. Fran, Deborah and Georgie (the Incomperellas) have been their usual fabulous selves, as have the Priceless Ladies (the two Joys, Jenny, Lisa and Jocelyn-Anne). Huge thanks to my three first readers, Jenny, Charlie and Jane, and to my husband who reads every word I write before anyone else does. My homegroup (Lauren's laugh-a-minute experience of hers is modelled on them) continue to offer coffee, home-made brownies, jokes about wax melts and encouragement; and my fellow writers at ACW are a constant source of inspiration and advice. My readers and the lovely people I meet at events are woven through Issy's further adventures, inextricably linked with her progress. Many of the character names are those of real people I've met along the way, and their reviews, comments and emails about their engagement with the UK's premier mumfluencer and her world keep me going when I'm flagging.

Thank you as always to everyone at Instant Apostle, and to all those who said, 'We want more Issy,' here she is.

A note on names

One of the hardest things about being a fiction author is finding believable names for your characters. Some of the names in *Trials* and most in *Continued Times* and *Further Adventures* belong to actual people I've met at events. They were most generous in allowing me to use their names for my fictional world. Some of them didn't make it into this book, but they can rest assured that they will feature in other books I write.

Also by Ruth Leigh

Meet Isabella Smugge – as in 'Br-uge-s', naturally! Instagram influencer, consummate show-off and endearingly self-unaware. With a palatial home, charming husband and three well-mannered children, she is living the *Country Life* dream.

Newly arrived in the country, Isabella is ready to bring a dash of London glamour to the school gate and gain a whole new set of followers – though getting past the instant coffee, terrible hair and own-brand sausage rolls may be a challenge!

But as her Latvian au pair's behaviour becomes increasingly bizarre and a national gossip columnist nurses a grudge, Isabella finds herself in need of true friends and begins to wonder if her life really is as picture-perfect as she thought…

'Recommended as a much-needed tonic, with a gin on the side.'
Paul Kerensa, stand-up comedian, speaker and writer

'Reminds me of Austen but with added Instagram, selfies and hashtags.'
Fran Hill, author of Being Miss *and* Miss, What Does Incomprehensible Mean? *and* Cuckoo in the Nest

Published by Instant Apostle, ISBN 978-1-912726-40-0

'Imagine Emma Woodhouse as a lifestyle blogger…'
Philippa Linton

The trials of Isabella M Smugge

Ruth Leigh

Life in the country isn't going as Issy Smugge planned it. However, the woman *Gorgeous Home* magazine once called 'Britain's Most Relatable Mum Designer' is nothing if not resilient!

With an unexpected baby on the way, a good-for-nothing husband and a mother who never seemed to care but now needs caring for, her hands are full. Her venal agent and creative socials guru keep work fizzing, but how will she cope with the mysterious village snitch and poisonous gossip columnist Lavinia Harcourt?

Discovering others' problems can be far worse than her own, she confronts bizarre church sub-culture and braces herself to use the NHS, rethinking all she thought she wanted. Could true happiness be just a few hashtags away?

'Touching, funny and cringe-making by turns, [Isabella] is a true (anti)-heroine for our times.'
Caroline Taggart, Sunday Times *best-selling author*

'Imagine Emma Woodhouse as a lifestyle blogger…'
Philippa Linton

Published by Instant Apostle, ISBN 978-1-912726-50-9

'If Austen was writing in the 21st century, she might have created Issy Smugge.'
S J Times

The continued times of Isabella M Smugge
Ruth Leigh

Now in her third year of living the rural dream, starry Instamum Issy Smugge is up against it. A single parent of four with an award-winning brand, a gin-swigging mother convalescing upstairs and a distraught relative craving a shoulder to cry on, her diary and listed Regency home are bursting at the seams!

Of course, she can count on lively support from the colourful playground mums – and then there's always Tom, the startlingly good-looking vicar, and his angelic wife, Claire.

But as pressure begins to mount, long-buried memories surface and difficult decisions need to be made. How will our heroine cope with painful emotions? (Clue: no filter!) And when the influencer needs influencing, who will show her the way?

'Compulsive reading in which friendship and laughter rise from disaster.'
Sophie Neville, author of The Making of Swallows and Amazons, Funnily Enough *and* Ride the Wings of Morning

'The expertly drawn internationally renowned influencer is a joy to spend time with.'
Helen Forbes, crime writer

Published by Instant Apostle, ISBN 978-1-912726-60-8